The Vagabond

Tracey Scott-Townsend

Wild Pressed Books

ISBN: 978-1-9164896-4-6

Published by Wild Pressed Books: 2019

Wild Pressed Books, UK Business Reg. No. 09550738

http://www.wildpressedbooks.com

To the Sons and Daughters

The Vagabond Mother

'I love being free. Empty pockets but a full heart. I'm so free, I can sleep on any street, under any tree, be who I want to be. Ain't got no money – my currency is creativity. Ain't got no food – an unlocked dumpster will lighten my mood. My choice is my master, my voice my broadcaster. I'm my own slave, I choose to follow me, and I choose how to behave.'

ZS, age 22

Disclaimer: not every Vagabond is a Castaway.

Part One

1

Maya

Melbourne, Australia. November 2014

Somebody brought them pale, sweet tea. Not *exactly* hot. Maya wondered how many corridors the tray had been carried down before reaching them. The remaining members of their family each held a cup between their shaking hands.

'But I don't take sugar,' said Lola. Her eyes looked enormous to Maya, bewildered. Just like when she was a toddler and the health visitor had given her a sugar cube after a vaccination. The sugar in her tea would no more take away her pain now than the cube had done then.

A woman – a nurse, perhaps – spoke to Lola in a gentle voice. 'You ought to drink the tea, darl. It'll help with the shock.'

Maya saw Daisy encouraging her twin by taking the first sip. It was always Daisy's mouth Maya had aimed for first with the feeding spoon when they were babies, as Lola would copy her sister. On Maya's other side sat a white-faced man whom she recognised as her husband. Con's hand lifted a cup to his lips in a mechanical sort of way, and brown liquid leaked down his chin. Maya found that she had taken tea into her own mouth. She watched her hand reflecting Con's movements.

'Are you ready, Sir?' The officer reappeared in the room, directing his question at Maya's husband.

'Yes.' Con placed his cup somewhere to one side. He stood but his body immediately collapsed back onto the chair. He tried again.

'Where are you going?' Maya surprised herself with the loudness of her voice. She snapped her mouth shut.

'Madam, forgive me,' said the officer. *What the hell for, he hadn't killed her son, had he?* 'I'm taking your husband to identify the body.'

The book, Joe's precious book, fell from her lap as she jumped to her feet, the cup in her waving hand slopping liquid. She yelped at the sight of outspread pages on the floor. The nurse picked the book up, closed the covers and handed it back to Maya with practised tenderness, gently removing the half-empty cup from her trembling fingers.

'There you are, darl.'

Maya clutched Joe's journal to her chest with one hand and reached with her other towards Con.

'I'm coming with you,' she said. 'You're not going without me.'

'Madam, I . . . '

'Let her come.' Con spoke in a distant voice. 'She's the boy's mother. We're in this together.' He reached for her with a trembling arm.

'But Sir, it's not. . . the water, you know.'

'She's strong enough,' Con allowed his chin to rise. 'We both are. We're in this together, aren't we, darling?' He tugged gently on her arm and together they made a move towards the door.

After a few steps Maya stopped and took a shuddering breath. Turning back, she beckoned the nurse with a hand

8

which wouldn't quite straighten from its former claw-like grasp of the book. When she opened her mouth to speak, words at first refused to emerge. But she tried again and eventually shuffled the words on her lips until she could get them organised. 'Will you give this to my daughters to look after, please?'

The nurse nodded and came forward. She carried Joe's journal like a crown back to the twins. Placing her cup on the chair next to her, Daisy accepted the book. Lola unravelled the scarf from her neck and offered it in her two hands to Daisy, like an open shawl for a baby. Daisy placed the book in the folds of the shawl and wrapped it tightly. With the book on Daisy's lap, both girls laid a hand on it. Maya felt her mouth practising the shape of a smile, aimed at her daughters. Turning her head stiffly to face forward again, she shuffled her feet a few more steps through the doorway. Con resumed his hold of her arm.

It was cold in the pale-painted lobby. Con and Maya waited before an internal window while the officer entered the room behind it. A white-sheeted figure lay on a bed, the face covered. Maya and Con grasped each other's hands. Maya could see that Con's jaw was clenched as tightly as hers and she made an effort to loosen her muscles. They should be smiling, she and Con. When they uncovered his face, Joe would want to see his parents smiling. An attendant stood on Maya's other side, perhaps ready to catch her if she fainted.

Pause, breathe. She focussed on Con, who had turned to her. She delved into him with her eyes. The moment stretched. *Do you trust me? I trust you.* Their favourite line from a film back in the eighties. Then they both returned their searching gazes to the window.

'Ready?' asked the attendant at Maya's side. Maya replied yes as firmly as she could. The attendant nodded at the officer behind the glass, who folded the sheet back with touching courtesy.

He'd been right about the distortion from the water but it wasn't too bad, not really. He was still no more than a boy. Someone had brushed his lightish hair. His beard was so much thicker than when Maya had seen it on their last video call and the person must have brushed that too – it could never have come out of the water that neat. Maya considered the poignancy of the hairdresser's job – or whomever had to perform that task. The boy's eyes were closed of course. Something swayed beside Maya, while her feet had taken root in the tiled floor. The swaying thing was like a tree in a gale: indeed, a wind seemed to be blowing down the corridor towards them. She felt hair lifting from her neck. But when she looked up she saw that the swaying tree on her right – sighing along with the wind in its branches – was in fact her husband. It was only Con, the breath from his lungs rising to a musical note of pain.

2

Maya

Melbourne, November 2014

Jet lag had kept Maya awake most of the night. Along with thinking, sobbing, pacing. She crept into bed just as the sky started to lighten. Con was lying on his side, the sheet tucked tightly under his chin as well as outlining his curved back, as though stitched in. Tentatively, she covered herself with the remaining edge of sheet and lay ramrod straight on the opposite side, her back to his. She couldn't remember falling asleep, but when she woke it was with sunlight blazing into her eyes through a gap in the curtains. Brain-fuddled and confused about where she was. Before the memory hit. *Slap*, in the middle of her forehead. The inside of her head felt like a rocking boat. *No, no, no. That poor boy.*

Tentatively touching the floor with her feet she pressed them harder into the soft rug beside the bed. Upright, she held onto furniture as she padded the apartment, finding it empty. *Relief.* To be alone, to continue collecting her thoughts. They must have gone out for breakfast. She searched the polished desk and tables but couldn't find a note. Never mind. *Breathe.* She wouldn't tell Con and the girls her plan today, nor probably tomorrow. It was so rare that the four of them got the chance to spend so much time together. She must try, despite their recent shock and sadness, to make the experience a good one. *Especially because of what I've decided.* A hollow pit opened inside her. How would she – what would she say? She glanced towards Joe's journal, lying on Con's bedside table. Pictured her husband holding the pages gingerly in his hands as he turned them – he'd refused to even look at their boy's precious book the day before. Like her, he would probably have appreciated some thinking time alone. *Oh, Con.*

She wandered through the three rooms of the apartment looking for evidence of her family. Lola's blue, flowered scarf – the one she'd wrapped Joe's journal in the day before, lay floatily along the back of a cream sofa. Daisy's embroidered dress lay discarded on the floor of the girls' bedroom. An open makeup bag spilled its contents onto the glass surface of their dressing table. A gnawing ache nibbled at her insides. *Her girls.* Back in hers and Con's bedroom she picked up Con's linen jacket and held the inside of it to her nose, trying not to think how he'd manage without her. He would have to. She felt iron around her chest. But he needn't know for a few days. Her stomach rumbled but she'd try and wait until her family returned before considering breakfast, or lunch – or perhaps it was even dinnertime by now. Time felt suspended.

A bath would help relax her. She padded along a short corridor and collected a large, fluffy towel from a slatted shelf. Before climbing into the wide bath which she'd filled with hot water and scented bubbles, she stood naked in front of the tall mirror in the bathroom. *Here I am.* Inhale, exhale. *This is me. Don't look away, however hard it is.* This was the woman who'd given birth to Joe. Her last baby. A medium-height, soft-bodied woman verging on overweight watched her from the other side of the glass. The woman's stomach sagged from

12

four births, forming a fold over her pubic mound. The hair down there was greying. Her thighs squashed together at the top and her breasts were empty and loose. She turned and scrutinised her heavy, swaying bottom. It was as if all the separate parts of her were readying themselves to let go. A line from a Disney song drifted through her mind, similar to something Joe had written in his journal – let them go. Her and Con. *His parents.*

Drawing in breath, she continued the inspection. The woman in the mirror had impeccable, professionally-coloured hair and expensively-moisturised skin. The parts of her that were visible to the outer world were carefully maintained.

Several of Maya's friends had been *under the knife* for one adjustment or another but she'd always felt the natural deconstruction of a woman's anatomy could be compensated for by a wise choice of clothing. Or simply accepted as part of life. She would never need to consider the opinion of another man, and Con seemed happy with her the way she was, so what did it matter? She looked at herself one more time. The woman in the mirror looked back at her with the same objective eye. Gouged underneath by hollows of sadness.

She climbed into the bath, for the first time in years neglecting to tuck a shower cap over her hair. Her inaugural renegade act! Sank beneath the hot water, allowing her mind to drift as loosely as her uncovered hair. She closed her eyes, steam shifting over her face. The encompassing warmth reminded her of the time she and Con had visited Joe in Iceland, *when he'd still wanted to see us*, and how she had sunk under the warm, steamy water of the Blue Lagoon. She longed for that again, for the three of them to be happy together. But that wasn't going to happen. She had to stop pretending that life could be all right again without her doing anything to make it so.

Snatches of Joe's words from the journal floated through her mind. *I hung my hammock between two of the trees and there you have it – I'm all set up. Home Sweet Home.* Maya

13

floated in the water of the deep bath and imagined herself gently rocking in a hammock. *Beauty to live for, beauty to die for.* And now he was gone.

Both of her sons had cut themselves off from the family. Could she – by following their examples, find out who she really was? Joe had said in his journal that he wanted her to fly. Perhaps it had in truth been a gift to her... but in accepting his gift she'd need to disentangle herself from the structure of her life with Con and separate herself from Daisy and Lola, too. She didn't know if she could bear to do that.

3

Joe's journal

I'm heading for Australia! This trip is much more exciting than the European trip my parents paid for. Then I stayed in hostels and ate in cafes and it was all carefully planned. But I felt as if I'd only had a taste of the kind of life I wanted. And when it finished my parents expected me to fit in with their plans.

But I'm not going to university.

I want to travel raw. In the words of Everett Ruess I want to follow my fortune to other lands. Adventure is for the adventurous.

I'm looking forward to just having nothing.

Seeing what I really need to live on.

Finding out what I'm actually made of. I need to cut the parents' voices out of my head.

Joe

4

Maya

Melbourne, November 2014

From a distance, Maya watched Con – an arm slung around each of his daughters' shoulders – move towards the barrier beyond which she couldn't go.   Daisy's hair, always a little untidy, hung down her back. It was tucked in at the neck by her father's arm. Lola's swung free in its short bob. Maya kept seeing them as little girls again and wanted to fuss around with a hairbrush and ask them if they'd had enough to eat. But they were grownups now and she had to let them go. Stripped of children, she needed to discover who she herself was.

Watching him go through the barrier, having ushered their daughters in front of him, the back of Con's neck was exposed by his collarless linen shirt. It was the one he'd worn on the outward journey but now paired with jeans instead of his linen suit.   The angry red boil that had appeared just below his back hairline was visible even from this retreating distance. She thought it might be painful when he leaned his head against the seat during the long flight home. *My love.* This felt like more than a temporary goodbye. *A ripping apart.* Already her insides ached.

'Please don't do this,' Con had begged. '*Please.* Please?'

The way his mouth had fallen open. His skin drained of colour. 'How can you leave me after everything we've been through?'

In bed. She stroked his hair as he pressed his face into her breasts. As he sobbed and coughed. Left smears of mucus on her skin. 'Shh, hush now. Shh, it'll be all right.'

Her own eyes burned, tearless. She held herself as separate as she could. 'Shh.'

Soothed him to sleep as she had overwrought toddlers in the past. Slipped out of bed and fitted herself into a chair on the balcony, knees drawn up to her chin, a soft blanket pulled tightly around her. Inexplicably, the chair rattled and it took a while to understand that it was caused by her trembling.

Con had insisted on transferring money into Maya's account to *keep her going* for a few months, after which he seemed convinced she'd come home. She didn't know whether she'd be returning home that soon (or after that long!) or not. Completely unleashed from her normal expectations of life and undergoing such a rapidly fluctuating series of emotions, she couldn't keep up with herself. She hoped to touch as little of the money as possible – after all, it had been Joe's aim to live without and she wanted to honour that. She just needed to work out how to start.

———

Back in the hotel room she cried for ages. Completely over-the-top howled. Midway through there was a timid knock on the door. She held herself rigid until she heard the voice of that sweet housekeeper asking if 'Madam' was all right. She managed to choke out an affirmative reply. At a second knock and another enquiry she snapped that she wished to be left alone. She held in the last of the sobs until the footsteps

18

retreated and released them in a final bout of howls. It was a spectacularly messy torrent. After it was finished she ran a bath. Snot and tears ran down her face into the water but it was easier that way than using up the hotel's supply of toilet paper and having to ask for more. For the second time.

It was Con and the girls she was crying for. Something had been severed by asking them to leave her behind. She'd never again be a reliable mum, an always-available wife. *That nice Mrs Galen-who-worked-at-the-doctor's.* Even if she did return and resume her job (the surgery had agreed to hold her position open for three months) she might not be considered truly reliable again. That had been important to her. In the future, if she went back, Con might always wonder whether or not his dinner would be on the table when he got home from the office. The girls might ring home and ask whether Mum was there rather than by default begin the conversation with their complacent *Hi, Mum.* She'd liked that.

She blew her nose one more time into the water and pulled the plug. Stood up and washed her hair under the shower and got out of the bath thinking of herself as a different Maya Galen now. An unreliable one. It was new territory.

Con had paid for the hotel room for one more night but Maya was aware her husband had spoken to the hotel manager when he settled the family's bill and that the manager had tacitly agreed not to let the room to another guest for now. In the spirit of going with the flow of her emotions she would wait until the following morning before deciding whether to check out or not. In the bedroom she lowered herself to the floor wrapped in her favourite fluffy towel, her short hair dripping jewels of water onto her freckled shoulders. She pulled the rucksack towards her and sat with it between her knees, cradling it for a moment. Touching it with her nose, she breathed its fresh, new smell. Purpose, outdoors and determination. A reason to go on. Pulling out the contents, looking through them with a sharper eye than when she'd packed it, she felt as if she was preparing for a new role in the village Amateur Dramatic Society of which she was an enthusiastic member. *She would miss so many rehearsals. They would have to find a new Wicked Stepmother for the Christmas production.*

She weighed cloth items in her hands. Two t-shirts – no three, they were only lightweight. Summer had just begun in Australia, the best time to be starting out, she supposed – although it necessitated several tubes of sun cream. Two pairs of lightweight calico trousers, the kind with all the pockets. A pair of (long) shorts; the young woman in the shop had suggested she might regret not taking a pair so Maya acquiesced. She rolled the beige cotton tightly and packed it into the bottom of the bag. Seven pairs of knickers and two stretchy cotton bras. Three sleeveless vests, chicken-wings be damned. She could feel the fat of her middle-aged belly resting on the tops of her thighs as she leaned forward. Hmm. Maybe all the walking would help her lose weight.

She'd been told she'd need a warm garment for the evenings and since she was planning on sleeping outdoors she'd need to add thick socks and a decent sleeping bag to her inventory. She ought also to have bought walking boots, but couldn't bear having her feet tightly laced up during warm weather. Instead she'd compromised with the pair of strong walking sandals recommended by the shop assistant.

Then there were the utility items. Dried food, basic cooking equipment and eating implements, all on a lightweight, miniature scale. An Australian phone loaded with credit, reading glasses, toiletries and first-aid necessities. A box of matches. A nylon hammock with a zip. A thin foam mat and a tarpaulin and bungee cords. She scrambled to her feet, still wrapped in the fluffy towel, not enough spirit to attempt lifting it right now. A different kind of weight from that of the rucksack hit her.

What the hell do I think I'm doing? Planning to sleep on the ground, under a tarp. In the Bush. At my age. Perhaps she really had gone mad.

5

Joe's journal

AUGUST 2012

TASMANIA is an island of wild and beautiful landscapes. You can see the sketches and maps I've made as well as the photographs I intend to stick in (that's what the currently blank pages are for - I need to wait until I can get some printed).

After I arrived in Devonport I asked around about temporary work as I was running low on cash. I got a lift to Hobart with an English guy who had a shaved head and a Union flag tattooed behind his left ear. I was a bit nervous but he turned out to be perfectly friendly. He's lived on the island for twenty years and he took me to a house off the main road where an elderly woman lives alone. The bushland reaches right up to the back of her property and she asked me to do some ground-clearing by the fence and build a new run for her chickens. My dad would be surprised to see me tackling such physical work - I only ever liked drawing or reading when I was at home. I feel a bit sad now, for all the times he asked me to help in the garden. Maybe I just felt a bit awkward being around him - it was like he wanted something from me and I didn't know what it was.

Jeannie, the old woman here, allowed me to pitch camp on her land for a few days and she fed me and let me use her kitchen and bathroom. She also gave me a small wage, enough to buy provisions.

I've moved on again now and I'm living on a beach. I've got this brilliant spot in a patch of scrubland, in the middle of a copse of trees. I just needed to hang my hammock between two of the trees and there you have it - I'm all set up. Home Sweet Home. There are so many different animals here. At night, all the bush creatures emerge from their hiding places. Possums, Tassie Devils. Kookaburras - or Monkey Birds, as I like to call them. There are many, many other birds besides. They each have their own song. Some are loud, some are quiet. Some are sad and some are angry. That's how they sound to me. I often lie in my hammock and wonder what they think of me.

There are millions of ants - muttering away to themselves in a tongue that has no sound but if you listen hard enough you can hear it anyway. The ants describe the path of their journey so that the following ants don't get lost. Oh yeah, and even more birds, many different types perching on their branches all around my hammock. They sit in groups, staring down at me as I sing my own songs, strumming my guitar. Sometimes they join in. ☺

Then there's the spiders. They sit and wait in their webs as the sun rises and sets. The spiders rarely go hungry (as I sometimes do) on such a fly-ridden continent as this. I sing my own little song to them - The flies, the flies, they live or die.

In the choppy waters of the great Oyster Bay, just down

22

the hill from here to the west, I watch seals swimming. Huge seals, bigger than Sumo Wrestlers! I've also seen stingrays wider than the span of a big man's arms, they are effing unbelievable! You can sit there and watch those rays gliding beneath the surface of water which is bluer than the bluest sky I ever saw. I go down there and pick mussels from the coral-coloured rocks. I stand and look out over the bay. I spent a whole day fishing, I never caught anything though.

Back in the bush, up on Paradise Hill, I watch the sun setting directly above the bay. I see the sky come alive with violent colour: purple, pink, gold. Beauty to live for, beauty to die for. If I descend the hill on the eastwards side I emerge from the wonderful wall of trees that protects my paradise from view. To the South I can see the Three Hazards.

That's what I call the three peaks. The people who once knew their real names have been gone too long gone to reveal their secret.

Just down the road from the peaks are the holiday homes but no guest from there ever comes close to the real paradise, my Paradise, up here on my hill. I've been living here for over thirty days and nights, and only one other human being has set foot here during that time to my knowledge. He's a fellow-vagabond who I met on the road. He has a job washing dishes in town and I might have to join him soon, earn some money to buy some basic supplies.

6

Maya

Melbourne, November 2014

Maya checked out of the hotel the next morning – it had to
be now or she might chicken out of her proposed adventure.
She left her linen dress and the smart sandals she'd been
wearing when she arrived in Australia, along with a few items
she'd deemed too heavy to carry – including a very expensive
handbag – in the room with a note for the kind housekeeper.
The one she'd snapped at. She was probably about the same
size and age as her.

Outside on the forecourt Maya wilted under the weight of
the rucksack. *Oh good Lord!* How was she going to manage
this? Because of the money in her bank account, to all intents
and purposes what she was doing was a game – true to a
remark Con had made. She could only prove she was serious
with direct action. She thought about Joe, taking his first
steps into an unknown future.

But where on earth to begin? What should she do – just
take off down the road and keep walking? With huge effort

she hitched the rucksack higher up her shoulders. It was too heavy to waste any strength just standing about. She placed one foot in front of the other and carried on, feeling back-heavy and unstable. Stopping and turning she saw that she'd reached the end of the hotel's drive and was now teetering on a broad pavement. *Don't stand still too long.* In full sunlight she negotiated a wavering trajectory between far more lightweight pedestrians than herself as well as other, more seasoned backpackers. Summer was in its early stages and the chairs and tables at the street-side cafes were mostly full already. She plotted her way between obstacles both animate and fixed, along the length of one, two, three, four, five seemingly endless blocks; rocking on her feet at the crossings and surging over with the amassed tide of pedestrians when the traffic paused. The rucksack's waist-strap cut into the soft flesh of her waist. It felt as if forceful fingers were digging into her shoulders. Blood pounded in her head and shock jarred through her feet and ankle bones despite the thickness of her walking sandals' soles. Joe had been an undernourished-looking eighteen-year-old when he set out on his journey. How had he coped with carrying his enormous rucksack? *Go on Maya, if Joe could do it, you can too.* It felt like carrying his cross for him. One, two, three, four, five more blocks. At a street corner, which opened out onto a market square, she felt sweat saturate her scalp and run down her back. The new sandals already rubbed the backs of her heels. *What on earth am I doing?* How long would it take to walk out of Melbourne and was such an undertaking even possible? She would have to sit down and study the street map. And what would she do when she reached those far-off imagined outskirts of the city. *Put up my hammock and go to sleep.*

On the hotel balcony Con had unpacked the brand-new zip-up hammock for her and attempted to demonstrate the way she'd need to erect it between two sturdy trees. He harked back to his late-teenage years when he'd gone on a (in his words) 'wild' camping trip with his mates. Her mind soon drifted to blankness with the tedium of his explanation. Like all the times in the past when she'd listened to his droned instructions for flat-pack furniture – while she'd already worked it out and half-assembled the item before he stopped to draw breath. Poor Con.

Reaching the other side of the apparently ever-widening square, lights flashed at the corners of her eyes. Her skin prickled. Taking another step she realised how dizzy she felt. She grasped the back of an occupied pavement chair to stay upright, swaying under the weight of the bag. Noticed the young man with red-gold hair who was sitting on the chair turning around to stare at her, his mouth half-open. Her blurring eyesight picked out in striking detail the crumbs on his bottom lip. 'Hey,' she heard him say as if from far away. 'Are you okay?'

Her mouth felt too dry to speak and she swallowed a few times. 'Not sure, I . . . ' Then blackness tunnelled her vision and contracted until there were only pinpoints of light left. She felt herself going.

'Whoa, there.' A pair of arms caught her just as she hit the floor. When she could see properly again she was lying on the ground with her head resting on her rucksack. A girl (who smelled strongly of sweat) held a bottle of water to her lips.

'Can you drink?'

Someone behind supported the back of her neck and helped raise her head towards the bottle. The gold-haired boy was crouching to one side of her, looking concerned. The scents of these young humans, pungent and oppressive, brought Maya's senses back into focus. The kids were similar ages to her children. Sadness welled in her chest but she forced it down. 'Thank you, thanks very much.' She swallowed a mouthful of water. They were kind, their mothers must have brought them up well. Tears pushed behind her eyes again. A rush of heat went to her cheeks. She was the same age as their mothers, they shouldn't be looking after her – she should be looking after them. 'I'll be fine now, thank you. If you'll help me get up?' She was glad they'd managed to extract her arms from the rucksack because she never would have been able to get to a standing position whilst carrying it.

'Uh-oh, steady on now.' The girl smiled, still holding the bottle of water close to Maya's face. 'How about another sip or two of this first? You look dehydrated.' Maya struggled back through hazy memories of relentless tramping and realised she hadn't had a drink for what must have been a few hours, since she'd left her hotel room. She was supposed to have bought one of those water carriers that fitted onto your rucksack and you sucked water through a tube. Con had made her promise she would get one after going through her inventory the night before he left. 'I worry about you, Maya. I don't think you've thought this through – of course you haven't, you haven't had time. It's been, what...' She'd stopped him there. 'But you'll never manage,' he'd added after she removed her finger from his lips. 'I'm sorry darling, but it's true. *You won't manage.*' She'd kissed away his tears then. Now she swallowed most of the bottle of water. 'I'll replace that for you,' she promised the girl. She lifted a shaking hand and pressed it to her damp lips. Saw the watery imprint of her lips on her the back of her hand before the shape evaporated in the sun. It had become a lot hotter since she left the hotel. She thought of the kisses she'd laid on her daughters' cheeks – only the day before.

'Don't be daft,' said the girl. 'If one traveller can't help out another, what's the world coming to, eh?' She smiled. Maya's vision sharpened and she noticed the open pores on the girl's sweat-sheened skin, the blackheads on her nose. All the skin treatments and potions her children had filled their bathroom cabinets with – how she'd teased Joe about this when he set off on his travels. 'How will you manage without your Acne cream?' The water swilled unpleasantly in her stomach. She'd acted towards Joe exactly the way Con had

28

acted towards her. Joe must have been holding his tongue, she realised. Courteous, like the young people helping her now.

'Well, thank you again. I feel such a fool, do you think you could help me up now?'

'Sure we can. Aiden, Ned, give us a hand, will ya lads?'

'Of course,' said the light-haired boy. 'What's your name, by the way?'

'Maya.' It was a relief to be on her feet. The lurch of dizziness passed quickly. *I must buy some more water.* 'How about you three? Well, I've learned already that your name's Aiden, and yours,' she turned to tall black man who had been supporting her shoulders, 'must be Ned.' He had short twists of hair sticking out all over his head. Maya wiped her hand on the leg of her trousers and offered it to each of them in turn.

'Jodie.' The young woman surprised Maya with a brackish-scented hug. Maya breathed out. 'Ya gave us a shock there mate,' said Jodie. 'Collapsing like that. But I'm guessing you're dehydrated, it happens easily – and quickly – in this heat.'

Maya smiled. 'You can't imagine the number of times I've said that to my children, and look at me. I feel such a fool!'

'Ah, well. You only learn by experience,' Ned smiled. 'Feelin' better? Stay and have some food with us, we were just beginning to eat.'

'Yeah, do, that'd be great,' echoed Jodie and Aiden. 'You can tell us where you're off to next.' Aiden pulled a seat out for Maya and propped her rucksack next to it. 'We might be able to help you, y'know, by sharing info and suchlike. Where've you been so far, Maya?'

Ned passed her a bowl of olives. She took one and popped it on her tongue. It tasted salty and brought a rush of saliva to her mouth. Jodie looked doubtfully at Maya's brand new rucksack and glanced over her pristine t-shirt and crisp trousers. Maya felt suddenly as though it was she who was

29

young, and they older. She could see what they were all thinking and it was what she was thinking herself, *should this woman be out on her own?*

'Okay, you got me,' she felt a laugh bubbling up. 'It's all brand new. I'm brand new to this. I've been nowhere yet and I have no idea where I'm going, either.' The laugh erupted from her mouth and they all joined in.

7

Maya

Melbourne, November 2014

Jodie held the door open while Maya shuffled inside, angling herself so she could get the rucksack – which had the sleeping bag fastened on top – into the room. Glancing around, she saw that the huge room divided into three distinct areas. There were two further doors besides the one she and Jodie had just entered through. A young man walked out of one of the other doors and she heard a toilet flushing – so that was a bathroom. Squinting at the last door across the room she thought she could make out the same symbol on its metal plaque. *Only two bathrooms.* The boy who'd come out swung himself up a ladder onto an upper bed and flopped onto his back, inserting earphones beneath his Beanie hat. He shuffled his hands about on the bed beside him and lifted an iPad up in front of his face.

Maya gulped at the sight of the twelve metal bunks. Some were occupied, either by a person, asleep or awake – reading or tapping at a laptop or tablet – or reserved by a rucksack or a pile of clothes. Other beds were empty apart from a rolled-up quilt and a single pillow placed next to a folded pile of white bedding. The bunks were arranged in clusters of four.

'We're over here.' Jodie guided Maya across the room with a hand on the back of her rucksack. 'In our own little enclave. It's as if you were meant to be joining us. Aiden sleeps on the top bunk here, and Ned's on the one below him. Oh look, he's left his hat here – he thought he must have lost it when we were out.' She picked up the cotton beanie and paused, draping it over the palm of her hand. Dropping it back on Ned's bed she continued, gesturing to the left. 'I'm on this bottom bunk but I'd be happy to move up and let you have this one. It might be easier for you – we can swap the bedding over.'

Maya fought panic. She hadn't slept in a room with anyone other than Con for years, not since Joe was a baby. Con often complained that she snored. Worse, what if she farted during the night? She was feeling bloated right now. And how would she cope with the sounds and night-time habits of so many other sleepers? And would there be a window open? She instinctively sought fresh air and saw that the huge windows along the side of the room, against which the heads of their bunks were set, were divided into small sections. Each opened separately. One opening was near the top bunk Jodie had indicated. But surely Maya would never manage to negotiate the narrow-runged metal ladder down to the floor and find her way across the room to one of the two bathrooms – and back – at least once or twice during the night? However, she was determined to be treated the same as everyone else, otherwise what would be the point of doing this? She heard herself demurring Jodie's kind offer. 'I don't want to put you to any trouble, I'll be fine on the top bunk, but thanks for the offer anyway.'

What have I done? She'd disturb everybody if she slipped and fell off the ladder. She saw Jodie's mouth open as if to protest but quickly close again. Jodie's freckled face seemed

32

to shutter. She shrugged off her long-sleeved shirt, baring more freckles on her shoulders, along with an orange vest that clashed with her hair. Her armpits sprouted gingery growth. Maya's neck grew hot and she looked down at her feet. Jodie lowered herself into the bottom bunk, unlaced her boots and kicked them off, then leaned back against a propped-up pillow with a small grunt. She pulled a phone out of her purse and started scrolling down the screen, keeping her eyes on it. 'Let me know if you need anything, okay? Aiden and Ned'll be back from shopping soon.'

Maya eased herself out from the grasp of the rucksack, which felt full of bricks. It slid down her back and crashed heavily onto the floor. Jodie had her earphones in by now. Maya got the feeling she needed a break from babysitting this mother-aged person. Jodie had shut off, like Maya's grown-up kids did when they couldn't *take any more of this shit.*

She squinted at the top bunk. It wavered above her. Stretching her arms, she managed to pull down the rolled quilt and the white cotton bedding and drop them on the floor. Moving away so as not to disturb Jodie she struggled to fit the quilt inside the cover. Despite a lifetime of such chores she messed up the task, at first inserting it wide-side in so that it bunched up in the middle of the cover. A woman, not young but not as old as Maya herself, sitting cross-legged on a lower bunk across the room gave her a wry smile before returning her attention to her book. *I wanted to be on my own*, thought Maya, *and so I am.* No Con to rescue her now. An eclectic mix of emotions rushed forward like a tide and retreated, leaving her empty. At least she had a focus. She folded the now made-up quilt and left it on the floor before tackling the pillow, which gave her less trouble. When that was done she unstrapped her sandals and placed them neatly under the bed, at the foot end. Jodie seemed completely engrossed in something on her phone now and Maya was glad the girl didn't appear to be watching while she tackled the ladder in a most ungainly manner. If only she'd

33

agreed to join the other women from the surgery at their weekly Zumba sessions. *If I'm this out of breath from climbing onto a bunk-bed what'll I be like after my first proper day of walking?!* Maya set about tucking the sheet around the edges of the mattress, lifting her knees and elbows alternately so she could pull it smooth. Then she had her first practise descent of the ladder to collect the pillow from the floor, swinging it up onto the bunk followed by her cotton tote bag which she pulled out of the rucksack.

She ought to visit the bathroom before getting herself settled. She wrinkled her nose at the splashes of urine on the toilet seat, wiping them off carefully with a sheet of toilet paper – trying not to gag. Now she knew how the cleaner at her home must have felt when she'd had to clean the growing boys' bathroom. Picking her way carefully back over the tiled floor between a pair of boots and someone's dropped clothes she bundled the quilt determinedly under her arm and tackled the ladder again. The quilt wrestled against her one-armed embrace and spilled out behind her. Reaching the top, she dragged the rest of it up. She heard a chuckle from across the room but chose to ignore it. She lay for a while on her stomach, elbows digging into the thin mattress, her chin propped in her hands as she gazed out of the window. Soon, though, her eyelids persisted in drooping – however hard she tried to keep them open – so she gave up and lay back on the pillow. She'd earned a rest. Waves of fatigue washed over her and she drifted on the tide, her eyes half-open.

From the window behind the bunk she'd seen the view of rooftops and eucalyptus trees and a public garden opposite. She could hear the sound of traffic from the main road two streets away. An unexpected shaft of joy entered her heart. This might be the first time in her life that she'd experienced any kind of freedom. Now nobody was there to call to her, asking *where's this?* Or, *what time is that at?* Or, *have you seen my shoes?* Nobody was expecting their dinner. She understood for the first time what Joe had been aiming for

34

most of his life.   It started when he began drawing complicated maps as a small child and insisted that those were the places he would travel to. She and Con had done their best to persuade him to go university – *you're a bright boy... waste of talent... complete your studies first, decide on a career – then take a year off...* but none of it had persuaded (or forced) him off his chosen path. A tingle of anticipation started in her fingertips and she tapped them softly on her chest as she lay on the bed. She'd always wondered where Joe's adventurousness came from, but now she wondered whether it had lain dormant in herself all along.

8

Maya

Late November 2014

Email from: Maya_Lifeforce@dmail.com
 To: Daisy Galen
 Subject: your vagabond mother

So, Daisy my girl, how are you? Write back and tell me all your news – your last email was so short I felt we'd been cut off mid-conversation... I'm sorry you've split up with your boyfriend, you must be feeling hurt and sad. But now that it's happened I can tell you I never thought he was good enough for you – and it's not just me as a mum saying that, it's true! He cheated on you, Daisy, and you don't deserve that.

You haven't lost your mum, honestly. I know it's hard to accept the different person I seem to have become since all this happened but I need you to, Daisy, and perhaps you need to as well, for your own sake. It's easy to get trapped into a single way of thinking.

Do you realise this is the first email address I've ever had of my own? It's always been Maya & Con at whatever, before. But this is *me* now. Self-discovery can never come too late and I'm only just beginning.

I do miss you all.

But I've got to admit I'm having an adventure – me – at my time of life! My hip-bones are bruised and battered from riding in the back of a pick-up truck, would you believe it? I ask myself all the time if these things are really happening to me. I had to do that thing I've seen on the movies so many times, when you chuck your bag up into the back of the truck – all right, I'll admit it – I did need some help to shove my rucksack over the edge – I can still barely carry it without collapsing under the weight – and I also needed some help to swing myself up after the bag. If I'm going to be honest it was a scrabble rather than a swing. My new friends Aiden and Ned were the ones behind me, pushing me up. I landed rather heavily in the dusty bottom of the flat bed and had to suck in my cheeks – yeah, both sets of cheeks (LOL) really hard – so as not to show the pain. Good job I've got some fat on my behind. But the strange thing is, I love this way of travelling! I can see why our Joe became addicted to it. ...

So, anyway. It was Jodie who got to ride in the front of the truck with the driver because she was the one he really stopped for. She's about your age and like you she's very pretty. The rest of us had more-or-less hidden behind a clump of bushes to give ourselves a chance of catching a lift for four and we had to wait a while for the right vehicle. Jodie didn't rush when she opened the door of the truck, she climbed in slowly – giving the rest of us time to get in the back. The truck was empty apart from a couple of sacks with a few kibbles of animal feed left in them so we weren't hurting anyone. And the driver wasn't all that bothered because he got Jodie's company – the reason he'd stopped.

Is it wrong, in the circumstances, to say I feel happier than I have done in years? Since Joe left home I suppose. The

38

Cottages felt so empty without you all and so huge. Too huge for your dad and me. If we'd done something adventurous like this together – well… but you know your dad – he enjoys his comforts too much. I would have said I did until I tried this different way of – not holidaying, exactly – it's a completely different way of life. A life in which I can go anywhere I want. The youngsters are teaching me how to live without much money, something I haven't had to think about since my mum was always telling us we could never afford anything when I was a child. Now I can't imagine going back to live in The Cottages. Sitting on our plush sofa in the middle of our vast living room. All by myself, mostly. Oh, Daisy. I'm sorry but… It's the endless rounds of dinner parties with the same people in different dining-conservatories. All painted in a slightly lighter or a slightly darker shade of what – let's face it – looks very much like Magnolia. Though the paint is ridiculously expensive and the colour has an exclusive-sounding name. How can I go back to that? I can't.

Not yet, anyway.

That first night at the hostel, the boys went off to buy some food and offered to cook our evening meal.

Reggae music played in the kitchen when we went down. A lovely, warm feeling filled me while we were all eating a meal together. There were not only us four (see how I feel I belong with my new friends already?) but several other hostellers as well, because we had so much food to share. I was glad to have been a part of providing such a feast even though I didn't cook the meal. I looked around the table at the laughing, chattering faces and it reminded me of when you were all small and I felt I had a purpose. But funnily enough I didn't feel like a mother to the group at the hostel, and they didn't seem to think of me as such even though I'm much older than them. There was a feeling of equality such as I don't think I've experienced anywhere else. Maybe it's an equality of purpose. Everybody here's *on the road*. A couple of people asked me why I'd decided to embark on such an

39

adventure (they were careful not to say *at your age*) but nobody probed too deeply. I'm not ready to communicate our family story yet, anyway. I simply mumbled something about if I didn't do it now, I was never going to, was I?

I never would have thought I was going to spend an indefinite period of time apart from your dad you know, Daisy. But it seems to have happened.

Okay, so I've got to go now as we're going to try and cover a bit more ground before it gets dark. I'll send this one off to you while I've got Wi-Fi, Daisy my darling, and write a bit more to you next time we stop.

Love you,
Mum xxxxxxxx

Email from: Maya_Lifeforce@dmail.com
To: Daisy Galen
Subject: your vagabond mother (again)

Hi again, love. I won't be able to send this one tonight but I just want to get it down on my tablet so I can send it as soon as I have Wi-Fi again. You can be the first to know – this is my VERY FIRST night in the hammock! When I met them, Aiden and Ned and Jodie – they asked me where I was travelling to and all that, but they didn't realise at the beginning that I'm planning to live rough and sleep out in the open. They imagined I'd be staying in hotels, or at least in hostels. So they insisted I stay at their hostel in Melbourne for a few nights while I became acclimatised to my new life. We took a train to a suburb of Melbourne from where I spent a day walking with the three of them. They wanted to see how I got on before they left me to my own devices. That was kind of them, wasn't it? It turned out to be a good thing because I nearly fainted again in the afternoon and Jodie had to remind me to drink water! (I've now got one of those water carriers with the drinking tube that your dad wanted me to buy before I started.) My feet were already covered in blisters. Aiden gave me his spare pair of walking socks – they were well washed, thank goodness. I insisted on giving him money for them though he was reluctant to take it. Aiden's a sweet boy. I suppose of all my new friends he's the one who reminds me most of our Joe. We've chatted a bit about his mum. He obviously loves her and he comes from a secure family.

Jodie is different, though. She comes from a difficult background and she was sleeping on the street by the time she was fourteen, the poor girl. Aiden's travelling to see a bit of the world in a secondment from his job but Jodie took off to escape – some kind of abuse I reckon. She doesn't like to talk about it. But she said she has no plans to return to the UK even when her Visa runs out. I do worry about her.

Ned seems a happy-go-lucky sort of lad. He also keeps his background a bit of a secret (let's face it, there's a lot I haven't told them about why I'm doing this either) but from what I've managed to gather he comes from the UK too.

Now for my 'homework'. I've been learning from the kids about how to live without money. Ned especially because he's lived on the streets in more than one country. He gave me a pamphlet that he's written, or rather we went to a local library to photocopy his because there aren't many of them about. Here are a couple of tips for keeping yourself fed (probably best not to mention this to Lola but I know you'll find it amusing, darling):

- Go to fooderies where people put their trays into racks after eating. You have to raid the trash racks before the staff clear them away. They call this table diving. (Ned made me rescue half a Panini this way to prove I could do it. I ate it and it was all fine, by the way.)

- Check for undamaged food in street bins – especially food still in its packet – someone may have only eaten one sandwich from a pack of two, for example.

41

I can't imagine raiding bins at the moment but Ned says I may need to one day. Just imagine if I went back to Navengore and started fishing about in the bin outside the chip shop! Hahaha! Imagine what Susannah Metherington would have to say about *that*! ☺

I bet you're laughing with me, Daisy. Oops, I nearly dropped the tablet then – and this hammock's not easy to get myself in and out of, I can tell you!

Anyway.

- Dumpster diving is the most effective way to find food in the 'urban-wild'. Supermarkets throw away a lot of food every day. Isn't that appalling? I never really thought about it before. As long as I can get out of the dumpster by myself next time I'm looking forward to giving it another go.

Don't be embarrassed about your mum, will you? I'm learning new skills, *don't cha know!* Ned says if for one reason or another you can't find any food, you either need to steal from supermarkets (which of course I don't plan to do!) or buy it. I actually wish I had the courage to clear all the money out of my bank account and give it away and then throw myself on the mercy of my own resourcefulness. But I don't think I'm ready for that.

Not yet.

By the way I just want you to know how much I enjoy these email exchanges with you. Your father prefers that we speak on the phone and Lola only wants to Skype. So it makes it special that my only email correspondent is you. Take care, darling. Love you loads xxxxxxxx

---

Email from: Daisy_halfcrazy@dmail.com
To: Maya Joy Galen
Re: your vagabond mother

Hi Mum,

You are funny! Okay, I have to admit, I'm loving the new you and all your stories and I like the fact you've put the "joy" back in your name with your new email address. Perhaps there's hope for me yet, yes me – Daisy – the steady one. Maybe I'll surprise everybody one day just like you have done!

I'm sorry about being a bit clipped with you before. I think I was still in shock after the reason for our trip to Australia, as well as finding out for certain that Daniel really had been cheating on me. Thank you for your comment about him not being good enough for me, although it does remind me of how Grannie always used to tell people I was too intelligent for boys! Well you can be sure I'm not about to dumb myself down to suit anyone. Maybe one day I'll find someone who *is* good enough.

I think you're right, not telling Lola about the dumpster diving and all the other ways of getting free food. Can you imagine her face? But I'll keep those tips in mind in case I ever need them. ☺

You wanted my news, well, there's not much to tell really. I bought Tink a new bed, it's furry and cosy like a little cave. It amplifies the sound of her purring! After I found out about Daniel, I wished I could crawl into it with her so I bought myself a furry blanket for the sofa instead, which is equally as comforting.

I'm getting to know the children in Reception better now and I must admit to having a couple of favourites – I know you're not supposed to – but besides Charlotte, who I've already told you about, there's this little boy called Jacob. He's always getting into trouble with the other teachers in assembly for singing too loud, or picking his nose or, I don't know, he just seems to get on their nerves for being too – *him* – if that makes any sense? But that makes me love him more. In art lesson I asked the children to draw me a picture of where they lived and Jacob actually drew a whole town! Like a map, and though it was completely imaginary (with a chocolate factory and a water park) it did include a pretty reasonable likeness of Newark castle. I couldn't believe the detail! When I showed it to the head teacher I could tell she was impressed but she tried to hide it with a sniff because I know she doesn't like him very much – ever since he wiped his finger on her skirt after she'd told him off for picking his nose. The best thing is, Jacob wanted to give his picture to me. I asked his mother if that was okay when she came to pick him up and she said I'd be doing her a favour as she already had too many pictures on her fridge (she's got five kids). So I've hung it up in pride of place in my flat.

Anyway Mum, I've just had a text from Lola and I promised I'd ring her, so I'd better send this off now in case I don't get a chance to do it later – or more likely I'd forget. I hope it reaches you soon.

Keep vagabonding, my lovely mum. I envy you, in part. I would have loved to do something more adventurous with my life, or more meaningful, perhaps like working with the homeless or disadvantaged youth – but primary school teaching does feel important, nevertheless (I love that word!) – beginning at the beginning, if you see what I mean?

Lots of love
From Daisy xxxxxxx

9

Maya

December 2014

Email from: Maya_Lifeforce@dmail.com
  To: Daisy Galen
  Subject: continuing story

Hi Sweetheart,

I'm glad you enjoyed my previous email. I really enjoyed your story about Jacob giving you his drawing of an imaginary city, too. Where did you pin it up? Between the bookcase and the mirror on your living-room wall is my guess. Am I right? From the way you describe him, that little boy reminds me a lot of Joe at that age and I'm glad you're helping to nurture his creativity. I wish Joe's teachers hadn't tried so hard to force him into a standardised box!

I like the sound of Tink's cave and especially your furry blanket, I could do with one of those for my hammock!

I'll resume my tale where I left off, shall I?

When it was time to settle down to sleep that first night in the wild I zipped the hammock right over my face. The top section has mosquito netting, you see. I could hear Jodie snoring (she had a slight cold) and Aiden and Ned having a murmured conversation. They'd set up a fair few metres away from me but the sounds of the night seem amplified in the bush – nature does that in the absence of traffic and maybe it's also the absence of pollution. They'd helped me set up my hammock in a separate copse of trees. They would be saying goodbye to me the following day and they wanted me to get a sense of being alone. Aren't they sweet? In the morning we planned to pack our things and the three of them would catch a lift back towards Melbourne. I would be heading towards Sydney.

I had a long talk with Aiden earlier that night. I told him the truth about this journey. He gave me a hug and said I reminded him a lot of his mum and that she'd probably do a similar thing if she lost him. He also gave me a few more tips about being a *vagabond*. A great word, isn't it? I'm glad you like it too. Aiden was leaving soon to return to the UK – he works for a firm of Eco-Architects in Newcastle – that sounds interesting, doesn't it? He hopes to become freelance in the future and travel the world. Perhaps I'll bump into him again one day.

So. I'm on my own now. I never realised how much capacity for thinking I had in this brain of mine. It was all tied up in organising when you children were young and I suppose it just went a bit dormant during the past few years. Now I feel my brain expanding. The space here, the space inside my head and the space out in the whole world is huge. I'm so alone, and I don't *mind*. I never realised what a luxury thinking time is! Back in Navengore I filled my time with general busyness, I never allowed my mind to roam free.

I regret now that during your childhoods I served you with a continuous battery of activities. Whenever you mentioned you were bored, I rushed to fill the hole with a suggested action or toy or game. I believed that was my job. I'm glad I was bad at it

46

sometimes. Do what you want with your life, Daisy. You have a special gift for teaching – I know that – but it doesn't have to be close to home. There are so many places in the world where you could be of use, and expand your horizons at the same time. But I don't mean to interfere. You have a perfectly good brain of your own and are able to make decisions by yourself, of course you are.

Anyway. I'm actually proud of Joe, and I wish we hadn't dissuaded him from following his dreams. At least he escaped from our good intentions. I wish he could see me now.

Lots of love to you my dear girl,

Mum xxxxxxxx

10

Maya

Sydney, December 2014

Maya was lucky enough to get a long lift all the way to the outskirts of Sydney in a car driven by a woman named Kylie, travelling with a sullen teenage boy. The woman chatted to Maya, making eye contact in the rear view mirror. The boy, next to his mother, kept his eyes closed the whole time, earphones plugged in. Maya sensed his mother was glad of some female conversation. She was fascinated by Maya's planned adventures and kept asking if Maya was doing it for charity. The real reasons felt too complicated to explain, especially with the driver's son in the car. On the radio a reporter spoke about a Twitter campaign, encouraging people to support each other after a terrorism incident. Racism had been heightened on the streets.

'Well, hon, this is as far as I go,' said Kylie, pulling onto a side road. She stopped the car. 'You know, the spare room's vacant. How about you stay with us for a night before you set off?'

The boy got out of the passenger seat and set off up the driveway of the nearest house, without saying goodbye.

'That's really kind of you,' Maya said, unclicking her seatbelt. 'But I'm keen to begin my proper journey. If you get what I mean? I need to do this on my own. Thanks so much for the lift, though.'

'Well, if you're sure?' Kylie got out of the car and helped Maya on with her rucksack. 'It's been nice meeting you. If you walk down to the end of the road, you'll find a station. You can get a train into the centre of Sydney from there. Otherwise there's a main road further on, where you can catch another lift.'

Once in the city centre, Maya chickened out of her plan to sleep outdoors that first night on her own. It felt too frightening to begin searching for a suitable place. One more night in a hostel, she thought. Googling, she found one close by and checked into a four-bed room with only one other occupant. The receptionist informed her the young girl she'd be sharing with wasn't due to arrive until the middle of the night. Maya had planned to spend some time in the recreational area downstairs but fell asleep on the lower bunk nearest the window as soon as she'd used the toilet and washed her face. Only to be shocked awake when the light came on just after midnight. It was her roommate arriving, accompanied by a clattering suitcase. She lay, pretending to be asleep still, counting under her breath until her heartbeat slowed and her eyes sealed shut again. She woke once more during the night, remembering in a panic to plug in her phone and tablet chargers.

In the morning she was much more considerate than the midnight intruder had been. The girl slept, her face pushed into the pillow and dark hair splayed out on the white linen of the bottom bunk opposite, while Maya crept from bed to bathroom, where she luxuriated in probably her last shower

50

for a while. Breakfast had just begun when she lugged her rucksack downstairs. She chatted to a Swedish couple of about her own age while she filled herself with croissants and eggs and toast. And coffee. When the couple had left she remained at the table, sending off a quick email to Daisy while she had Wi-Fi. She sent Lola a message too, saying they would Skype or FaceTime as soon as she was able. It was time to check out of the hostel. A light breeze seemed to flutter at the back of her neck as she fitted herself back into the rucksack straps and prepared to leave. *This is it. I'm really doing it this time.*

'What are your plans today?' the receptionist asked, rifling through leaflets stacked in a display unit by the window. 'Anything I can help you with?'

'Just a general look around, I suppose,' Maya felt embarrassed to convey her intention of sleeping rough. 'I'll let my feet decide where to take me.'

'Are you staying in the city for long?'

'I haven't really decided,' Maya said. 'I'm trying to go with the flow, if you know what I mean?'

The young man with an earring in his nose laughed. 'Good idea. I tell you what, if you go over to Central Station, just across the street there, you can get a locker where you can leave your rucksack for the day. That way you can explore the city weightless.'

'Thank you,' said Maya. 'I don't know why I didn't think of that.'

Moving effortlessly, now carrying only her lightweight tote bag, Maya had no desire to read any guides or find out the 'best' thing to do in the city. She wanted simply to wander – follow her heart and let her unconscious footsteps take her where they would.

Her feet took her from Railway Square to Pitt Street Mall, where she lingered only briefly – she had no interest in

51

shopping. Already she felt like a different person from the carefully groomed Navengore mother whose idea of fun was a shopping day at Nottingham or York with the two Sues and the two Carolines. *If they could see me now!*

She took a ride on an overland train when her feet were too tired to walk any further. The train let her out onto a platform that overlooked the ferry terminus, with a view of Sydney Harbour. Maya's feet felt sorer after the sit-down on the train. The practise walks with Aiden and the others hadn't yet rendered them hardy, it seemed. She'd disembarked at Circular Quay – more square than circular – and stood gazing at the blue water. Tall, glassy buildings pierced the skyline. She allowed her mind to drift along with her footsteps and became almost absent from herself until – leaning on the railings of the Sydney Harbour Bridge – a man took her arm gently and asked if she was all right. She thanked him and said that she was, but she felt as though a part of her had broken away, caught up in the wake of a sightseeing boat that was heading off towards the Opera House.

If her daughters had been with her they would have wanted to visit the Museum of Contemporary Art and she would have enjoyed the activity with them. Above the tall buildings the sky was an opaque blue. A heat haze shimmered over the traffic. Maya walked around a small park, fingers trailing unfamiliar foliage in the path's borders. She shivered at the thought that she would need to find somewhere to sleep tonight. Perhaps the hostel near the station where she'd left her luggage. . . ? Or a hotel, even, just for one night. But no. If she didn't tackle rough-sleeping this night she might never do it. *I don't have to do anything I don't want to*, she reminded herself. But she *did* want to, that was the point. To be free of the bounds that had always constrained her was the only thing that made any sense now. In her mind she saw Jamie and the way she and Con had tried to mould and guide him. Nothing had ever seemed to work. She considered Joe's singular path – again nothing she or Con did had ever altered him, only held him back until the elastic leash they'd had on him finally snapped. Now it was time to loosen the bounds of conventionality she'd kept on herself.

She treated herself to lunch at a restaurant overlooking the harbour. In the washroom she studied her reflection in the mirror. After a month in Australia, her face was browner than she could ever remember seeing it and the freckles she'd been teased for as a child had broken out in force across the bridge of her nose and sprinkled both cheeks in the absence of a mask of makeup. Her pale auburn hair seemed to have grown two inches – but that couldn't be possible, surely? The goodbye with her family at the airport seemed so long ago now. And so did their experience at the hospital. *I'll never stop thinking about you, Joe.*

Sighing, she retied the colourful cotton scarf around her hair – the scarf was a present from Jodie – *keep your hair wrapped for a month or so and you'll never have to wash it again*, her young friend had said. Maya's present image was overlaid by an impression of the pale-skinned woman with tinted gold hair in a neat, chin-length bob, who wore a cream linen dress that stretched slightly over her well-fed stomach. The woman who had newly arrived in Australia. Maya placed a hand on her stomach. Even though she'd just eaten, she could feel that she'd lost weight.

She loosened her shirt and slipped her arms out of it so that it hung around her waist. Cupping water in her palms she washed under her arms and dried herself with paper towels. She was buttoning up her shirt again when a group of neatly-dressed women walked in. They were heavily made-up and wore sunglasses on top of their glossy hair. She noticed them eyeing her as they gathered at the mirror, applying another layer of mascara and lipstick. Their flicked glances were curious rather than distasteful. Maya knew how naive they were – the ilk of her cohort back in

Navengore. *Why would a woman of her age let herself go like that?* They'd be wondering. *Why doesn't she go back to her husband?* Maya smiled in the mirror as she passed behind them. Only one of the women smiled back, a tortoiseshell comb suspended in the air by her head as she said 'Hi'. She glanced worriedly at her friends afterwards as if to check whether she'd done the right thing.

Maya took the train back to Central station and determinedly retrieved her rucksack from the locker. The weight of it had doubled, or so it felt. Her heart beat erratically in her chest. She was ready to do this. She would lay her waterproof hammock on the ground, the foam mat inside it. She would erect the tarp over the makeshift bed by attaching it with bungee cords from overhanging branches, just as Ned had shown her – so that any precipitation would run down on either side and not directly onto her. And she would wrap herself in her sleeping bag and lay down on the ground. She'd be safe... what was the likelihood of anyone discovering her, if she waited until dark to set up her bed and dismantled it in the morning before anyone was about? Maya's heart raced even faster with terror and anticipation. But she had a destination in mind that she'd chosen that morning, a closely-wooded park not far from the hostel.

The early-evening streets were still crowded. Where once Maya would have automatically made confident eye contact with the preened middle classes such as she had been in her old life, she avoided them now. They would not recognise her anymore. She smiled instead at a tall Rastafarian with heavy grey dreadlocks. He had a joint balanced between his forefinger and thumb, poised at his lips. They nudged shoulders in passing. He carried his worldly possessions just as she did. He flicked his eyes back at her as he passed, an eyebrow cocked, the joint proffered back towards her but she shook her head and then nodded thanks. His lips opened in a wide smile as he went on his way, humming. Warmth spread from Maya's solar plexus into her neck and cheeks.

She still belonged, only in different company now. *Sorry, sorry*, she mouthed as she bumped into members of a jostling group emerging from the railway station. *Sorry...*

A man sat, begging with a cardboard sign propped against his blanket-clad knees outside the station. Maya emptied her pocket of coins and dropped them into the man's cup, meeting his eyes with a smile. 'Bless you,' he said.

Walking the paths in the public gardens until the park emptied somewhat, the rucksack became increasingly heavier. The light faded but there still seemed to be too many people around to set up a camping spot. Maya stopped in front of a park bench and wrestled her arms free of the rucksack, allowing it to drop onto the slats behind her. She'd begun to panic. Where would she hang the tarp? What if someone saw what she was doing and came over and abused her? Though it was still warm, Maya shivered so hard she could feel the rattling of the bench on which she had slumped. To calm herself she unbuckled the top section of her rucksack and lifted out the bread, cheese and grapes she'd bought earlier. She drank water from her metal cup.

After finishing her simple meal she looked around again. Over by a nearby fence a couple kissed. Two men. Maya wished they'd move on so she could make her preparations to settle down in privacy. They didn't seem keen to disentangle themselves in a hurry so eventually she got up from the bench, fastened the rucksack again and hoisted it onto her back, feeling breath leave her body as she readjusted her posture to the weight. She set off along the path but her feet hurt too badly and she'd had enough. A metre or so away from the path, and out of sight of the kissing couple, she noticed a thicket of bushes whose branches curved upwards and then over, almost meeting the ground. Their trunks were thick like the thighs of the wrestlers her grandma used to enjoy watching on TV. She checked whether anyone was around, then slid her rucksack off once again and dropped to her knees beside it. She crawled into a gap in the bushes, pushing her way into the tent-like space beyond and dragged the rucksack in behind her. The ground felt dry and faintly warm. She lay the tarp on the leaf-mulched earth and unzipped the hammock. She placed the foam mat inside the hammock and her sleeping bag on top of the mat. She had a tiny pillow that made more difference than she could have imagined when she found it in the camping shop. Deep within the arc of the branches, she unfastened the Velcro straps of her sandals and tucked them into the unzipped hammock with her – if anything got stolen she didn't want it to be her shoes. She wriggled into the sleeping bag and pulled the zip of the mosquito net up over her body and face. She heard the footsteps of what was probably the couple passing along the path close by and the murmur of voices. But she was too tired to care. Before the murmurs had fully died away, Maya was asleep.

11

Joe's Journal

The bushland here is filled with bigger trees than those on Paradise Hill. I walk barefoot through the undergrowth at all hours of day now. At first I was fearful of ants and spiders because I've suffered bites while wearing sandals. As time flows by though, I've become increasingly aware of all the other bare feet that have walked this beautiful red earth for eighty-thousand years - since the very first feet ever touched this land. Sometimes you can find a large patch of tall grass that has been crushed flat by the long back feet of kangaroos. They do this to insulate themselves from the cold spring earth at night. In the day, temperatures rise to over forty degrees.

I glory in my isolation but at the same time I wish I fit better into the company of other people. In the words of Everett Ruess: "My tragedy is that I don't fit in with any class of people."

I feel a sort of nostalgia already for a time in the future when I'll no longer be experiencing this blissful lifestyle, and I'll have only words to remember it by. Or perhaps the nostalgia is for the old me who dreamed of the day I'd be free, as I now am: I can't really explain the reasons but I only know it makes me feel conflicted.

12

Maya

Bali, February 2015

Maya sat on the concrete lip of the pool, wrapped in a
brightly-coloured sarong. Her newly-shaved legs dangled in
the water looking browner than she'd ever seen them before –
she was a habitual 'peely-wally looking bairn' as her
Glaswegian grandmother had been keen on remarking. Until
she discovered fake tan as a teenager. It was appalling,
smeary stuff in those days. She'd replaced one of her pairs of
long trousers with a second pair of shorts at a clothes-swap
on a hostel stopover in Sydney, after returning from a hiking
trip to the Blue Mountains.

Having spent the morning sifting through a myriad of
emotions at being about to see her husband and daughter
again, she now drifted in a trance of no thoughts or feelings
at all, hypnotised by the light-catching ripples on the water's
surface and the turquoise tiles inside the long, narrow pool.
Tropical plants tucked against the walls of the compound
sent long fingers of shadow across the paving stones. The

sky was white-hot. When Maya leaned forward as she did now, rousing herself from her stupor, she could no longer feel her stomach resting on her thighs. She was enjoying a temporary respite from her now accustomed lean lifestyle, in a villa in Kuta Bali. It had taken a while to adjust to the abundance of variety – of food, of leisure activities, and of what seemed to be pure luxury on offer in exchange for the handing-over of coins and notes. She felt caught in a no-man's land between her old and her new selves.

Lola had wept on the video-call.

'You didn't come home for Christmas. It was horrible.'

Maya frequently had to remind herself that her daughter was twenty-three years old, not a baby.

'I'm sorry, sweetheart.' Lola's face looked distorted on the screen (a snot-faced toddler having a meltdown). 'You could have stayed in Australia with me. I wanted you to.'

'I didn't want to be in Australia,' Lola said. 'I wanted to be at home, and I wanted you to be there, too.'

'I know, I know,' was all Maya could think of to say. But being away made it much easier for her. At the time Lola called, Maya had recently landed in Bali. Her trip would be short, a tour of the beaches mainly. She'd had a brief meet-up with Ned, who took her all the way around the island on a little motorbike known as a tuk-tuk. She was making sure the extra money Con had transferred to her account would last a lot longer than the three months he'd anticipated she'd be away – which she had been already.

She eyed her guitar, propped against the wall in the corner of the villa's garden. She'd bought it at a flea market in Sydney before her flight to the islands. It had taken a bashing in the plane's hold from Australia, despite being wrapped in her jumper within its zipped case, and now had a small hole on the front of the body. She would make a patch for it – give the instrument some character. The guitar was child-sized but it had a good tone and was easy to carry. It felt good to own a guitar again.

She hummed as she hunched over the pool – *swing low, sweet chariot.* Her hands itched for the neck of the instrument, to hold its smooth body close to hers, tucked under her right arm. She lifted her feet from the water and pushed herself to her feet. As she walked slowly across the paved garden to the guitar where it was half-hidden under an overhang of lush green foliage, she glanced over her shoulder and saw her wet footsteps disappear under the sun. Reaching for the guitar, she slipped the strap over her bare shoulder, settling the instrument comfortably against her body and fiddled adeptly with the tuning pegs. When she was satisfied she strummed experimental chords and sang softly, relishing her temporary solitude. She felt the thrum of the guitar's hollow body against her stomach, felt herself unifying with the notes. Straightening, she closed her eyes to the sun and opened her throat. She sang an Eva Cassidy song that reminded her of a wet autumn back home. The strings twanged as she jolted at the sudden interruption of a man's voice.

'Excuse me.'

Back in the present, Maya looked up, squinting against the sun's glare. Although she'd been expecting him, recognition still came slowly – Con. *Someone from another life.* In turn he hadn't yet understood that she was his wife. He stared at her a moment, confusion knitting his eyebrows. Lola pushed through the door behind him and when she saw Maya she dropped the bag she was carrying.

'Oh. My. God. *Muuum!*'

Con rocked on his feet. He lowered his bag to the floor. In contrast to his daughter he moved towards Maya in extreme slow motion. Lola bowled herself across the slabs and it was thanks to Maya's newly-sharpened reflexes that she was able to swing the guitar onto her back in lightning motion. She guided both herself and Lola, as the girl made heavy contact with her, away from the edge of the pool.

'Mum, Mum, Mum,' Lola buried her face in Maya's neck.

61

Maya pressed her lips hard into Lola's scalp as she'd done on the day her family left Melbourne. At first she'd tensed but now her arms relaxed around Lola and pulled her closer. *My baby.* Her body had forgotten what it was to be a mother and the feelings hurt as they flooded back. She and Lola sobbed and rocked in each other's arms.

'I missed you.' Lola burrowed in deeper. 'Daisy said she was sorry she couldn't get time off work, well, that she has too much planning to do. But she wants to arrange a holiday with you at Easter if you haven't come home by then.'

Her voice lifted in hope. Maya tried to keep her muscles loose. She was afraid of pulling away, knowing she'd have to make physical contact with her husband. *I've got used to being my own self. I'm afraid I'll lose the essence of the new me as soon as Con touches me.* That it'd be absorbed back into his skin and that his hands would remould her. But she knew Lola would never pull away of her own accord.

'Come on, darling,' she broke the suction between herself and her daughter – as, a long time ago, she'd had to insert her little finger into the corner of Lola's mouth to detach her from the nipple when Daisy had long since finished feeding on the other side. 'Let your dad have a turn, hey?'

She kept hold of Lola while the girl used the backs of her hands to brush tears away from her face. 'Here,' Maya bunched a corner of her sarong. 'Use this.' She smiled over Lola's shoulder at Con.

'Hello.'

'Hello. Dear God, look at you... Good lord, Maya, I...'

'You look different, too, kind of.'

Hot fat spat inside her. Fear of rejection. Fear Con would want her to come home. The frank, unashamed emotion of Lola she could deal with, but since November she and Con had been circling each other like vultures, picking snippets off each other's carefully-maintained masks of control. Now there were no screens between them and no internet to fail and cut the pain short.

'I can't believe it, this... these past few months...'

Maya glanced at the sky and back again at Con, who was turning a strange colour, rocking on his sensible shoes. Oh, no.

'Lola,' she yelled. The girl rallied. She and Maya caught Con before he lurched towards the pool and lowered him backwards into a wicker chair. The guitar banged on Maya's back.

'Put your head between your knees, darling.' She stroked the back of her husband's neck, where she saw a circular patch of paler skin. The boil that had been about to erupt when they parted had lived its life, died and disappeared in the months since then. Her stomach clenched. 'Now, now. You're okay. It's the shock, that's all. Keep your head down a minute.' Conflicting emotions and physical sensations sparked and flickered inside her. Con let out a deep sigh. She wondered if this visit was a good idea for herself or for him.

'Mum, is Dad all right?'

'He'll be fine, sweetheart. Go and fetch a bottle of water from the fridge, will you? The kitchen's just through there, to the left.' She kept her hand on Con's neck. At the same time she slipped the strap of the guitar over her head and lowered her beloved instrument carefully to the ground, leaning it against the wicker table. Con raised his head at the sound of wood scraping wood. His focus had sharpened. His gaze was level with the tops of her breasts. Colour came flooding back into his face. She shifted, only slightly but she sensed his awareness of her withdrawal.

She seemed to split into two, one half of her looking ahead already to the time he would have left and she'd be on her own again. It was easier on her own. After only three months apart she wondered if she had it in her to resume being a wife. Yet she did experience a rush of tenderness as she let her hand settle more firmly on the tops of his shoulders. That was the other half of her, aware that he was a man, strange enough to

63

her now to set off a faint tingle in her body. She sniffed – the air around him smelled burnt.

'You okay?'

'I just. . . ' he coughed, his breathing still slightly ragged. She lowered her face to his. Their cheeks touched, his breath coming at her sideways. It was bitter but she held her face there and let herself become accustomed to it. All she could think of was how much of a stranger he seemed, and yet her body knew he was familiar, too.

'It was a shock. You amaze me, Maya. I don't know where to begin.'

Maya put her arms around him awkwardly. 'I can't get to you from this angle.' she laughed softly and lowered herself to her knees. Their foreheads rested together. 'There, that's better.'

Footsteps announced Lola, emerging from the villa with three bottles of water. She placed them on the table and Maya saw from the corner of her eye the guitar rising out of her sight. She heard it land somewhere further off and hoped it hadn't been damaged anymore. She watched the swish of Lola's blue and pink skirt advancing and receding and the legs of two more chairs appeared around the table, scraping along the ground. Lola could be organised when she wanted to be. She did work with children who had additional needs, after all. Maya allowed her chin to sink into Con's shoulder – rediscovering him by scent and tactility. His hands flattened against her back and she thought of how, again, there would be a breaking of suction when the two of them separated.

'Shall I help you up, Mum?'

She recalled the solemnity of her young twins when she'd asked them to help her out of a chair – their two sets of hands patting and pushing her, cheeks puffed out with the effort. How their eyes had shone when they'd managed to get her onto her feet. Especially when she was pregnant with Joe and had such a bad back.

Simultaneous timelines ran through her mind and it felt as

64

if she was living them physically. The children were babies and then they were no longer babies – they were with her and then they'd gone. Maya herself was a young woman and then she was heavy with fertility. She became empty. Finally she had ripened again with the fulfilment of middle-aged purpose. Now the timelines tangled together and she wasn't sure who she was anymore.

'Thanks, sweetheart.' She put her hand out to Lola, keeping the other on Con's shoulder. He looked up at his wife and daughter as Maya rose to her feet and she saw a light like hope in his eyes. Meanwhile she struggled to keep her two worlds separate.

We have two weeks together, she thought. A holiday. After which her husband and daughter were going back to their predictable lives. *When I wave goodbye to them at the airport, that's when I'll be able to continue rediscovering my new self.* She tried not to long for it too greedily. It felt like an addiction – solitude, independence of thought and action. Time to breathe and think. The new Maya was the one she now felt more at home with than the one Lola and Con still hoped she could be.

13

Maya

Bali, February 2015

'Seriously? Only twenty pounds a night?' said Con. 'For a villa like this? That's crazy. Why haven't we always taken our holidays in these kinds of places?'

They were in the yellow bedroom with glass doors that looked out onto the pool.

'You were always too busy to go on holiday,' she said. 'And you said this kind of holiday was trashy. All that money we had, what a waste...'

'What do you mean? It wasn't wasted. I made sure it was saved up for the children's futures.'

'Yes but—' *two of our children have gone.* 'I just wish we'd had more fun together as a family. Imagine Jamie diving into that pool out there, when he was younger. If we'd taken holidays like this. He swam like a little fish, Jamie did, didn't he?' Her insides fizzed. Their older son was a sore subject but she was sick of pretending he didn't exist.

'When he wasn't getting banned from his swimming lessons for bad behaviour,' Con said in a controlled voice. 'Why are you bringing him up now, Maya? Shouldn't this holiday be about *us*?' He shifted on the edge of the bed. After his swim he'd taken a shower followed by a short nap while Maya and Lola caught up with their news. Now he was dressed in a white t-shirt Maya had never seen before and a pair of longish cotton shorts.

'It's hard to separate *us* from the people and things we're connected with,' she said quietly. She mustn't become subsumed by Con's more dominant personality, sharing a house and a bedroom with him again. Her skin itched. 'Nothing's just about us. Everything we produce or consume has a consequence. Nothing's abstract, even though it's easy to pretend it is when you're cushioned from the consequences by privilege.'

'Oh for heaven's sake, will you listen to yourself? What do you think is paying for the *privilege* of your self-absorbed *journey of discovery*, Maya?' he tapped his head with a forefinger. 'Have a think. Yes, that's right, money. You'd never have been doing this if it wasn't for money. Get over yourself, will you?'

Maya blew out air.

'I might not have lost both of my sons if it hadn't been for money, either,' her lip trembled. She pressed the back of her hand briefly against her mouth. He wouldn't make her cry. She was different now. 'Always threatening them with cutting them off. They didn't care, Con, did they? It was because of those kinds of threats that we lost them both.'

There was a pause. Maya patted the scarf covering her head, worried at the nubs of hair beneath it with her fingertips. Con's back stiffened.

'Oh, so it's all my fault they both disappeared, is it? You being the perfect mother and all. You know, the kind that walks out on her children.'

Another pause.

'Children? The girls are twenty-three, Con. You're most probably talking about yourself.'

She imagined steam coming out of his ears. He flung himself upwards from the bed and paced towards her, sidestepping as she reached to open the door to the bathroom. She felt his hot breath by her cheek as he passed.

'Well *if* I was, and I wasn't, I was merely referring to the way you babied our children, even today, moaning on about what Lola's been eating since she moved back in with me. But if I *had* been talking about myself I may as well not have bothered. You don't give a shit about me, anyway. You haven't even asked what *I'm* eating. Usually I grab myself something from the supermarket or buy a takeaway, for your information. Lola eats before I get home and I don't keep tabs on her. Don't you care about me?'

'Oh, Con.' Maya felt suddenly tired. 'Stop fishing.' She shook out the towel she'd collected from the steamy bathroom and spread it over the back of a chair. 'Of course I care but I'm not your mother, am I? You're big and ugly enough to look after yourself. Your mother taught you to cook didn't she? I remember you cooking after I had the twins.' She moved around the bedroom, picking up Con's peeled-off trunks and another towel from the tiled floor. She stopped to look at the damp articles in her hands and shrugged.

'You didn't have to when I had Joe, though, I'd prepared meals for all of us for a whole month. Even Jamie's packed lunches and the twins' nursery snacks. I bought so many of those plastic tubs with lids – it was a good job we had a huge freezer. I labelled everything and even had to borrow friends' freezers for the overflow once I'd filled ours.'

'Did you? I never realised,' Con sat down again. He picked at the fringe of the cane-coloured throw on the bed. 'I thought it was great that you'd managed to carry on as usual. I didn't really think about how you did it, I suppose.'

'No,' she moved the long white curtains aside and pushed open the glass door, draped his swimming things over a chair outside. A thought flashed into her head. 'Do you remember that you wanted to go travelling before we settled down and had children?' *Funny how things turned out.* 'I wish we had done, now.' She glanced at him as she moved over to the dressing table and sat in front of the mirror. Hoped he wasn't sulking. 'Once we had Jamie and then the twins we became so settled in our expectations, didn't we? Especially when we moved to Navengore.'

A bigger conservatory, another ensuite bathroom. Keeping up with the Jones's and the Harwells and the Keartons. She'd believed she was happy.

'Con, you know, we could sell the house – we don't need it any more. Con,' she half-turned. But she stopped when she saw his expression. The groove between his eyes had deepened as he stared at her. She finished rubbing moisturiser on her face and unwrapped the turban from her hair self-consciously, tying a fresh white linen scarf around it. She had on a white cotton sundress. They were going out to dinner at a restaurant on Malioboro Street where she would introduce her husband and daughter to the best noodle dishes she'd ever tasted. She felt the burn of Con's gaze and glanced at him again. 'What?'

When he answered, Con's voice had thickened. 'You look like a different woman. It's weird... it's like I don't know you. You sound like Maya but the wife I knew has disappeared. You're not her... Maya, you're just – so different. How did this happen?'

'You know how it happened,' Maya said softly. 'You didn't expect I'd stay the same, did you?'

Con patted the bed beside him. 'Look. You haven't stopped buzzing around since Lola and I arrived. Take a break, Maya love. Come and sit down beside me.' He paused, tight-lipped at her hesitation. 'I won't touch you if that's what you're concerned about.' When Maya had showered and put on her dress it was in the bathroom with the door closed. She'd shied away from intimacy with him since he and Lola arrived two hours ago. Lola was having a nap. In the past they would have taken advantage of such an opportunity.

The last time they made love was a few nights before Maya took the phone call from Australia. They'd been for dinner in the new glass-walled dining extension of one village couple or another – she couldn't remember which. Looking out over their swathes of yellow-lit lawn ringed by expensive solar lighting. Anna or Caroline B. – or perhaps it had been one of the Sues – had cooked Maya's favourite dish which used to be beef hotpot. They'd all drunk copious amounts of wine and played a game where you had to cover the bottom half of your face with a grinning paper mask. After the game they had the usual conversations about the private tutors who'd enhance their teenagers' exam results. Nice people, lucky to live in such a picturesque village. Later she and Con had walked home arm in arm, both of them swaying, aware that when they reached The Cottages they would hurry upstairs, undress and have wine-fuelled sex. It had been enough – then.

But what do I feel for him now?

She pictured herself washing under her arms at the sink in a public toilet building. She'd done the same thing in the restroom of a restaurant. She'd pooed in a hole in the ground while on the bushland trail in the Blue Mountains, and covered it over using her folding spade. She drank water from a stream. She hugged strangers on the road and shared crowded bedrooms with both men and women she would never have met in her previous life. *Yet I feel afraid of being alone in a room with my own husband.* In case the intimacy he desired somehow turned her back into the woman she'd been before. She wasn't ready to be that Maya again – wasn't sure if she ever would. And if she did transform back into the old Maya it would feel like a betrayal. Of Joe. Of herself.

'Come on, love,' Con said again. 'I only want to talk to you. There's no hurry to go out is there? I'm not really hungry if I'm honest. Come closer. Talk to me. Tell me about the

71

amazing thing you're doing with your hair – no, honestly – I'm fascinated.'

Maya tucked the ends of the scarf under her hair and glanced back at the brown, toned, older woman in the mirror. The sundress was pretty but she'd hesitated to spend the 420,000 IDR at the market that morning. In her old life the equivalent £23 would have been throwaway – less than a lunch out. Now each coin she parted with was precious.

'What d'you want to know?'

Con smiled, palms upturned in his lap. She saw that his nails were bitten down to the quick and she felt a stab of guilt. Now that she looked at him properly he was thinner, too. She wouldn't let the guilt consume her, she mustn't. Her hands dropped to her sides. 'It's not that amazing to be honest. I haven't washed it, that's all. Well, I rub coconut oil into it but I haven't used any kind of shampoo for months now.'

'I like it though,' Con said, trying hard. He had tears in his eyes. 'I like you being different. You seem *more* the old Maya, if you know what I mean. Like the girl I met at university.

She sat down on the edge of the bed. Edged closer so that her bare arm connected with his. If she closed her eyes they could be *them* again. It frightened her. A vast hole – full of material possessions and commitments – opened up as if to swallow her. She inched away just enough to break the connection between the hairs on their arms. She saw that the golden hairs on her arm were still leaning in the direction of his darker ones, which in turn were reaching out to hers. It was only static electricity. His fingers curled into his hands. His knees looked bonier than she remembered. She should try and work something out.

'What would you think about not going back to the UK just yet? I mean, buying a rucksack and filling it with everything you'd need for the road, like I did. Do something totally different. Oh, Con. We could do this together – or even, if you wanted – travel separately. You could set off by yourself. It sounds corny but you could, you know, find

72

yourself. I feel as if I'm beginning to. It really works, honestly.'

'What are you talking about?' his hands clenched tighter, leaving his knuckles white. The tendons in his wrists stood out. 'Why would you say such a thing?' Out of the blue, in the way it had, his fury descended. He thumped the bed with his bunched fists. 'I've been patient, Maya, you can't say I haven't. But I hoped you'd come home with me and Lola. I thought when you saw us again you'd realise how much you needed us. I can't believe you're suggesting I'd do something as stupid as you have.'

Maya got up and walked to the door, closing it gently. She placed a finger on her lips as if Con was a child. It infuriated him more. 'She's not a fucking kid, Maya. When will you realise... they've GROWN UP. I thought these years would be our time together.' He lowered his face onto his bunched-up hands, growling into his knuckles. 'Bringing them up was an important job, I know that. And there are difficulties, and sad things happen, I've accepted those too.' His shoulders shook.

His voice continued, low-toned. Maya stood by the door, arms clasped around her waist. She felt detached and pictured herself back in the Blue Mountains, her pack heavy on her back. Sweat dribbling between her breasts. One more step, and one more. She had forced herself to reach the summit of each hill before she allowed herself a gulp of water from the dromedary tube hanging over her shoulder...

'... Are you even listening to me?'

She found her voice.

'Sorry I've fucking changed. What the hell did you expect, that I would just go on as normal? After everything that's happened?'

In the pauses between their shouted accusations Maya heard Lola moving around in the room next door. But Con was right, Lola was an adult. Maya had wrapped her in cotton wool for too long. Still, she lowered her voice slightly. 'We both have to accept that we've probably altered beyond recognition. The question is what do we do now? I'm inviting you to join me on my quest, if you want to call it that – or suggesting the alternative of embarking on one of your own.' She moderated her tone of voice further but not her words. 'There was no need to jump down my fucking throat. If you want to stay cocooned in that enormous, empty nest – living a life of triviality – that's up to you. But it isn't what *I* want anymore. I'm not coming back with you. I'm sorry but the sooner you understand that, the better.' Her voice broke. She sank into the wicker armchair by the glass door. Ripples from the pool reflected wavering light across the ceiling of their bedroom.

Con straightened his back.

'I'll cut your fucking money off, then.' His eyes were red and his voice hoarse. 'You're not a teenager, Maya. It's about time you grew up and started living a responsible life again – quest? For God's sake, woman, you're living in a fantasy movie.'

She breathed deeply. She'd climbed a mountain in blazing heat. She'd hallucinated from near-dehydration on the mountain path, seen Joe standing in a shimmering heat-haze on the bank of an almost dry stream. She'd slept outside, alone, under a jewelled sky in the Australian bush – despite her fear of spiders (she hadn't reckoned on the ants). She'd dug a hole like an animal in the bush and buried her scent. She'd cooked a meal on a tiny camping stove for a bunch of youths she met on the trail. She could stand up to him.

'You may accuse me of acting like a teenager if you wish but listen to yourself, threatening to cut off my allowance – as if you're my father. The Great Authoritarian – that was your attempted method of parenting wasn't it? Well, it didn't do much good –.'

She'd seen his face. 'Con, I'm sorry. That was a cruel thing to say. You're a good father, you've always done your best. Let's stop this now.' But Con wasn't listening.

'Don't tell me when it's time to stop. Don't you think I've wanted to have this out with you for a while? If I was the authoritarian, you were the doormat, Maya. Never able to say no or refuse your little darlings anything they wanted. And like you say – look how *that* turned out.'

'Yeah, right. Okay, enough.' It was hard to breathe. 'We were both wrong. We can't change what happened.' She pressed her palms into the woven wicker arms of the chair and pushed herself to her feet. Grasping the edge of the frame, she felt her way through the open patio door into the nearest corner of the garden. A full-length mirror had been built into the crazy-paving of the pool's surrounding wall. There was that tough-looking woman in a white dress instead of Con's wife. After a moment Con followed her out. Maya walked to the edge of the pool and turned to see her shadow stretching back towards him on the ground. 'I don't need any money from you, Con,' she said. 'Just so you know. I can do this by myself.'

Con's physicality swallowed her shadow as he moved forward, heavy on his feet. His knuckles brushed the fabric of her dress. With the pool behind her, she felt her body tense. But he only held her eyes for a searching moment before turning away. He moved to stand with his back against the wall, facing her again, the frown between his eyes deep.

'I know.' He let out a slow breath. 'Of course you can look after yourself, I never thought for a moment that you couldn't. I gave you the extra money because I wanted to have some control. It felt important to still be in your life even if it was only in the occasional meal you treated yourself to or a couple of weeks of luxury in a hotel.' He gestured with his arms at the villa. He pushed himself away from the wall and walked around the edge of the pool towards the doors that led into the kitchen and living area, at a right angle to their bedroom. He lowered himself into the poolside chair he'd collapsed on earlier. 'Can you understand any of that?'

She followed him and sat down too, laying her arm on the table beside his. 'Of course I can, and I appreciate it. I know everything's messed up. We were happy before, weren't we? I still love you – I do.' She made eye contact with him as she grasped his arm. 'But I can't help that it's changed now. I can't go back to that life. It feels soulless.'

Con nodded and squeezed her hand. There was a movement from the door behind them. A slant of sunlight fell over the top of their daughter's head, bringing out the hint of red in her dark hair.

Maya remembered pushing her two girls on the swings in the park. Joe was in his pram. Jamie – where had Jamie been? The late afternoon sun shining on the girls' hair had turned it reddish. The memory was lucid and the emotion of it filtered through into the present. At the time, she had never wanted anything more.

Lola plucked nervously at her dress.

'Have you two finished having your row? Because I'm hungry. Are we going out to dinner yet?'

14

Maya

Bali, February 2015

On the second day of their visit, Maya walked with her
husband and daughter on Jalan Mataram in the old town of
Kuta Bali. The humid atmosphere created a haze that both
seeped up from the ground and hung in the air, and also
radiated down from the sky. Bright light cascaded off stalls
and signs and vividly-coloured fabrics as well as fruit and
vegetables. Lola wafted her face with an information leaflet
she'd picked up at the airport and insisted on bringing with
her as a guide. She hadn't got used to her mother being a
go-native traveller yet. Maya wore a scarf pulled over her
nubs of hair, wrapped around and fastened at the front of
her neck – the delicate place that was still prone to burning
however tough she thought her skin had become. Con joked
that she looked like a Muslim woman – but hatless, he was
the one suffering now. The lack of breeze had led to a
stagnant heat. Sweat dripped into Con's eyes and created
damp moons below his armpits, causing him to walk

self-consciously with his arms pressed to his sides. Meeting Maya's eyes, Lola stifled a giggle, a hand held over her mouth.

'This bag seems to have got heavier,' Con was carrying the knapsack containing Lola's requirements of a cardigan, a delicate scarf and several bottles of water.

The life of the street was dense and vibrant. Maya felt that if she could rise above street level the pressure would ease and she would be able to take in the maelstrom of sounds and activity, but for now she was overwhelmed by the pressing environment, the constant hum of mopeds and small trucks. She was used to quiet tracks and empty spaces. The traffic seemingly had no regard for pedestrians. The air was filled with a ceaseless pipping of horns. She'd been informed by a receptionist at the hotel that this constant tooting was known as *making attention* and was applied to any driving manoeuvre – turning, driving straight on, slowing down, speeding up, warning pedestrians not to cross and telling pedestrians it was okay to cross. It could mean *thank you* or *fuck off*. The noise was an integral part of the proper functioning of Indonesian roads – an organized chaos that from the outside seemed impenetrable. But the flow of the traffic was like a school of fish, moving together in harmony. Mostly.

'Look out!' Con grabbed Maya's arm. 'You almost got run over.' Some streets had a narrow walkway of ornate reddish slabs but they were often cracked, twisted or completely absent in places, exposing the open drainage and the rancid smell of sewage. Most of the time it was simply easier to walk in the road.

Lola made them stop at a stall which sold crafts, looking for a present for her sister. The various shops and stalls flanking the narrow lane formed a patchwork of colour, woven with unique styles and scents. Plastic signs hung about ten feet above each one, most of them faded and torn. Exposed wires and cables criss-crossed overhead, too. Maya had the sense of being in a tunnel – one that led from her past to her future as well as taking her down a street in Bali. She felt uncomfortable as a tourist. Predatory, almost.

Con stopped at a motorbike repair shop, no more than an open fronted shack with a corrugated metal roof. Oil saturated the concrete floor. Machine parts and tools hung from the walls and ceiling on hooks and brackets which looked unstable. Perhaps he was pondering a mid-life motorcycle acquisition. But the remark he actually made was with regard to the abundance of health and safety transgressions. Men in the repair shop sat around smoking and tinkering, shooting glances at the foreigners in their doorway. A line of *Absolut Vodka* bottles filled with petrol stood in front of the shop. Con shook his head while Maya pulled him away.

'Are you hungry, yet?'

Lola was prone to forgetting to eat and then overcompensating, she'd been the same as a child. Maya might as well mother her while she was here. They were standing next to a *warung*, the principle eating establishment of Indonesia – cheaper to buy the homemade dishes than fresh ingredients from the supermarkets. A glass cabinet displayed the food on offer, a few plastic chairs and tables stood around and a friendly local made and served the dishes. Maya chose *nasi champur*; rice and a mix of vegetables. They seated themselves on the plastic chairs, Con sliding the backpack off and threading his foot through it on the floor. Maya frowned at him. The pleasant smell of food was mixed with oil and distant sewage. Flies buzzed around their heads in swirls of dust as they ate.

After their meal they continued walking the crowded lane, Lola with her arm looped through her mother's. Maya hooked an errant strand of hair behind her daughter's ear, enjoying Lola's recent tendency to tactility. The neediness she seemed to have developed was at the same time touching and a cause for concern. *I just want to enjoy my time with her and save any worries for later.* Maya breathed the humid air, enjoying but slightly disorientated by the juxtaposition of her family with her new independent self.

They passed clothes shops with racks of branded sports gear spilling into the street. One owner called out to Con. 'Hey mister, come look in my shop, very good price for you sir.' Con waved an imperious hand and urged his womenfolk on. There were phone shops in which the attendants perched on stools behind glass cabinets filled with gadgets and sim card deals. 'Boss, do you need a sim card? Best prices here, mate.' Con's chin rose higher and Maya and Lola exchanged another smile. Lola squeezed Maya closer with her arm.

They came upon yet more food stalls, the sound of a hissing pan, the fragrance of peanut sauce drifting past, and again more shouts from vendors to buy from them.

Yet it was possible to find peace amongst the mayhem. Behind a twirling ornamental gate was a Hindu shrine. At the base a stretch of grass – a rare and welcome sight in the city. The centrepiece of the shrine was an eight-foot statue of the Hindu monkey god, made from black stone and expertly carved in the traditional style. The statue's eyes bulged and it had a protruding tongue. A pagoda made from the same black ornamental bricks shaded the statue from the glaring sun. Lola breathed out in wonderment and Maya was again reminded of the little girl her daughter had been not so long ago. In the strange environment the moment felt lengthened, as if Maya's brain was trying to prolong the sense of peace and tranquillity in this oasis of calm.

———

It was early evening when they entered the cool dark of the villa-complex lobby, an open space blessed with fans. Imaginary lights burst like fireworks in front of Maya's eyes after the brightness of outdoors. When the faux-fireworks settled the dimness was a welcome respite from the oppressive heat and the hectic atmosphere of the streets.

Later that evening Con and Maya ascended to the roof of their villa where they sat drinking wine. Lola had gone to bed early with her bottles of water and a cool, damp cloth on her forehead – suffering from mild heat stroke. On the villa roof they had a view across the city of pagodas and angled rooftops silhouetted against the still bright yellow sky while the sun set behind them. Maya could see into the street below, now lit up in the gloom. It was still busy. Men sat in front of their shops and stalls, smoking, laughing and observing the flow. Their distant voices floated up with the other sounds of the city. In their heavenward haven Maya luxuriated in the strong breeze and the fact that the humidity had receded.

15

Joe's journal

OCTOBER 2012

I'm back in mainland Australia. Working on a potato farm in a place called Bundaberg. It's relentless, hard work and my muscles are growing, which I find I'm enjoying. I've never been bothered about going to the gym or anything before but it seems to be happening all by itself now.

Also I've been spoilt by my time in beautiful Tasmania, where I felt free. But I need some dosh, so here I am. We have to get up at stupid o'clock in the morning to catch the transport from our hostel to the farm. It means we're all half-asleep as we rattle and bump and jumble together on the journey. The other day on our way there I spotted a huge spider on somebody's jacket (The jacket was on the floor) We had to sit as still as we could while the truck jolted along, and then we had to wait for the driver to remove the spider from the vehicle before any of us could disembark.

There's a great community here though. I seem to have found the people I fit in with after all. Maybe a little solitude was the thing I needed to discover my true self. We sleep in bunkhouses, and just down the road from here is a bar where we let our hair down at the weekends. My roommate's called Will. He's a bit older than me but we get on so well.

A group of us play music together in the evenings - Will's a much better singer than me and he's also sensible enough to carry a harmonica instead of a guitar. At least a harmonica fits in a pocket - my guitar is a bit of a hassle to carry around along with the rest of my stuff. I may trade it for something else.

Will and I have been writing songs together. When we both get back to a big city we may go and record something in a studio. Will's from County Galway in Ireland. Funny that I'm all the way across the world in Australia when I've never even been to Ireland, just a stone's throw away from my own country. Will's issued me with an open invitation to do a round trip of Ireland with him one day when we're both done with our 'rest-of-the-world' quota. But before that there are so many places to visit.

To paraphrase Everett Ruess once again, I am among friends. I'm surrounded by the beautiful land and I have music and food a-plenty. What more could I want?

Okay, so Will's just come into the room. I'm gonna put this away now - he likes to tease me about writing in a journal.

Ciao, guys.

16

Maya

March 2015

She waved Con and Lola off at Jakarta airport. Con wore shades to hide the redness of his eyes. Maya swallowed nausea and tried to make sense of her confusion. Did she want to go home with him, after all?

'I might visit again, Mum,' Lola nudged between them with her strong shoulder. 'I might get Daisy to come with me in the school holidays. Wherever you are by then.' She swallowed several times. 'I know it's more expensive then but we can't really take any more time off work.' Her eyes were puffy but they shone unnaturally bright. She was making a good effort not to cry. Hesitating, she pulled Maya towards her, rested a hand on the back of her mother's neck and kissed her hard on top of the scarf that covered Maya's twisted nubs of hair. A reversal of the kiss Maya had given her at Melbourne Airport. Maya put her arms around her and held her breath until specks of light swirled under her closed eyelids.

Lola wrestled free and stepped backwards, keeping her eyes down. Her jaw looked tight and Maya sensed anger within her sadness. 'See ya then,' Lola said as if it didn't really matter. She moved away in her pretty floral dress, walking backwards, the braids at the sides of her dark hair swinging. 'I love you,' she said before turning and walking into the WH Smith outlet. Maya's stomach clenched. She half-closed her eyes and allowed her chin to sink into Con's shoulder. Con squeezed her tightly. An age passed. They stood in the middle of a constantly moving channel of people, a human river in which they were frequently bumped and jostled. Wheeled suitcases knocked the backs of Maya's heels. Con hardly noticed but Maya felt constricted within his hold and scrabbled for release, panic building in her chest. An announcement blaring out on the tannoy caused her ears to ring as she tried to decipher the words. She pushed at Con's shoulders. 'Come on, love, let's move over there – out of the way a bit.' A chance to breathe. 'And in a moment you'd better head off. I need to check my bag in, too.'

Con dragged her rucksack across to the windows for her while she carried her guitar. They glanced at the planes rolling in and out on the concourse below. Con took off his dark glasses and dabbed his eyes.

'Don't forget how much I love you. I know you feel you need to do this but if you change your mind – if you want to come home then let me know straight away. I'll sort it all out for you Maya, I promise.'

'I know, I know. I promise to call if I need you. Now, goodbye love. Goodbye. Look, Lola's waiting for you over there – we've already said our goodbyes and I'm not going to put us both through that again. Goodbye, love...' She peeled her lips away from Con's again. 'Goodbye. Kisses. I'll be thinking of you... goodbye.' A sob caught in her throat. Con turned and marched purposefully away to join Lola, who hadn't returned to her mother, at the security barrier.

Maya crouched on the floor and fiddled with the straps of her rucksack, battered now and covered in dust and stains. She strained and hefted it onto her shoulders. Rising almost-gracefully into a standing position – thank goodness her knees were still in good working order – she cinched the waist strap tighter and adjusted the buckles at her shoulders. She closed her eyes for a moment, breathing deeply, shutting off the airport sounds all around her. Transformed herself back from Maya who was Con's wife – the erstwhile mother of Jamie and Joe and the overprotective one of Daisy and Lola – into the vagabond she strove to be. She patted her pocket, feeling the outline of the harmonica Ned had given her when she met up with him on her arrival in Bali. It was easier to pull out and put away than her guitar and she sometimes used it on its own for busking. Since leaving home music had become important again. Maybe she could use it as a connection to Jamie... If he ever contacted her again.

Another announcement came over the tannoy. Blinking, she glanced around. The crowd had swallowed her husband and daughter. She took another deep breath, put one foot in front of the other and headed back towards the check-in desks. Women with glossy hair and ironed clothes passed her and she swallowed down any residual nostalgia for her former self. She searched the information boards and counted along the rows of desks until she found the Nordic section – wondering what spring would be like in Iceland.

17

Joe's Journal

I woke up twice last night. I unzipped my tent and looked out at the stars. A drop of water fell on my face as I disturbed an overhanging branch. I don't think I had the best idea when I decided to sleep in a park in the middle of Reykjavik but at least I have the best winter-grade sleeping bag - my belated Christmas present from Mum and Dad. They flew here to meet me at the end of January, and the three of us stayed in a hotel. They brought me Jaffa Cakes from England and some of my old winter clothes, though the jumpers are tight on me now. Mum insisted on buying me a new North Face jumper and we gave some of the ones they brought from home to the clothes-swap at a hostel. I was treated to five days of luxury. Did all the usual tourist sights. We went for dinner at the Pearl, visited the Saga Museum and went swimming in the Olympic-sized pool, where we tried out the different hot tubs and saunas. We also climbed to the top of the cathedral tower. Before Mum and Dad left they paid for a hostel for me for an extra five days. Dad tried again to get me to come home. But Mum didn't. I think for the first time she got me. I think she gets me in more ways than she wants to admit - or maybe she just doesn't know what to say about my sexuality. I'm not ready to broach it just yet.

After my days of hotels and hostels it felt good to make contact with the ground again. And - here's another quote from Everett Ruess - there is splendid freedom in solitude. Just after sunrise I was woken by traffic passing by on the road above. So I got up and spread my sleeping bag out to air in the sun before too many people came into the park. Later I packed everything into my rucksack and headed downtown. I walked past the harbour, overlooked by the concert-hall (which Mum loved, especially the glimmering lights on its sides). Then I took a long, snowy walk slightly uphill towards another hostel which has a campsite. Covered in snow, but at least with some facilities. I thought I may be able to do some washing-up or something in exchange for breakfast - I've run out of money already. A pair of headphones I couldn't resist ... what can I say? Anyway, my luck was in. They've given me a room in the hostel because they're not busy at the moment. Well, I can lay claim to one bed in a four-bed room, but I currently have the place to myself. In exchange I do some cleaning and some night duty on reception. I'm grateful for the indoor accommodation, for the free shower and the laundry facilities. I'll sacrifice my splendid solitude for this. And I get to eat breakfast every day - if I manage to get up on time.

18

Joe's journal

Halló!

The snow's still thick on the ground but the worst of the blizzards seem to be over. About time, too. You take your life in your hands when you get caught on the highway in one of those white-outs, as I discovered on the way back from a trip to Skogafoss last week. There were five of us in a van. It was bright when we set out but half-way back to Reykjavik the snow fell, driven horizontally across the road by a strong wind. There was no visibility at all and the traffic came to a standstill. Eventually a snow plough arrived and got things moving. It was pitch dark by that time and I did wonder if we'd spend the night out on the road in the middle of nowhere.

We - the hostel staff - also took a coach trip to a horse farm (on a day when there was no blizzard). We drove through the stark landscape of rolling hills backed by steep mountains. All covered in snow. I went riding

91

for the first time since I was a kid. The horses here are totally different to the ones Daisy and Lola used to ride at the stables in Navengore. Daisy once insisted that anything under 15 hands high is a pony, not a horse, but it's considered offensive to refer to the tiny Icelandic equines as anything other than the ancient breed of horse that they are. These horses live outside all winter. They stand in a circle during a blizzard, their backs to each other, thick manes covering their eyes. Their coats are deep and shaggy. In Will's words they're hardy as fuck.

Yes, Will's here! He's my room-mate again. I heard on the grapevine that he was leaving Australia, so I suggested he join me in Iceland. I was so pleased when he agreed because I know he'd been planning to do Italy and Spain instead. Maybe he likes me more than I realised. He's teaching me to play all this crazy stuff on the harmonica - I never knew such a diminutive instrument (a bit like the horses, eh?) could sound so rich. Or maybe it's just Will - he's such a good musician.

He reminds me a bit of my brother. Jamie was the one who first got me into music. I wonder where he went when he left home, I haven't seen him in so long. I wish we could get in touch.

Anyway, Will and I have started busking together. He persuaded me to buy myself a harmonica from the World Music Store. He borrowed a ukulele off someone here at the hostel and we went out to the Botanical Gardens, catching the last couple of hours of daylight. Will sang. He has one of those soulful, bluesy voices, and it helps that he's Irish. We played Neil Young, Joan Baez and Bob Dylan songs that I recognised from my mum's record collection back in the day...

We saw the Northern lights last night. I was lying on my back in the swimming pool - yeah, in the middle of winter because all the pools are geo-thermally heated - and I watched green and red lights race across the sky and

across Will's face like some crazy disco at a kids' party.
It takes your breath away.

Takk Fyrir, Nature, you're awesome.

19

Joe

April 2013

Email from: Joe.Galen@Cusp.com
   To: Maya Galen
   Subject: I got a job

Hey Mum,

I hope you're all well back home. I'm glad to tell you – and you'll be pleased to hear, I've been offered 6 weeks full time paid work cleaning rooms at the hostel. You know I've been living in my tent on the campsite since my work in reception finished, right? (I thought about you working as a receptionist at the doctors when I was doing that and I tried to be as professional as you, hehe.)

Today I waved off my friend Will. You remember I was telling you about him and me working together in Bundaberg – we were writing music together? He stayed here for a while, too, but he got itchy feet and decided to head off to Italy. He's the best friend I've had in a while and I'll miss him.

I was thinking of buying an electric moped – they're very popular here. I wouldn't have to pay for fuel because I could just plug it in at the hostel where I work. But then I would need to stay in Iceland and I'm not sure I want to.

I have so many other ideas as to what to do, after I finish work. I could travel to Africa. Or to the Canary islands. Or I could go to another part of Scandinavia. I'll probably go to France and then Germany. Or the other way around. Funny to think how much money you and Dad used to give me as an allowance *every single week* – but it didn't mean anything to me then because I had everything I wanted anyway. Now the thought of having money makes my eyes pop out of my head because of the things that I could do with it. But sometimes it's best just to dream – as soon as you get the thing you wanted it loses its power anyway.

In the end there isn't any material thing that satisfies the spirit more than the "cool, sweet grasses where I have lain and heard the ghastly murmur of regretful winds" – in the words of Everett Ruess. Have you read *A Vagabond for Beauty*, yet?

Love,
Joe xxx

20

Joe's journal

MAY 2013

This is a (short) summary of a (long) walk I did with my friend Nick, who I met in Bali. Nick's American dad runs a business in Indonesia and Nick's mother is half-Balinese. Anyhow we linked up again in Belgium and together we had this crazy idea that we could walk through Germany. It was only winter after all, huh? Well, if you want to get somewhere, use your own two feet - as my dad once said when I asked for a lift home at 2 in the morning. And that was a one-off thing - I hardly ever went to parties, not like the girls.

Okay, I didn't have much time for writing when I was on the road with Nick, so bear with me. I was too busy putting one foot in front of the other, admiring the amazing views of forest-covered hillsides and feeling incredibly lucky to be alive. Every night Nick and I needed to find somewhere to lay our heads, someplace we weren't too likely to freeze to death. The best place we slept was in a hunting tower, a small, square shed-like structure placed above the landscape on strong wooden stilts (with a ladder to climb up). You see them everywhere at the edges of the forests, they're used as hides for hunting boar. But the police turned up with the landowner to find out what we were doing there, having seen the smoke from our fire. After listening to us, the landowner decided to let us stay. I was already in bed (on the floor under a wooden bench in the tower) wrapped up in my sleeping bag. I had to disentangle myself and get down the vertical ladder to the ground while only half-dressed, my heart thumping. Nick was still sitting by the fire when they arrived.

Another good place that we slept was inside a church. The women who looked after the church brought us some food and coffee. They thought we were refugees. I was pleased they'd treat refugees that way. Nick and I also spent a night sleeping in an abandoned greenhouse. We woke up in the morning and observed the intricate ice-patterns on the glass. Another time we slept in the centre of a subway tunnel under the road.

It was so cold walking by the coast. The sea didn't freeze but most else sure as hell did - including parts of my body! The bitter Baltic winds cut through our skin like it was candy floss. Sheesh! We wrapped ourselves in layers of wool and polyester. The previous night's fire had been hot because we'd found some logs nicely cut up into thick chunks, all ready for us it seemed. We cooked a stew of salvaged vegetables on it. We stank of smoke the next day - the night had been windy and there was no escaping the smoke around the fire. When I woke up that morning I poked my head out from the bivvy-bag to find myself surrounded by snow. I looked around for Nick and found that he was buried under his tarp! He'd become soaked and it was a miracle that he didn't freeze to death. We packed our things, stamped our feet and walked.

We crossed many white winter hills south of Köge, hills that stretched into the distant blur of the sky. Mounds of snow made good rest spots where we sat and nibbled our daily ration of salami and watched the birds circle in the sky, a worthy alternative to sitting slumped in front of a TV. We fantasised about creeping down to the water and hunting a duck, how we'd roast it on a spit over a crackling fire. One late afternoon we came across an old, partially-burnt-down cottage. We entered the still-smoking property and collected tins of food from the cupboards. We climbed the rickety stairs, treading carefully, and claimed some undamaged pairs of socks and a spool of string from broken drawers. It was an odd experience. Walking around, we discovered that ZAKI and LAIPI had been there before us and had left their graffiti all over the building. We gathered some ruined pieces of furniture and carried them out to the barn where we made a fire. Nick hung his sleeping bag from the rafters and we lit the fire beneath it to dry the sleeping bag out. The next morning we woke. We packed our things, stamped our feet and walked on.

Between two hills, the frozen lake opened up suddenly, stretching way beyond our view. Müritz. We played harmonica - the silver metal becoming sun catchers. The sun set over the ice at night and it was beautiful. In winter all Germany's outdoor venues are closed - this gave us a nice pick of places in which to squat. We made our home in the bar of an outdoor adventure park for a few days. Each night we walked through the woods in stealth, sneaking into the park and sleeping behind the bar. The final morning there, we woke and we packed our things, stamped our feet and walked on.

When lacking something, I've learned to improvise and repurpose. I find there's usually a way. We needed to get through Germany in the cold. A pair of thermal long Johns, a pair of thick socks, a warm blanket, a new hat. I made those things myself from old jumpers and a poncho. Everything else I needed, I scavenged. That's what a vagabond must do.

21

Maya

Iceland, March 2015

Snow plastered the ground as the plane came in to land. The airport buzzed with the activity of snow ploughs clearing the runways, creating great banks at the sides. It was such a contrast to the hot climates she'd recently left. Maya's walking sandals – however thick the socks she wore them with, would be useless in these conditions. Swallowing bile at her lack of forethought, she paid airport prices at a North Front outlet and bought herself a pair of lightweight snow boots. *What would Joe have done in this situation?* Walked in his sandals, regardless of the snow, probably. She had hoped to follow his re-purposing ethic and wore a sense of failure along with her new down coat. Still, there'd be no point in getting frostbite out of stubbornness. She walked out of the airport in her new boots and climbed onto the bus the woman in the tour office had pointed out to her.

On a blue-white landscape, clouds of steam rose into the thick sky. At first, her limbs refused to move when she got off the bus. The rest of the passengers spilled out of the vehicle and set off down the crunching path before her. She'd been to the Blue Lagoon once before, two years ago when she and Con flew to Reykjavik to meet Joe. She took a deep breath and blew it out like the puffs of steam thickening the opaque air. Now she was alone. *Come on, Maya.* She forced herself forward, entered the building and bought a ticket. She left her rucksack and guitar in one of the tall lockers and carried only a small bag into the changing rooms. Stripping off without a thought, she showered naked as per the requirement of every swimming pool in Iceland. Attendants kept an eye out to make sure the rules were followed: clean bodies means no disinfectant needed in the water. Freely washing under her arms and between her legs she imagined standing beside her Navengore persona of two years before, huddled into a corner fearing that everyone was looking at her.

Having struggled to push her damp limbs through the arm and leg holes of her swimming costume, she made her way downstairs as icy cold blasts of air funnelled upwards and brought the hairs on her arms to an upstanding salute. Emerging into the open air of the Lagoon she blinked back the hot tears that were pressing behind her eyes. She couldn't help searching for Joe. This was where she had last seen him. *Joe, my lovely boy.*

Why, Joe, why?

'Your complacency,' Joe's final email had said. 'You'll never listen to me. This is the only way I can think of to make you both see that I'm not the boy you wanted me to be.'

She sank beneath the encompassing, milky water of the Blue Lagoon. Into the warmth of a creamy, lapping element. She tipped her head back and felt the water fizzing between her fledgling knots of hair. When she stood, cold air cloaked her shoulders and arms, penetrating the fabric stretched over her torso. She gulped and sank back under, floated on her back while ripples of hot, sulphurous water washed gently over her body and limbs. The sky had turned velvet, rimmed by the lights that flickered to life around the edges of the pool. Maya swam to the hot waterfall and stood underneath while the heavy cascade needled her shoulders. When she'd had enough of the pleasure/pain she swam through a tunnel into a watery cave, crowded already with floating bodies, causing her to swim straight out through an opposite opening. She plastered her face with mud from the wooden boxes placed around the edges of the lagoon. Closing the lid she turned and caught the eye of a young woman wearing a hijab, giggling with her friends. Maya smiled at them and moved on, content at this moment to be alone. She no longer missed Con – or anyone.

She swam into a deserted, almost unbearably hot bay under an overhead light and watched her skin turning beetroot until she could stand the heat no longer. Swimming back into cooler waters, she held her wristband up to be scanned at the bar at the edge of the pool and bought an ice-cold fruit smoothie. Floated away on her back, holding the drink above the water with one hand. In this atmosphere of hazy slow-motion, lulled by the licking waves and the silty floor of the lagoon, images and memories of the family life she'd left behind drifted through her mind. She allowed them to ease out and be replaced by vaguer, more existential questions and answers that seemed to come and go of their own accord. *What did it mean to be alive? How could people remain so inextricably connected, even when away from each other? Was she, in fact, inextricably connected to anyone at all, even her children?*

She existed in isolation from them right now and had done for several months before the visit from Lola and Con. She felt like a lizard sloughing off an old skin. The hot water a baptism of yet another rebirthed Maya. Did anyone need anyone in particular? Or would any convivial companionship – or what was it? Comradeship – that was it. Would comradeship do, when the need to no longer be alone arose?

Maya finally began to understand Joe and perhaps Jamie, too. Some of the hurt eked away. They were never hers in the first place, were they? She longed to communicate to her boys, wherever they were, that she could start to see what they'd been trying to show their parents all along. A plan began to float through her brain as she in turn floated in the milky, warm water. The plan consolidated without her really having to formulate it.

22

Joe's journal

COPENHAGEN - JULY 2013

Okay, I'm breaking a pattern here. This journal is supposed
to proclaim my enthusiasm for the vagabond lifestyle, but
truth to tell I'm feeling down right now.

This is going to take some working out... It's about
my older brother, Jamie. I wish I knew this guy, but I
always felt kept away from him, including when he lived at
home. Kept from getting close to him at least. I shared a
bedroom with my big brother until I was four years old and
even from back then I can remember Dad always shouting
at him. I remember being scared of Jamie. By the time
we parted bedrooms he was almost twelve. A boy of that
age is a lot stronger than a four-year-old and it used to
hurt when he - took out his frustration on me, I guess.
He must have been more than ready for a room of his
own. Even though he sometimes bullied me, I felt sorry
for him. I had this undefined sense that Jamie was the
outcast in our family.

Jamie and I were like the pauper and the prince in terms of parental affection - Dad's, especially. I know I was spoilt rotten by Mum. I guess Jamie had the same material privileges as me, only his talents weren't valued the way my supposed ones were. I had two big sisters who babied me like crazy as well as an adoring Mum and a mostly-proud dad. He thought I should do engineering or something because of my technical drawing skills. I sensed the slightest reticence in him though, like he didn't want to be impressed by the things Mum showed him that I'd done but he couldn't help it.

But Dad didn't think Jamie was anything special and that wasn't fair. I sometimes didn't know how Jamie could be Dad's son at all but you could see he definitely was. The same dark colouring, the same knitted eyebrows. Whereas I look a lot like Mum. So maybe it was himself Dad was railing against. Is that why he didn't love Jamie? And did Mum love me so much because I was / maybe I am - like her?

My brother was a talented musician. And now I know he still is because I've discovered his uploads on YouTube. I wonder if Mum and Dad have ever bothered to look him up and listen to his stuff. I can imagine Mum saying

- yes, I'd love to darling and I will, I promise I will, but I'm just a teensy bit busy doing such-and-such at the moment. I promise I'll listen later, yes I will, I promise. -

If she'd only stopped and really looked at - really listened to Jamie the way she did me and the girls.

When I was a kid Jamie had a guitar and a keyboard in his room. As I got older, if he was in a good mood he'd invite me in and let me listen to a song he'd written. I remember the tingling feeling I'd get when I watched Jamie singing with his eyes closed. I'd watch his fingers dancing on the guitar strings and I'd want to cry. But I held it in until I got back to my own room. Those same fingers that played the guitar so delicately were often scratched and scuffed on the knuckles. Even though I was a kid, the stories about the fights my brother was involved in during his last year at school got back to me through the angry conversations Mum and Dad had after I'd gone to bed.

In the end Jamie left home and didn't tell them where he was going. He stole some money - quite a lot- and he just left in the middle of the night. It was after a massive row with our dad and everybody in the house heard it.

Jamie wouldn't have realised how much I missed him after he was gone. But the other day someone - it was Will in fact: yes, he's here in Copenhagen - Will shared a link to a song he found on YouTube and the song was by Jamie. My brother. He doesn't use his real name but I know it was him because it was a different version of the same song he once played to me in his bedroom. And I recognised his voice - the voice that made me cry. My brother. And I realised how messed-up our family really is.

So. Fuck. I live in a cool community on a huge boat here in Denmark and there are a few other people from my days back in Oz here. Lisa and Ben. And Will. That's right, Will. I came to this place because Will told me about it. He heard I was walking from Germany to Denmark - that crazy walk I did with my friend Nick. It's great being here, part of the community on the boat. We work in a salvage yard three days a week in exchange for meals and a bunk in a shared cabin. I get plenty of time to write - because that's what I'm mainly doing these days. I've loved it here in Copenhagen and I've been on a high from getting to hang out with Will again. But it's all changed. I'm succumbing to depression because... I can't write about that yet. And now I also suddenly miss my brother. Maybe it's being so close to Will that has made me feel this way about Jamie. Maybe. But I think our parents should have encouraged us to be closer. Instead I remember Dad telling me Jamie was a bad influence and that I'd better not turn out like him.

My down mood is worse because I've been getting loads of hassle from my dad too, yeah, and my mum because she always goes along with what he says. Come home now, they keep saying. You're wasting your talents. You should be doing something with your life. What the heck was that education for if you're only going to throw it away? Well, it was for you, Mum and Dad. You asked me to finish school and so I did. You asked me to do those A' levels, so I did. I never said I wanted to, did I?

I wish that just for once Mum would stand up to Dad but she always wants to keep him happy. Sometimes I try to picture her if she'd never met Dad. I think she'd be a bit like me. I used to go into my bedroom while she was supposed to be tidying up or making my bed and I'd find her standing at the wall with her back to me and she'd be trailing a finger over one of the maps I drew on the lining paper. And when she turned her head and noticed me she hadn't quite managed to get the look of wistfulness off her face yet. I think she encouraged me with those maps, with following my own heart on the one hand even when backing Dad up with the other, because I was expressing a longing for the kind of freedom she longed for herself. Don't get me wrong, she loves my dad, I know she does, and having a family was what she always wanted. But I still get the feeling she has a pair of invisible wings that one day she wants to open up and fly away on.

(It's made me feel better, writing that. My mum's a grown-up so I've got to let her go. She's not my responsibility and I want to be free. So I'll let her fly.)

I think I'm going to do something. It hurts, but I think I'm going to have to do it. I need to let them go... and find myself.

23

Maya

Denmark, June 2015

Copenhagen was where Joe had been when Maya last heard from him. *Oh, God, going on two years ago.* How could he forsake her? She'd loved Joe more than any of the others, deep in her bones. Losing him was her punishment. Losing two sons was utter carelessness. She'd neglected one boy and smothered the other.

The backpack straps bit into her shoulders as she tramped the streets leading towards the harbour. Her boots and the down jacket she'd bought at Keflavik airport three months previously weighed the bag down. It hurt to think of getting rid of them but there was no way she could carry the extra weight through summer. She'd been lucky in Reykjavik because of her temporary job and her room at the hostel which meant she hadn't had to carry her rucksack around with her.

The blister on her left heel had broken, rubbed raw, and the strap of her thick-soled sandal was stained with blood. *Good, I deserve it. I want my Joe.* As her footsteps slowed people crowded past, rivers of noise and colour flowing in opposing directions. She stopped, blinking back tears.

She was hungry too, which didn't help. She had a packet of sandwiches in her rucksack but now the scent of chips and vinegar drifted up to her nostrils and her stomach tightened with longing. *Chips.* Turning her head from side to side she discovered the source of the vinegary fumes.

The folding cardboard box lay invitingly open on top of a pile of rubbish in a bin outside a mini fish restaurant. Someone must have only just dumped it there because she'd been dithering on the spot for a while and hadn't smelt the rich pickings earlier, although she'd noticed the tempting display of ice-bedded seafood in the window and the names and prices penned on the glass in different colours. She edged sideways on the pavement and checked around before lifting the takeaway box from the bin. Most of the chips looked in pristine condition. Several others were mushed into an unrecognisable mess at one side of the box, these she shuffled casually into the bin and moved off, closing the box and slipping it carefully upright into her tote bag. She re-knotted the thin straps together and walked away as quickly as she could with her sore heel.

Preoccupations weighed back in as she continued along the cobbles towards the harbour. It wasn't only Joe. Memories gusted through her mind like a tornado that must have been gathering strength the whole time she'd been wandering and had time to think.

Jamie.

She sees herself back in London, tired and feeling like an incompetent mother amongst the baby-wearing clique of their leafy neighbourhood. She misses Jamie's first steps, his first solid food, while someone else looks after him. She never carries him in a sling. By the time she picks him up from nursery at the end of a tiring day he is falling asleep against her shoulder. She straps him into his buggy and bumps him down the steps onto the street, sliding her briefcase into the plastic tray beneath his warm weight in the canvas seat. Even as she pushes him home she grieves for their sporadic contact.

She has him home, grumpily woken up and fed, cursorily bathed, dressed in a Babygro and settled into his cot with the nightlight on and the mobile wound up by the time Con arrives home. The schedule's relentless.

The next morning Con will have left the house before she crams her hurriedly-washed and dressed baby back into his buggy, a rusk clutched in his fist, and wheels him the length of two streets back to his day nursery.

'Look, Jamie –' She sometimes remembers to talk to him if her mouth isn't stuffed full of hastily-buttered toast. 'Look at the colours of the leaves on that bush. They're orange. Can you say that? Orange.' But it's already time to drop him off at the nursery door with a quick kiss on his cheek. Though she's unable to resist smoothing the black curls away from his face while he's taken out of her arms by a nursery nurse. His face crumples, and she has to ignore his spurting tears – his wet, pink, opening, needing mouth.

My baby. If he's truly hers, why does she hardly spend any time with him? But she needs to hurry to the tube station and she prays she isn't going to be late for work again. She and Con work so hard to provide the things for their son that they never had when they were children.

The smell of the sea dispersed into the air and a flurry of seagulls circled overhead under a puzzle of stone-coloured clouds. Rays of light shone through the moving gaps between the jigsaw pieces, sprinkling the backs of the wheeling gulls. A single bird flipped towards the sea like a puzzle piece knocked off the edge of the table. Maya cast her head from side to side, scanning colourful buildings and covered stalls along the edge of the street. She was going to buckle under the weight of the overloaded pack at this rate. If she spotted a charity shop behind the market stalls she'd be inside it like a shot and offload the expensive, extraneous winter gear. But it was mostly the windows of bars and restaurants her eyes lighted upon.

She planned to set out from Denmark in a few days, but she had allotted herself a short break from vagabonding, some time to explore Copenhagen. She'd booked herself into a hostel for two nights. *A proper bed. A warm shower.* Bliss.

Letting go of the chest straps she succinctly adjusted her posture. Stretched out her arms, wriggled her fingers. How free she'd feel to walk along this picturesque street unencumbered by the weight of the only belongings she needed these days. Fewer and fewer *things*. If only she and Con had understood this when they were younger. Their youngest child – brought up in the comfort of materiality – had opted for a life of weightlessness anyway. She didn't know what Jamie had opted for.

She hadn't heard a word from him for almost ten years.

Someone huddled on the street ahead, beyond the market. Maya felt in her pockets for some Danish Krona but discovered she'd already used the small amount she'd drawn out on arriving in the city. She'd bought a new gas canister, now tucked into the bottom of her rucksack, and some dried food. Instead of tossing coins she dropped into a crouching position, maintaining a careful balance with the weight on her back. The stranger was a young woman who sat against the plate-glass window of a busy bar. Her knees, in dirty jeans, were huddled up to her chest and her arms wrapped around them. She wore a dirty grey hoody – the hood up despite the warmth of the day. After a moment she lifted her chin and met Maya's eyes.

A cold flush went through Maya's body – for a half-second she'd recognised the girl as Jodie – but this was a different girl with violet-underscored eyes and hair a paler shade of ginger. She wrinkled her nose and let out a stream of unintelligible words. 'I'm sorry, I don't understand,' Maya said helplessly. It wasn't only that she was speaking a different language – there was something odd about her speech. The girl unlocked her fingers to make rapid, fluent shapes in the air and Maya understood she was deaf. The girl gestured towards Maya's clothes and hair. It was then that Maya noticed her own reflection in the window. Her unwrapped hair spiralled in all directions – she looked like a wild woman. A sour taste flooded her mouth and a phrase of her grandma's came to her – *you're no better than you ought to be.* She clambered unsteadily to her feet and stood swaying for a moment. Then she twisted her arm to the side pocket of her rucksack, popped it open and pulled out the pack of sandwiches – one with a single bite taken out of it – that she'd rescued from an abandoned tray at the airport cafeteria. She offered them to the girl who took them and turned the opened packet over suspiciously. She didn't look up at Maya again.

What if it was Jamie she found on the next corner? What if Joe had lived like this?

She hobbled on. It was noon and she wasn't allowed into the hostel until two. She couldn't be bothered to walk all the way there to drop off her backpack before returning to Nyhavn, which was the area she was making for. The last place she'd heard from Joe. She supposed she could find a bench somewhere along the cobbled harbour-side and sit down with her tablet but first she wanted to be rid of the winter items in her pack. Reaching the end of the street, she still hadn't seen any charity shops. Did they have such a thing in Copenhagen? But at least here was an empty bench. With the backpack planted firmly between her knees she used it as a table. First she polished off the cooling chips. Then she wedged her tablet in place and drafted out an email that she would have nowhere to send than to herself. But one day, she wanted Jamie to read it.

First and foremost, I should have protected you from that vile-tongued mother of your school friend. You were only a little boy. It was harmless fun, I knew that then and I know it now. It was only the adults who interpreted your child's play as something vile. And most of all I should have defended my

113

little boy from the things Con said. The twins were a year old and you adored them. And your father asked, in all apparent innocence, if our little girls would be safe as they got older. But I mustn't blame him for your emotional neglect, I'm your mother. I should have sat down with the other mothers and discussed it straight away, directly after the birthday party. You're telling me that *he* had *her* pants down? *I should have said.* And it just so happens that she had his pants down too? So why is it my son who's being labelled as some kind of pervert? They're barely five years old, for God's sake. She's a girl and he's a boy, they were examining each other's differences, that's all – their curiosity is totally normal. *But I didn't rush in to your defence. You know all this already, Jamie, or maybe you've blanked it out as I have for so long. It feels important for me to write it down now, though, and perhaps one day I'll be able to send this to you. It was another mother who collected you from the party, as pre-arranged, and it was her who was given the story of your supposed crime before anyone spoke to me. As planned, she had taken you home with her until I could pick you up later because I had a hospital appointment with the twins. This woman made you sit in a room on your own until I arrived. In case you interfered with her daughter. I don't know if you remember any of this, Jamie, but I want you to know how sorry I am that I never spoke to you about it.*

You were shivering when I arrived to take you home. Pale with the shock of the adults' reaction to your innocent game. White-lipped, I bundled you into your coat and fastened your hand around the handle of the double buggy and bustled all three of my children along the streets to our home. I see now that you probably thought I was angry with you, too. You must have felt so hurt and confused.

The incident blew up the telephone network between all those infant school mothers by the end of that evening, even those whose children had not been at the party. I didn't find this out until the next day. All the mothers apart from me had

114

been telephoned and they all had an opinion on my sexual deviant of a son, who had not yet celebrated his fifth birthday. In the coming weeks – because I didn't speak up – I was frozen out of the babysitting circle and was no longer invited to coffee mornings in the various mothers' homes.

My best friend became my enemy overnight as her daughter was the same age as you and her mind had been poisoned. The little girl found playing Mummies and Daddies with you – with the other children watching – was treated as a victim. I heard later that her mother had sought counselling for her. There was no such provision for my little boy – for you, my son – when you later became subject to bullying because of the things the other children had heard their parents say about you.

Jamie, I'm sorry. I failed you. Maybe I can discuss all this with you one day. I promise to try.

Her nose was thick with snot and her eyes blurry with tears. She wiped her sleeve across her eyes and paused to read her scurried thoughts over. It was the first time she'd ever put what happened into words. It seemed important to explain more.

I suppose it would have been easy enough simply to change schools. I could have bundled you and the twins into the car every morning and driven you halfway across London to a school where none of the parents knew us. I could have, if I'd had the energy. But what kind of life would it have been for us all? My depression didn't help. I was no longer even confident enough to take my two baby girls to the toddler group in our area. I should have got the school to call some kind of meeting – requested that they invite a child psychologist in to explain that you were not the dangerous monster the mothers of girls seemed to think you were. I should have done. But the situation bubbled and brewed out of all proportion. The little girl's mother was probably embarrassed about her daughter's behaviour and she proceeded to distribute lies with her whiplash tongue.

By then you and I had already been tried and convicted. Life in our cosy terraced house was ruined. I visited several estate agents who had national branches and from them I discovered what kind of property we could buy with the sort of money we'd get for our London home. If we sold it and moved to a different area of the country we could buy a mansion. Your father had relatives in Lincolnshire. . .

For once I put my foot down and because he was weary of my depression he gave in to my wishes to move.

She hadn't realised quite how hard she was crying until she choked on the sobs – coughed so much that a blob of mucus landed on the pavement next to her guitar, strapped to the back of her rucksack. *I'm sorry, pavement.* She wiped her nose and lifted her chin. Slipped off the elastic band that she wore on her wrist and gathered her knobbly mass of hair onto the back of her head. No more time for crying – she had a journey to complete.

She would start with Joe. At least she might be able to talk to some of his friends. Following his trail was an act of atonement – it was the least she could do to try and make up for her failures as a mother.

Joe had lived on a section of the river somewhere away from the main tourist area of the city. She turned the tablet off and slid it carefully back into her rucksack. Balanced the weighted bag against the bench and stood, stretching her back and arms. The different-coloured houses surrounding the water looked so pretty, especially in the early afternoon light – startlingly defined against the sky and juxtaposed, from her position by the bench, with the masts of ships that added a mediaeval flavour to the view. *I need to imbibe every experience, this is all there is. No more time for crying.* Her nose was still running. The tissue from the airport rest room had disintegrated so she felt in her pockets and then rummaged in the top of her bag where she found a lightweight headscarf to use as a handkerchief. She would use the laundry services at the hostel later.

116

24

Maya

Berlin, December 2015

The dishwasher had broken and Maya's hands were roughened and red from the relentless washing up. But it was worth it for a place to stay and all the food she could eat. At least it felt good to have her hands warm instead of always cold. Like her mother's and her granny's before her, her circulation was poor. During the past few weeks her fingers had spent a lot of time white and numb and she often felt an aching pain in her joints. As for the numbness, the pins and needles she suffered when the blood returned made her jaw clench. She hadn't realised Berlin would be so cold.

As the supply of pots lessened she drifted into a brief daydream of the kitchen in her quiet former home, after the children had left for school. She swished her hands in the hot suds and idly watched bubbles pop. In the corner of her vision Abebi's brown hands descended on the washed pottery, lifting and drying each item and stacking it on the shelves. When the draining board emptied, the movement stopped. Maya remained in place, her vision swimming out of focus. The kitchen was steamy. Chattering noise from a party of school children and the clattering of pots from the dining room was punctuated by an occasional hiss from the grumbling coffee machine in the corner. As she stared unseeingly into the bowl the pattern of washing-up foam with its popped bubbles and mountainous turrets transformed itself into the 3-D map Joe had once constructed on the professional drawing table they'd got him for his bedroom.

Now she felt that sickening lurch in her stomach again. Nobody could explain what happened to Joe. Someone she'd been put in touch with by someone else who still lived on the boat in Copenhagen had suggested he'd moved to Germany not long after leaving Denmark but that was all. It wasn't much help now she was here. And it had been two years since the informant had last seen or heard from Joe. So how did the drowning in Australia happen, his journal so carefully protected in the leather satchel? *One year ago, Joe.*

Maya washed the few new pots that had appeared with a clatter by her right elbow and Abebi picked them up from the drainer by her left.

'That's all for now,' Jenna smiled at her co-workers. She moved back across the room and popped her head around the door to the dining room, checking a final time. 'The monsters have finished eating. I'll stick some toast in for us, shall I?'

Maya dried her hands and rubbed them together, feeling their sandpaper texture. 'Do,' she said. 'I'm starving.'

She and Abebi stretched their backs. Abebi grinned widely. 'Thank goodness for that. I think we've definitely earned our breakfast.'

Maya poured the coffee and they all sat in the morning brightness of the primrose-painted kitchen, listening to the thud of footsteps and excited voices overhead. The youthful guests had made their way upstairs to their dormitories. Maya flexed her fingers, noticing again the slight swellings around the joints. She pictured Granny's crooked fingers and remembered Mum rubbing ointment into hers as the bones ballooned. Maya really needed to start looking after her joints – this European winter was taking its toll on her certain propensity to arthritis.

'Where are they from – the school party?' Abebi lifted a crumb with her fingertip.

'England.' Jenna glanced at Maya. 'Lincolnshire, their teacher said. Isn't that where you're from, Maya?'

'Yes, it is.'

Perhaps they were children of families she was acquainted with. She'd thought earlier that a girl with long dark hair, joking over the table with her teacher, had looked a bit like the youngest daughter of that artist in Navengore. But the perceived familiarity could have been down to the girl's resemblance to Lola and Daisy at a similar age. The way they all straightened their hair and flicked their eyeliner at the corners. And anyway of course that girl – the artist's daughter – would have left school by now. Other people's children grew up too.

'Lincolnshire's a large county,' she focussed on the butter knife as she spoke, drawing it across her toast.

Jenna pushed a strand of blonde hair behind her ear. Abebi glanced at Jenna before fixing Maya with her liquid brown eyes.

'Jenna tells me your daughters are coming for a visit at the weekend but she says you're not going home with them for Christmas. Do you think you might change your mind when you see them?'

The way they both looked at her felt like an intervention. Maya munched her toast, then took a sip of coffee. She could feel Abebi's eyes. The younger woman had sobbed in her sleep again last night and no doubt would have done anything to be back with her family in Nigeria – if only their home still existed. Both Maya's new friends had poured their secrets out to her while the three of them drank *Heiße Schokolade* – made with solid bars of Swiss chocolate (bought from that gorgeous shop on Tauentzienstraße) and hot milk, topped with whipped cream – in the off-duty night kitchen. But Maya was guarded about her family concerns. Her reluctance to return home even for a visit was hard to explain without going into detail.

'Trust me, if I did I'd get trapped there. I just know it. And I haven't finished doing what I'm doing yet. I have a quest to complete – if it helps you think of it that way?' She could see from their expressions they weren't convinced. They didn't understand what her quest was and she was no longer sure she did, either. All she knew was that going back to Navengore would transform her back into the old Maya. Flexing her arm she inspected the bobbles on the sleeve of the second-hand jumper she wore. Her former self would have been draped in cashmere, chosen from a range of colours neatly folded in her dresser drawers. It was simpler to have no choice.

Neither of the other two had the option to re-join their families. Jenna's American parents had both died of cancer and Abebi's mother had only had enough money to smuggle one daughter to safety. Consequently Abebi lived with survivor's guilt. Maya finished another half-round of toast, feeling defensive. 'I've talked to my daughters and they tell me they understand my reasons.'

Abebi looked disappointed. Maya swallowed the grit in her throat. 'I'm looking forward to introducing them to you. Now, we'd better get ready for our sightseeing trip if we're going to be back in time for evening duties. Come on, chop-chop!'

The young women rolled their eyes at each other. They often called her Mother.

Maya had holed herself up in Berlin for the winter. It was easy to find a hostel job as the summer workers were moving on when she arrived and the school parties had flooded in. There was enough work to earn her a small wage as well as a bed and two meals a day.

A few weeks into her stay she'd joined the younger women for the first time on their weekly culture trip, that one to the Berlin Wall Memorial. In their company she was reminded of hanging out with her young friends in Australia a whole year before.

Standing shoulder to shoulder with Abebi and Jenna at the top of the metal-gridded tower behind the Documentationszentrum, they looked down at the former death-strip, the ugly observation tower sealed inside the double barrier of wall. Bile churned in Maya's stomach. *This was all going on during my childhood and youth.*

Back on the ground, on lawns of vivid green, rusted-metal displays featured photographs of East Germans who'd died attempting to escape. The three women read some of the names aloud to each other, meeting the photographed gazes head-on and pausing for a moment of respect.

'Hans-Dieter Wesa, 19/01/1943 – 23/08/1962,' Maya read, her throat tightening. An angel-faced boy, as she'd perceived her Joe to be, as his mother must have thought of him. Retrospective bravery embedded in his outward innocence. *Dear God.*

'Dorit Schmiel,' read Jenna. 'Also only nineteen years old. Look at the light in her eyes. So beautiful and alive. How can she have been cut off like that, just for wanting her freedom. Unbearable.'

Maya glanced at Abebi, who raised her chin, scanning the row of photographs. 'Erna Kelm,' she read out carefully. '21/07/1908 – 11/06/1962. She reminds me of you, Maya. Perhaps she was trying to help some younger people escape, her family, maybe. Or perhaps she was a teacher. Fifty-four years old, she was so brave.'

Abebi continued to stare at the image of Erna Kelm. Her eyes had gone stark, the scent of her fear almost palpable. Tense seconds later Jenna broke the spell, slipping her arm around her friend's shoulder. 'Shall we go and see Checkpoint Charlie now?'

Six weeks later the temperature had plummeted. They wrapped themselves in warm clothes and set off for Museum Island, Maya's choice. Not yet back to full strength after a cold, she'd probably only manage to get round one museum – two at the most. 'Perhaps the cathedral,' she told the others. 'If we only have time to look around one place. There's a wonderful cathedral in Lincoln, you know, and I'm always interested in comparisons.' Apparently Museum Island itself was a work of art with its arrangement of stunning mediaeval buildings, whether or not you entered the museums. And they would go to one of the restaurants across the river afterwards – she was almost looking forward to that more than the *culture*. After being confined to the stuffy kitchen at the hostel, it felt good to get out into the crisp air and join the crowds on the pre-Christmas streets. There was a hint of blue in the cold sky, maybe the sun would come out. Scanning a colourful window display of toys and wrapped presents, she blinked away tears and blamed them on the brisk wind that blew dust into her eyes.

They walked and then ran for the bus at Potsdamer Brücke and climbed to the top deck. Maya sat quietly behind the other two, nestling her hands into the folds of her recently-acquired scarf. Someone had left it behind in one of the dorms. She felt a pang of regret for the almost-new coat she'd donated to a charity shop in Copenhagen only a few months before but that was an unhealthy attachment. This was the way of her life now – everything was dispensable. Luckily most hostels had a well-stocked cupboard of unclaimed property and at her current one the staff had first dibs on its contents. She rubbed her hand up and down the sleeve of the black wool jacket she'd also procured and felt grateful for her continual progress towards an easy-come, easy-go attitude to *things*. Before she left Germany for warmer climes she'd make sure this jacket got a new owner.

The brittle branches of the trees lining the road seemed to shiver in the cold. She glanced up and noticed a mother with a child, standing on the balcony of one of the pale grey apartment blocks. The mother pointed something out to the child, perhaps a bird, and the child flapped its arms at the sky. Christmas lights were strung along the edge of the balcony. They passed the *Museum für Kommunikation*, which they'd visited two weeks before. Maya had loved the palatial atrium with a glass ceiling and the theatre-like balconies. She'd wished she had small children again so they could explore the vast array of old telephones and typewriters together. The bus crawled past the oldest church in Berlin – St. Nikolai Kirche –the lower half built of ancient grey bricks and the upper section in red as if picked up from elsewhere and placed on top. Two porthole windows above the arched door resembled hollow eyes. Nine centuries ago the mediaeval version of herself might have come here and prayed for her lost sons. *Joe. Jamie.* Two pointy, silvery towers pierced the wispy cloud that hung in strands in the faintly blue sky. The sun made an appearance, highlighting the upper portion of the church and coating it with gold.

Maya drifted inwards with thoughts of Christmases past, when the children were young and they'd attended the Christingle service at the village church. Further on, Jenna stopped chatting to Abebi and turned to Maya, pointing towards where the pale grey stone pillars of Brandenburg Gate glowed faintly yellow in the watery sunshine. 'You should see those Linden trees in summer,' she said. 'A whole avenue of them in bloom.' She paused before returning to her conversation with Abebi. Maya smiled and half-listened to the girls chatting, a tune her mother used to sing to her and her sister going through her head. *Linden Lea.* Flowery-gladed, she hummed. The bus trundled on. Stopped and started again. Passengers alighted and more came upstairs. Maya felt a bump in the back of her seat as what sounded like English tourists settled behind her. The bus slowed, barely crawling through a crowded shopping area. Idly, she followed Jenna's profiled direction of gaze. A family walked along at much the same speed as the traffic-jammed bus. A handsome young man with a beard and dark curly hair poking out from under a beanie hat walked on the road-side of a petite woman with blonde-streaked dark hair. She held a dancing dark-haired child by the hand. Another young man – muffled up in a scarf and wearing a felt hat with ear-flaps covering the sides of his face – walked on the inner edge of the pavement next to the little girl. He seemed to be making her laugh and she kept taking swipes at him with her spare hand. *So young, their whole lives ahead of them.* She wasn't quite sure what it was about them that tugged at her insides. *Maybe I'm still shaky from the cold I had.* Jenna exploded into laughter at a comment from Abebi that Maya couldn't quite hear and didn't want to.

She focussed completely on the family on the street. She couldn't see any of their faces clearly as they were slightly ahead of the bus but something about them made her feel raw. Perhaps it was that the nearside man's hair reminded her of Con's when he was young. She found she was pressing a hand to her chest under the blue wool of her scarf. Or maybe it was the little girl – as the girl in the Lincolnshire party of students had done – this child also reminded her of Lola and Daisy when they were toddlers. Perhaps all little girls would from now on. The burn of tears pushed at the backs of her eyes and her vision blurred, so that when the bus moved forward and she turned her head to look back at the oblivious family on the pavement it was through a veil of salty water. She couldn't see them properly! Pressing a hand against the glass, the bus turned a corner and she wiped her eyes. It was only a few days until she would see her daughters again.

Part Two

25

Jamie

Berlin, November 2013

Multi-coloured lights flickered on the ceiling and walls and the beat thudded through the speakers on either side of Jamie, throbbing through the booth and his whole body. On the decks he was in another world – one in which he'd always felt he belonged. Darkness buzzed with light. He gazed out over the writhing mass of dancers on the floor below and energy shot through his body. The club was in a grand old building, a brutally-designed, concrete cathedral of sorts. The interior consisted of the vast cavern of the room in which Jamie was playing, and a maze of corridors opened off it into smaller spaces. People crammed into all of the spaces, most dressed in extraordinary costumes and some dressed in nothing at all – their skin painted in bright colours. You were weird if you looked normal. Jamie wore a fluorescent tie-dyed t-shirt and red leather trousers. A necklace of amber beads jumped on his chest, pumping along with his heart. A yellow bandanna held back his dark hair. His feet were bare, the way he preferred when he was working, despite the floor's stickiness. As the rhythm crescendoed he took one hand from the decks and punched the air, letting out a yell of joy. The dancers crowded onto the floor below mirrored his action and he felt they were one, a many-faceted entity.

Lejla stepped up to the podium and touched Jamie on the arm. He grinned and carried on spinning, took his eyes off the disks for a second and mouthed a greeting. She smiled and continued standing by his side until he gave her his attention again. She pointed to the floor below the booth but all he could see was the churn of bodies. He pulled an earphone away from one ear and cocked his head towards her. The beat increased in intensity. Lejla cupped a hand to Jamie's ear. 'Some kid,' she yelled. 'Wants to see you!' Jamie brought the set to a fade-out, caught Bruno's eyes and jerked his head towards the decks. Bruno gave him a thumbs-up and rammed his headphones on – stepped in front of Jamie and started his shift early. There was a slight ripple of disappointment from the crowd – Jamie's crowd – but then they were off again, fickle in their loyalty to anything but the beat.

Jamie pulled Lejla to one side, couldn't help running his eyes appreciatively over her breasts in the neon crop top and her hips in the short, fringed skirt. She wore chunky-soled sandals but still only came up to his shoulder. He couldn't get enough of her.

'What is it, babe?' He stroked her hair, knowing she wouldn't interrupt his work for nothing, just as he wouldn't have when she played her set earlier. Lejla inclined her head slightly to one side. 'You know this boy?' She had to shout above the beat. 'He say he need to see you.'

Jamie found it hard to shift his gaze from his lover to any point beyond where she stood. She looked too damn cute with her hand resting on her hip like that. He loved her new rounded shape as much as he had her old skinny one – even the silvery scars that now marked her belly. But with an effort he pulled his gaze away and saw the tall guy standing with his arms wrapped around himself, looking out-of-place. The picture of mundanity.

Limbs jerked and whirled around him but the boy stood immobile, staring kinda desperately back at Jamie. Jamie refocussed his eyes. The kid appeared amber-haired in the flashing lights and was definitely familiar. He had a growth of pale hair on his face but it couldn't be called a beard yet. Even in the fluctuating lights it was the boy's eyes Jamie recognised most of all. The last time he saw him, he'd only been about twelve years old. Now he was a man.

Lejla stayed behind to assist Bruno. Jamie pulled Joe by the arm into a dim little room that stood in for an office off one of the corridors, flicking on a light switch as they entered. Under the lightbulb Jamie felt like a butterfly to Joe's moth.

'Come on in, man. Oh, wow.' He drew Joe against him with one arm and pushed the door shut with the elbow of his other. 'Christ, look at you. All grown up!'

They were equal in height. Jamie squashed Joe's face against the side of his own with his broad hand, which encompassed the back of Joe's head. He felt the sweat of his bearded cheek bleed into the soft hair on his brother's face. Then he released him, pushed him away slightly so he could examine him properly.

'This is amazing! You found me. You came to see me, I can't believe it! But hell, what're you doing here, lad?'

While Jamie's voice caught in his throat, Joe sobbed openly, gripping his own upper arms with both hands as if holding on for dear life. Snot plastered his upper lip and tears ran copiously down his cheeks. Jamie nodded to himself, turning away slightly. He ripped the bandanna from his hair and felt his hair spring up around his head. He used the yellow fabric to wipe sweat from his face and neck while Joe struggled to get himself together.

'Take your time, man.' Jamie grabbed a length of toilet paper from the roll hanging by a string from a nail on the wall and shoved it at Joe's chest. Joe uncurled his gripped fingers and pushed the balled-up mass against his face to hide behind. Jamie turned to a cupboard against the wall, considered for a moment, then pulled out a bottle of whisky and two dusty glasses.

'Here, man. Look, sit down over there will you? Have a gulp of this, it'll either kill you or cure you. Remember that time I tried to get you to have a sip of the whisky I kept hidden in my room?' Jamie was amazed at how easily the memories returned. 'If I remember rightly I tried to persuade you to have a smoke as well. Of weed.' He laughed harshly. 'You were a good little laddo then though, weren't you? Let's hope you've toughened up since.'

He watched with satisfaction as Joe tipped the first swallow of whisky down his throat, pausing to take a shuddering breath before finishing it off.

'Thanks.' Joe choked on another sob. 'It was just a shock, that's all. Actually seeing you, you know?'

'Yeah.' Jamie's head buzzed. His t-shirt was soaked through with sweat. He rummaged in a leather bag that hung from a peg by the door and pulled out another rumpled t-shirt, also tie-dyed. Lejla had a stall on the market. Every item made of cloth in their apartment was brightly coloured, even the baby's clothes. Jamie stripped off his t-shirt, feeling the sweat cool on his back as his skin was exposed to the comparatively chill air in the makeshift office. He tossed the sweaty shirt to one side and pulled the fresh one over his head, tugging it down over his hard stomach. He caught the flash of admiration in his younger brother's bloodshot eyes. Last time Joe had seen him Jamie was running to fat – a total loser in everything. At least, that was how his family had viewed him.

Joe now sat folded almost double on the wooden chair opposite Jamie. He'd wrapped his arms around his knees. Jamie waited until his brother's breathing evened out. They'd be able to chat soon. Jamie leaned forward with the whisky bottle and poured some more into Joe's glass where it stood on a small table.

'Had a fight with the family?' The kid must have found out where his big brother was – somehow – and packed his little bag and fled here to Berlin. He probably had enough pocket money each week to pay for the flight. Still, it was nice to see Joe again – great, in fact. The kid had taken a lot of shit from Jamie in the past and never seemed to hold it against him. And Joe had liked his music. Jamie's parents were always too busy to listen, or they didn't think his music was important. The twins were always off doing their girly stuff but little Joe could usually be found hunched over that huge drawing table in his room, working on some map or other. He would come running into Jamie's room at the click of his big brother's fingers.

'What? No.' Joe took a swig from his replenished glass and Jamie had to admire him. What would the folks back home think about that? Their precious lad swilling it back like the best of them. 'I haven't seen the family for a while,' Joe said. Jamie felt his eyebrows jolt upwards.

'You mean you haven't come straight from home?' Maybe there was more to him than he'd anticipated. After all, it had been a good few years. He took a deep swallow from his own glass.

'No,' said Joe again. 'I haven't been home in eighteen months. I've been on the road. I live on the road, stopping here and there sometimes, you know?'

'What?' Was this the same spoiled prince Jamie had been brought up with? Jamie had still been living at home when he was Joe's age. What a turn-up for the books, as their dad used to say. 'Do you mean staying in hotels or, like, rooms in people's homes – are you on some kind of funded gap year?' That must be it. An extended gap year, maybe. Joe must be about – what, going on twenty by now, Jamie guessed. But they would have given Joe anything his little heart desired, Mum especially.

'No, not funded at all.' Joe surprised him again. 'I can see why you'd think that about me, Jamie. In fact to be fair, my first-ever trip around the main cities of Europe... I visited Berlin you know – to think you were probably here all the time and I didn't know – well, *that* was funded by Mum and Dad. I had a place waiting for me at Durham Uni. But I let them down, as they put it. The funded trip was supposed to *get it out of my system.* But having swallowed the bait I decided not to go to university after all. Their bribe didn't work.' Joe sniffed hard. 'After that two-month trip I couldn't bring myself to settle down like they were pushing me to. I didn't fucking want to go to university.' Jamie jolted in his seat in mock-shock at the swearword coming from his brother's mouth and Joe managed a shaky grin. He swallowed the last of the whisky and took a deep breath.

'So I emptied my savings account of every last penny and yeah, it was quite a lot of money since they'd insisted I didn't spend my own money on that first trip. The money in that account was supposed to go towards a deposit on a *mortgage* after I finished university – if you can believe that? Yeah.'

Jamie nodded. He sure could.

'They were going to keep putting money in it for the three years I'd be at university – like they did for the girls. But I took the money that was already there and it was enough to buy a flight and a visa and have the requisite amount in my bank account to go to Australia, so that's what I did.'

Jamie almost cheered. But it was fucking sad as well. Recently he'd seen a programme on TV about the rise in depression in young people. Hard-core oldies saying stuff like, *it's because they have too much these days, that's why they all get depressed.* As if material stuff was the only thing you could want. It wasn't like that at all. It wasn't having too many material possessions that had caused *his* depression, it was that his parents seemed to want him to be a different kind of person. And he'd been willing to give up all that *stuff* to try and find the person he was inside. He'd had to steal money – they'd apparently had the mortgage-deposit idea *after* he left, with one less kid they must have decided they could afford it – for a flight abroad. Jamie had been in Berlin for eight years now and made a life for himself. His parents didn't know their grandchild had been born earlier that year. Jamie decided to wait and see what Joe was planning to do before he told him about the baby.

26

Jamie

Berlin, November 2013

Jamie didn't often drink these days and the whisky's warmth had spread from his stomach into his chest and all the way down his arms into his fingertips.

'So are you in touch with Mum and Dad at all?' He swallowed a bubble of air and immediately coughed out a belch, placing his hand over his diaphragm. 'Sorry. Or, uhm, the sisters, do you keep in touch with them? Man, they must be... what, twenty-four or so by now?' He pictured the two girls in their jodphurs and riding hats. Or on the landing in their pyjamas on the last night he'd seen them. When their father had blasted Jamie for arriving home late, for being a waste of space and a deep disappointment to his family. He wondered what his sisters looked like now. 'I can't believe you've all grown up.' There was a moment of stillness while time adjusted itself. Then the lightbulb in the ceiling fixture buzzed. Jamie hoped it wasn't going to pop, but it only flickered for a moment before it stabilised again.

'They're twenty-three,' Joe said. 'I'm nineteen. And four months. You've grown up too, Jamie. You seem like a – you know – a real man now.'

'A real man.' Jamie laughed. 'Yeah, I suppose I am. I wouldn't do the things now that I was doing when you last knew me. Look,' he showed Joe his knuckles. 'No more fighting. So you don't keep in touch with the parents and the twins?'

He held his breath while a flood of nostalgia for the two baby girls he remembered being born washed over him. Yet at the same time he supposed he hoped Joe had jumped into the deep end like him. That would make him, Jamie, not so much the outcast after all. He rubbed at a scuff on the knee of his red leather trousers with his finger, thinking how incongruous he looked next to Joe, here in the dull room. He could just imagine his father's face if he saw him. *Waster –* he could almost hear his voice as well. Though the beats still thrummed through the walls and floor and ceiling of the tiny space, Jamie felt distanced from the life of the club now, as if his former life had opened its mouth and was about to swallow him back in. He edged forward, scraping chair legs over the concrete floor. The shadows beyond the glare of the dangling bulb felt dangerous. Was Lejla still out there, spinning the discs with Bruno? And did they truly have a baby who slept soundly at home with her grandmother watching over her? He'd never doubted these things before but Joe's presence made them tenuous.

'I was in touch with home right up until a couple of months ago.' Joe sniffed twice. 'I had to cut free for a while, you know? It won't be forever but... I wanted Mum to see... to see they've got to leave me alone. Stop hassling me.'

'Hey, man.' Jamie leaned back and grabbed him another handful of tissue. The floor seemed to be rocking under his feet even while he was sitting on the chair. Lejla would know what to do. 'You can always give her a call if it upsets you.'

'I can't,' Joe said, still sniffing hard. 'Nothing will ever change if I do. I miss having Mum there at the press of a button but I've realised I've been relying on her to keep me going, you know. To encourage me and tell me how well I'm doing. And then the minute she persuades Dad to come on FaceTime with her she's all like, oh, Joe, your father's probably right. Like she's balancing on the fence between us both.'

'Yeah, she's always been like that.' The face of Jamie's mother materialised in faded pixels in front of his eyes. He blinked and the image dispelled in a rush. He held his head for a moment before glancing back at Joe. 'So what is it you want to do so much? I mean, *my* plan was to get away and become a musician, which is what I've done. I still play the guitar, you know. I do an acoustic act and I play keyboards in a band as well. And of course there's my spot in this club, which is probably what I love most of all.' He wanted his young brother to be proud of him, he realised. Like when Joe had admired his tunes as a little boy. 'It's taken me years to build all this up though. I mean, what is it you want to *do* Joe, that they're stopping you from doing? You said you went to Australia, so how did you end up here?'

"My visa ran out and I hadn't done enough hours of farm work to renew it. And also I... there was someone who...' He stopped. Coughed and blushed.

Awareness spread through Jamie. He saw it now and perhaps he'd also been able to see it when Joe was a young boy – he'd vaguely guessed by the time Joe was a pre-teen. All sorts of signals. Like, at the age of twelve Jamie remembered feeling embarrassed to leave a mate's family's dining table because his friend's sister was sitting opposite and there was an embarrassing tightness in his trousers. In retrospect he recognised similar behaviour from Joe with his school friend. The way Joe blushed when he looked at the boy. Jamie met an eclectic variety of characters in his work and he'd had long conversations with two or three young guys who had recently come out.

137

'What's his name, mate?'

Joe jolted. 'What, who. . . how did you –'

'A lucky guess. But now I come to think of it. . . '

'You don't mind? You're not, like, disgusted with me? I thought you'd be, well, the kind of boy you were, I thought you'd be. . . '

'Joe mate, have you seen where I work, the crowd who come to listen to my music? Have you seen how I'm *dressed*?'

'Oh my God,' said Joe. 'You mean you're. . . as well. . . ?'

Jamie guffawed. 'Christ, mate, no, not me. I'm married. To a woman. But you – well, you're my baby brother. You might not think I was that bothered about you but it meant a lot to me when you used to come and keep me company and listen to my music. Sometimes I was raging inside. You were my calming influence, did you know that?'

There was a silence, if one could call it that with the thrumming of the muted music and the intermittent buzzing of the lightbulb and the hammering of Jamie's heartbeat. And Joe's noisy, astonished breathing. Joe was the one to break it.

'I never thought it would be this easy being around you again. But when I was in Denmark recently –' he must have noticed the way Jamie's left eyebrow had shot up – this kid got *around*. 'Yeah, so when I was in Denmark, after I'd flown to Brussels from Reykjavik,' he was grinning now, the kid was, at Jamie's obvious amazement. 'Get this, Jamie,' his cock-of-the-hoop brother said next, 'I walked across Germany with a friend, Nick. No, not the one I – we're only friends. But we did this big walk from Hamburg all the way to Copenhagen. Hitchhiked some of the way of course but mostly we walked. So anyway, it was after I'd moved into the boat community in Denmark. My friend Will,' here the colour flooded into his brother's cheeks and Jamie knew that Will must be *the one*. 'Will played me this tune he'd found on YouTube. It was an acoustic song, just a voice and a guitar, but I recognised it as yours.' Joe squeezed his eyes shut.

Jamie took the opportunity to empty the last of the bottle into their two glasses. They both took a sip, after which Jamie felt himself filling with the kind of poignancy he thought he'd left behind a long time ago.

'Shit, Jamie,' Joe said, then stopped.

Jamie sat up straighter on his seat. 'Yeah?' he noticed his foot tapping to the bass pounding through the fabric of the building. He'd never been able to sit still.

'My feelings should have been about you, and they *were*. Hearing you sing made me want to see you again. But I messed up. I had these feelings for Will, you see. I think he must have known – well, I assumed he did but I must have got it wrong. We'd been close when we both worked on the farm in Australia, although nothing... But I thought he knew. I always thought maybe, he, you know... But nothing happened between us in Australia. Or in Iceland. We were just friends.'

After another pause Jamie made an encouraging noise and Joe continued.

'It was the second time we went to listen to your music together. We were both on his bunk in our cabin. We were sitting with our knees bumping into each other and I felt so grateful and warm as I listened to the music. Grateful he'd led me back to you, through your songs. It was like a sign. And everything that had been under the surface between us, between me and Will I mean – as I thought – it all bubbled to the top. I thought the same thing was happening with him as it was with me but I was obviously wrong. So fucking wrong. Shit, Jamie, I made such a fucking idiot of myself.'

Jamie saw his brother shiver as he evidently recalled the precise moment. Jamie empathised, he'd misread women's signals, or in retrospect lack of them, so many times before he met Lejla. Perhaps it was a trait the brothers shared. Perhaps they'd inherited it from their father. He picked up Joe's glass and encouraged him to empty it of the last few drops of whisky. Joe swallowed.

'I looked him in the eye and I leaned over to kiss him,' he said, his knuckles whitening around the glass. 'And he was shocked. He didn't want it. I made a mistake.' Joe banged his forehead with the heel of his other hand, then covered his eyes. Through his fingers he blurted out, 'He was so shocked, that he punched me. It was a gut reaction. I had a black eye for more than a week after.'

Jamie whistled a long note through his teeth. 'What did he do then?'

Joe placed the glass carefully on the table next to him. Sucked in a breath. 'He scrambled off the bed and left the room. He tried to apologise for hurting me later when he came back onto the boat but I already had my bag packed by then. I couldn't stay there anymore, it was too embarrassing.'

Jamie didn't know what to say. 'You live and learn,' were the words that came out of his mouth at last. 'It's all you can do. You can stay with us, if you haven't got any other plans. . . '

He was looking forward to introducing Joe to his niece. 'Where's your stuff, anyway? You must have a backpack or something with you.'

'I left it at the station,' Joe wiped his nose, the tissue scrunched up in his hand. 'It's in a locker. I didn't know whether I'd actually find you.'

'How did you know I worked here?'

Leaning to look under the table, Joe tossed his soggy clumps of tissue into the metal litter bin.

'After I saw you on YouTube I followed a couple of links to your profile on Sound Cloud. It said you worked here, in your bio. So, after a few delays and stop-overs with friends between Copenhagen and here – well, here I am.'

Jamie took out his phone and checked the time. It would be light outside. He rose from the chair, stretched, and began to vaguely tidy the room while his mind ticked over and over.

'I'll take you out to meet Lejla properly in a moment and I've got a little surprise waiting for you back at our flat.'

140

Joe got to his feet while Jamie unhooked his bag from the peg by the door and switched off the light. He locked the door behind them. As they walked out into the corridor the beat throbbed louder. People pushed past them but Jamie felt exposed, away from the intimacy of the small room. His brother suddenly a stranger. He fished for a question to keep the connection between them flowing. 'What are your plans long-term?'

'This,' Joe said. He straightened his shoulders. 'What I'm already doing. Travel, see the world, meet people, write, draw maps.'

27

Maya

Navengore, July 2013

A year had gone by since Joe had properly left home. He looked like a different boy each time they saw him on screen. Aside from his savings, he hadn't accepted any money from his parents. He told them he was proud of himself for living the life of a vagabond. 'Look it up in the dictionary,' he said, borrowing a well-worn phrase of his father's. 'It's a real thing. I'm practising the craft of vagabonding.' *Piffle*, said Con but Maya spied him looking the word up on his computer later. 'Having no settled home,' he spluttered. 'Joe knows he can come home any time he likes.'

Maya and Con flew out to meet Joe in Iceland in January. The three of them had a lovely holiday – did all the touristy things, beginning with the Blue Lagoon. They took the Golden Circle tour – Maya especially enjoyed the geysers – and they did a tour of waterfalls. Maya found Skogafoss the most beautiful; in the snow a tower of tumbling, cacophonous water encircled by black rocks and arms of ice.

In Reykjavik they attended a concert in the Harpa building by the harbour, *Oh my goodness, look at that mirrored ceiling!* And perhaps the best thing was the boat trip to see the icebergs and the glaciers. It was magical. To be able to put her arms around her boy again had felt so good. He was still only eighteen, just a child really. The feel of his smooth cheek against hers. He was her precious, final baby.

More recently Joe had met up with a friend in Belgium – an American boy he'd first connected with on Bali. It seemed quite common amongst young people to take off around the world and re-encounter each other in different countries as though the world was a house with so many different rooms. *Who knew?* Joe kept in touch with Maya on FaceTime and sometimes he spoke to Con, too. Maya tried to hold Con back from criticising Joe, but his messaging sessions with his son usually consisted of exhortations to come home by the end of summer and prepare to take up his deferred place at university. 'Enough's enough,' he'd say. 'Show some sense, boy.'

'It won't work,' Maya told Con. 'The more you push him, the further away he'll go. Think of Jamie.' Heat flooded her cheeks. Their oldest son was hardly ever mentioned in The Cottages and strangely enough, not much by friends and neighbours either. The black sheep of the family – his character had been labelled and signed off by their community just as it had been in London when he was a little boy.

Occasionally Maya received a hand-drawn postcard from Joe, a map of the course his latest adventure had taken, or sometimes a letter with a larger, intricately hand-drawn map torn from the pages of the A4 journal she'd bought him when he first went away. A beautiful book, with a relief map of the world on the cover. She had a special box in which she kept everything Joe sent, along with all his emails, printed out. She planned to staple and stick everything into a scrapbook one day.

She eventually found her own special book at *Paperchase*. The hardback cover was richly embossed with intricate, silvery detail on a ruby-red background. She left the first double spread blank so she could ask Joe to draw a map of his complete travels into it when he finally returned home. Secretly she couldn't help hoping that would be at the end of the summer and that Joe would decide to go to university after all. What would he do in the long-term if not?

Joe was currently walking from Hamburg to Copenhagen. Maya sat at the computer watching his words appearing on the screen and thinking of his cold fingers, typing. She would save everything he wrote and print it out later for her *Book of Joe*. Browsing the months' worth of material was almost more satisfying than when she had him *live* at the other end of an internet connection, when he might lose patience with her overwhelming questions. Her son typed quickly with a variety of emoticons – tears of laughter, a wow face, a walking figure and a thumbs-up. Telling her about his journey with his friend, Nick. *Of course*, he continued writing, *we'll hitchhike when the going's too difficult and maybe jump the odd train as well but mostly we'll be walking.*

Where will you sleep? Maya typed back. *Will you be warm enough? What will you eat?*

'Mother!'

Maya jumped as Joe suddenly appeared on FaceTime, his dear face instantly filling the screen and his sing-song voice giving her ears a delightful surprise. 'I'll do the same as I always do. There are always cast-offs to be had. There are lots of cabbage fields round here you know. We have a tiny stove with us and a saucepan.'

'But Joe. . . ' She couldn't take her eyes from her boy's dear face. She hit the button and captured stills from the screen as she examined every detail, every nuance of his expression. He'd changed so much since she saw him at the end of January. His face had lengthened and he'd grown facial hair. He didn't look so much like her own little boy anymore. 'But

Joe,' she leaned her chin on her hand while she gazed at him. 'Where will you go to the toilet? It's one thing to be digging holes in the Australian bush but in the European countryside, near farmland – what if you get arrested?'

'Oh, for... Everything's fine, Mum. Don't ask so many questions. Do you really want me to give you details? No, don't answer that.' She could sense his exasperation over the miles and whatever magic it took to get his living image on her computer screen. He was a good boy for holding back, she must be an irritating mother – she could see that. Her older boy intruded into her thoughts – again – his face a cartoon picture of fury on the night he left their home for the last time, after an appalling row with his father. Jamie had never held back. Once Joe was born, she'd completely failed Jamie as a mother. No point denying it. Baby Joe had screamed while she was in the head teacher's office discussing Jamie's rudeness to a teacher or his getting into a fight with another boy, so she'd begun leaving it up to Con to deal with those meetings. Then she'd had to accept Con's punishments of Jamie. Now when she tried to remember her oldest son's childhood she found she'd almost erased it from her mind.

And yet his room was upstairs. The bed was stripped, his things put away. The curtains had been washed and rehung and the carpet vacuumed many times. Sanitised. Her heart pounded uncomfortably and she tapped her fingers on the desk in a calmer rhythm than her pulse could produce.

'So anyway, Mum,' Joe said. 'I gotta hit the road. Break over. And you know, I need to conserve my data. Hey, but say hello to Nick before I go.' Joe's face disappeared from her screen and she saw thick undergrowth with a gap in it and a sloping, empty field behind. The sky in the place Joe existed sat above the landscape, a leaden grey. She had just begun to think the image had frozen when another boy's face appeared, most of it covered by a beard.

'Hi Mrs G.' the mouth in the midst of the beard grinned and

146

she had to smile back, he looked such a friendly boy.

'Hello, Nick,' she said. 'Are you keeping warm enough?' she could hear Joe chuckling in the background, saying *that's my mum.* But what else was she supposed to say? Nick was surprisingly fair-haired for someone who supposedly had Balinese blood on his mother's side. But maybe his American genes were stronger. She would have said Scottish if she'd been asked to guess but then nobody (except the Indigenous population of the USA) was originally American anyway. Now that she thought about it, the other lad was not unlike Joe. Quite similar in appearance to her son in fact. The screen rocked and her own dear boy was in view again. 'Not gonna draw this out,' Joe said. 'I'm off now, Mum. Love you, bye.' And he was gone. They both were. The silence rang out.

Maya glanced around her at the vast, insulated emptiness of her home. The bare hallway with the huge living room (sectioned into two with a folded-back room-divider) through a door on one side of it. She sat at the computer desk in its niche under the stairs where it had been installed back in the days when the house still consisted of the two original cottages and they only used one. On the other side of the hallway was an enormous kitchen – with a massive conservatory leading off from that. A corridor off the other end of the kitchen contained the boot room (though all the boots in there had been outgrown many years ago and yes, Jamie existed at least in boyhood boot-form). There was also an *ironing room*, a second sitting room or play room, a capacious cloakroom and a fully-equipped office that they had once called the *homework room.* But of course, the children had preferred to do their homework at the scrubbed-pine table in the kitchen with their mother in close proximity.

She stretched as she moved out of the computer chair and pushed the kitchen door open. Stood looking at their old table. She strained to remember Jamie sitting there, bent over his reluctantly-done homework, dark hair curled on the nape of his neck. She could see the knot at the top of his spine and the grubby collar of his shirt poking out of his red school jumper but she was afraid she might have been inventing the memory. A much more vigorous image of the girls jumped out at her. Their pigtails swinging, the roundness of their faces and the way their eyelashes lay on the pale area above the rosy skin of their cheeks as they looked down at their exercise books on the table. It was so real she thought she heard the twins chattering and arguing, saw the bloom of red appearing on Daisy's cheek as Lola lost her temper and hit out at her sister. Heard Lola's scream as Daisy pricked her with the tip of her pencil. *Where were her babies now?* Maya struggled constantly with the loss of those small people who had once been her whole world. She now rattled around The Cottages as if the house was the empty box left over from the best present ever – which had been stolen away.

She would go back in time and live in a log cabin with them if she could have them back as children.

———

Joe didn't get many more opportunities to communicate with his mother during the long walk from Hamburg to Copenhagen. Every now and then he would find a bar or a café whose free Wi-Fi extended to the street outside but their attempts to connect often failed. There was a worrying few weeks when Maya heard nothing at all from her boy. She rang Daisy.

'Have you heard from your brother, love?' Felt a sting in her heart when she realised it hadn't occurred to her to state which brother she meant but Daisy knew. She hadn't heard. And neither had Lola.

'He'll be fine, love,' Con whispered against her ear, holding her close in bed. 'Don't worry so much. You've got to let them go. They're all grown up now – this is our time.' It may be, but Con was still working until seven or eight each evening. At least. Maya finished work at five. She often found herself in Joe's room, tracing the lines of the maps on his wall or leaning on the wide drafting-table, studying the giant atlas he kept there.

She had her laptop open on the kitchen table one evening, checking the contents of her bank account online when the call signal came up on the screen.

'Joe!' *Thank God!* There was her boy's beaming face. It had been almost two months since she'd heard from him. He was indoors and appeared to be sitting on a sofa covered with a patterned rug. She could see metal pipework climbing a wall behind him.

'Hi Mum!' Joe looked happy, if a little thinner. He seemed more grown up than the last time he was on her screen – perhaps it was the achievement of his rugged walk or maybe it was that he'd now grown what could reasonably be called a beard.

'Where are you, darling? Are you safe? Are you keeping warm? Sorry.' She squirmed on the kitchen chair. Joe hated such fuss.

'Yeah, I'm fine, I'm good, Mum. How are you and Dad?'

'Good, good. The same, nothing to report here. But what about you, tell me everything. Where are you now?'

'I'm in Copenhagen. Ah, Mum, I'm staying on this really cool boat. It's a massive old coal barge – the kind with a concrete base. It's moored on the river where all the old warehouses are. I'm living in a community of about fifteen people, although people come and go.'

He turned his face away from the screen and seemed to be speaking to someone out-of-shot. He was smiling as he shifted his gaze back to camera. She smiled in return, he was definitely happy. Still, she felt concerned.

'But who does the boat belong to, darling? Are you squatting? Because, you know, you could get in a lot of trouble from the authorities for that. Or the owners of the boat. They might send the heavies in.'

'The heavies? Mum, don't get me wrong, but you don't know what you're talking about. Everyone who stays on here has to work three days a week in the salvage yard that belongs to the owner of the boat. So we get free rent. But we still have to dumpster-dive for our food and we hold a sale of the stuff rejected by the salvage yard once a week to bring in a small amount of cash, you know? It's all you need to live on.'

Maya smiled again at her son's image on the screen. Con must have come in the front door very quietly because it was the change in Joe's face, shadowed by a faint reflection on the screen that alerted her to her husband's presence at her shoulder. 'Hello, darling.' She half-stood and twisted to kiss him on the cheek. Con looped an arm around her and kissed her forehead in return.

'What have we here?' He let go of her and pulled up a chair next to hers at the table, leaning towards the screen. 'Hello, youngest. What are you up to, then?'

'Hi, Dad,' said Joe. 'I was just telling Mum –'

'He's living on a boat in Copenhagen! Isn't that amazing?'

She felt Con stiffen beside her. 'I'm sure our son can speak for himself,' he rubbed his cheek with his knuckles. 'How's it going, Joe, what kind of boat is it?'

'Great.' Joe wetted his lips, his eyes flicking from one to the other. 'It's an old coal barge. I'm living in a community and we each have to work in a salvage yard three days a week to earn our board.' He went silent.

Con's shoulder twitched. 'For God's sake, Joe. Salvage work? You could do so much better for yourself.' He shrugged himself out of his jacket, folded it neatly and laid it over his lap, all the time keeping his eyes on the screen. Maya searched her husband's face in profile, watching emotions flicker over it. She saw love for his son, exasperation. She berated herself for irritating him.

'If you must stay in Copenhagen,' he said. 'Why not

150

continue your studies there? That could work. Or look into getting an apprenticeship – engineering, perhaps. You're worth much more than labouring.'

Maya could feel her heart lodging itself in her diaphragm. She slid her arm around her husband's back, feeling the warmth of his skin through the thin fabric of his shirt. *Shhhh,* she was thinking. Heat pulsed from him into her fingertips, electrical signals that she struggled to interpret. *Love,* they seemed to transmit. *Apprehension, loss, helplessness, envy, anger.* She concentrated on decoding the signals one by one.

Beside her his voice continued in a rising interchange with Joe's and she couldn't hear any of their words. She closed her eyes, tried to telepath tranquillity to both of them. Some kind of snap in the air made her open her eyes again. They'd both gone silent. She looked at Joe on the screen. His face had closed up in that familiar way. She glanced at Con and saw the glitter of tears in his eyes – emotion that would make him even angrier.

'Do you agree with him, Mum?' She saw the challenge in Joe's pixilated glare. 'You always back him up, whatever he says, don't you?'

From the corner of her eye she noticed the first tear free itself from Con's lower eyelid and was acutely aware of its slow descent down his cheek. Joe wouldn't notice. Annoyance at Joe for playing them off against each other erupted in her chest. He didn't seem to think his father had feelings too. Emotions only Maya ever got to see. She was tired of fielding shots from both sides. She'd always protected Joe at the expense of Con's emotional security.

'I think you should listen to what your father says,' she told Joe, coughing a little to make her voice come out.

28

Joe

September 2013

Email from: Joe.Galen@Cusp.com
  To: Maya Galen
  Subject:

Dear Mum

Unfortunately I think it's going to be quite a while before I'll be in touch with you again. As for coming home, ever, I don't know. I don't know what to say to explain this. I know you never meant me any harm but I just think we need to get out of sync with each other for a while. Maybe some space will give you time to think, as it will me.

You've always been torn between Dad and me and not wanting to upset Dad. Since it's time for me to live my own life now – maybe it's time for you to devote yourself to Dad if that's what you want to do. I'm tempted to suggest all sorts of things you could do but it's not my place to write your life for you, any more than it's yours to write mine. You think you understand me but you don't.

If we carry on the way we've been since I went away – well, since before that really – since I was born, maybe? I'm sure we'll just repeat all our arguments again as we have during these last few months. So even if I do return home it's only a matter of time before I leave again, before I feel the need to push my Self to a new limit.

You need to read the book *Everett Ruess: A Vagabond for Beauty* like I suggested ages ago, and maybe you'll understand me better.

I love you as always but I can't do this thing anymore where I try to keep everyone happy all the time. Stuff has gone on in this family that I don't think is right and I need to go off and get my head straight so I can work out what it is I need to do to make things right again.

Love you,
Joe

29

Maya

November 2014.

Maya had been running on auto-pilot for more than a year. She'd heard nothing from Joe. Out and about in the village, embarrassment was the most difficult thing to cope with. At the everlasting rounds of dinner parties and fancy balls in aid of this or that, at the summer fair and the *Children in Need* cake-bake days, from her place behind the window of the receptionists' office at the village surgery – she had to fend off questions about the adventures of her golden boy of whom she'd boasted so proudly. Most people knew by now that Maya had lost touch with the apple of her eye.

When Joe first left home Maya sang praises of his adventurousness, his courage and his resourcefulness. He'd done well in his A' levels – which deflected potential criticism that he was throwing away his talents. 'He has a place waiting for him at Durham,' she'd boasted. 'He'll be back in the autumn and be a more rounded student, richer in experience for his travels.' She could see how smug that must have come over as now. She must have been insufferable. Then, when he'd refused to come home and follow the path his parents – his father – had set out for him, Maya changed tack. 'He can take up that university place whenever he chooses,' became her strapline. 'He's learning so much out there in the world. We're so proud of him. He was always such an individual child.' She noticed the covert glances, caught the trails of whispers behind hands, of course she did. *To lose* one *son is careless*, people would be thinking, *but to lose two...* Pursed lips completed the unspoken inference.

If only Con hadn't continued to harass Joe about his life choices when she'd warned him... But how could Joe have just cut them off like that?

Maya grew to hate her home. She hired a cleaner again, paying her from her own wages – because she no longer wanted to stroke and caress the surfaces. Solid wood, marble and slate that she'd once loved. The girls lived in their own places: Lola in a house-share in Sleaford because she worked at the girls school and couldn't drive and Daisy rented her own tiny flat in Newark, where she worked as a primary school teacher. Daisy had her own car and could easily have driven to work from the family home but she chose to live alone. They'd bought The Cottages when the twins were two and Jamie six. Maya had pictured all her children continuing to occupy its spaces as young adults. They could easily have divided The Cottages into separate cottages again – three units if necessary. They could have had connecting doors. Now it was empty. All those fancifully-named rooms never used.

The towns where the girls lived were equidistant from Navengore, each about sixteen miles away. Maya saw Lola every weekend, sometimes during the week too if Lola was having one of her crises. She knew it was selfish but alongside her concern for Lola, Maya was grateful of an excuse to feel needed. Daisy was generally busier and Maya had to catch up with her at odd times but the three of them met up for lunch all together at least one weekend a month and both girls came home for Sunday dinner at least once every six weeks. Sometimes Con visited one or other of their daughters straight after work on a weekday, and on those nights Maya spent even longer on her own. She took as much overtime as possible at the surgery and wondered whether she ought to train as a nurse. The plan cogitated at the back of her mind.

On an ordinary Friday in November when Con had still not returned home by 8.30pm (a short text had let Maya know he was visiting Daisy) the house phone rang. It would be a late invitation to a weekend dinner party, Maya supposed. She and Con would be required to make up the numbers after another couple had dropped out. Or perhaps it was one of the very rare calls she received from her sister, Jen, who lived in Sweden. It wouldn't be Joe because he'd never called the landline. He would have emailed if he wanted to get back in touch. Lola and Daisy only communicated by mobile. *It wouldn't be Jamie because. . .* because she'd abandoned all hope of ever hearing from him again. He was as good as gone, she'd accepted it. Maya made her way downstairs with an armful of towels and bedding for the wash, treading carefully in her slippered feet because she couldn't see over the top of the pile.

She almost didn't answer. It was the girls' Sunday for dinner this weekend and Maya and Con had planned a rare trip to the cinema for Saturday evening so it would have to be a polite decline for the prospective dinner party anyway. And Jen would ring back later if it was her. But manners prevailed. She dropped the washing at the bottom of the stairs, moved over to the phone and lifted the receiver.

'Hello, Maya Galen speaking.' There was a pause and a crackle before a voice responded. A voice which belonged, apparently, to an Australian police officer.

A period of time passed after the phone call when Maya sat on the floor in the hall. The lights seemed to have gone out – or rather, more oddly, she was sitting in a tunnel with only a pinpoint of light at the end. It was cold in the tunnel and there was no sound.

Then an all-encompassing light and a wave swamped her and she started shivering fiercely. It was while she was trying to swim back to shore that the front door opened and Con walked in. The wave receded. Maya scrambled to her feet, surprised to find she was not dripping wet.

'What the. . . ?' said Con. The look on his face was so alien – *he* was so alien – it almost made her laugh.

30

Maya

Melbourne, November 2014

A car had been sent to collect them from the airport when they landed in Melbourne. Maya insisted only she and Con need attend, they could arrange for the girls to follow later when they knew what was happening. She didn't want her darling daughters – the remains of her children – to see their parents falling apart. But the twins, especially Lola, had begged to come too.

Con had undergone a full-scale breakdown and subsequent recovery during the three days between the phone call and this moment. He'd sobbed in Maya's arms and she'd sobbed in his. Then he stiffened in rigid shock. She watched his face go grey. *Don't you dare have a heart attack*, she heard her angry mind mutter. *For once this is about Joe, not you.* Nevertheless Con seemed incapable of speech, although he shook his head when she asked him if he was in pain. When his teeth started chattering, his lips peeled back in a rictus grin, she felt forced to lead him upstairs to bed, tuck him under the duvet and call the village GP, who was a friend of the family. While Con slumbered under the influence of the sleeping pills Dr Harwell prescribed, Maya wound up the clockwork key in her back and had to arrange everything by herself. Con was now at least outwardly back to normal, although she sensed that like her, he was only a shell of his former self.

Maya saw Joe everywhere. Sometimes he was a baby, sometimes a toddler. Then he was the four-year-old who had just moved into his own bedroom, gazing in wonder at his crude drawings of maps that she'd had blown up all over his bedroom walls.

'I wish we could have got hold of Jamie,' Daisy said. 'It's only fair that he should know.' Her angry eyes released more tears. 'I can't believe you haven't searched for him before now.' They stood in line waiting to have their passports checked at Arrivals. 'I miss my big brother.'

Maya set her mouth in a hard, miserable line. For once, Con didn't say anything. Yesterday he'd made some enquiries as to Jamie's whereabouts among the boy's old friends but came up with nothing, and that was that. Maya had been too busy organising everything else.

'You don't even care about Jamie, anyway,' Daisy accused Con. Losing one brother seemed to stimulate an urge to find the other. Lola cried steadily. A gap widened around their family in the airport line, apparently emanating the fumes of grief like a bad smell.

From what the officer said on the phone Maya had been left with no doubt in her mind that it was Joe.

Daisy's flint eyes, now dried, sought out the cap-wearing chauffeur holding up a sign with their name on. Later, Maya couldn't remember much about the transition from the crowded airport concourse into the taxi or Embassy car or whatever it was. Their bags, which had appeared from somewhere, were thrust in the boot. The journey passed in a whirl of heat and lights and colours, from a landscape of aridity to leafy suburbs, to brightly-painted buildings in the city. It all ran together. All Maya knew was that sweat had pooled in her armpits and her thighs had stuck to the back of her skirt. The car slowed and they were driven around to the back of a hospital. Somehow, Maya was now walking down a cool corridor, surrounded by the remains of her family. She glanced behind her and then turned again to face front. The corridor stretched on forever in both directions. Everything was painted the palest green. She kept her arms pressed against her sides, walked shoulder to shoulder with Con. Daisy and Lola walked behind them. They were all traipsing after a person who wore grey clothing that resembled pyjamas.

The book was placed in Maya's hands. It felt as heavy as the whole world and her knees buckled beneath the weight of it. Con held her up. She confirmed to the officer that it was Joe's book. He had inscribed his name and home address on the inner cover. And their telephone number. *In case of loss, please return to. . .* He'd showed her the pages of this book many times during their video-messaging sessions. Drawings, route plans, one-pot recipes, journal entries, (which he'd sometimes shielded with his hand as he showed her something else) the odd brochure or ticket stapled onto the paper. Best of all were Joe's hand-drawn maps, created with different coloured pens – the isograph set of pens she'd bought him for his seventeenth birthday. The book had been meticulously wrapped in polythene and sealed in a Ziploc bag, the officer told her, which was why it had survived the water. Maya heard Con swallow all the air in the room. Struggling to breathe, she found she was standing on a rock in the middle of the Universe, holding her son's book in her hands.

161

31

Maya

Melbourne, November 2014

At her side, Con let out a groan like the wind in the trees.
Shock, grief, she supposed. But Maya knew at a glance that
the boy wasn't Joe.

They travelled all over the world, these kids. Maybe Nick
had been returning to his home island of Bali and had stopped
in Australia on the way. Joe, her most generous boy, must
have given his friend the journal as a kind of travel guide.
Perhaps the reason Nick had the book was something along
those lines. Perhaps Nick had promised to send it back to
Joe when he'd completed his travels in Australia. She didn't
think Nick would have stolen the book from Joe. The lad was
friendly when he said hello to her on FaceTime. Scottish, she
thought he looked. He had laughter-lines around his eyes,
she remembered those.

She'd asked him if he was keeping warm enough. *Oh, you
poor boy. What made you. . . ? Why?*

Maya's knees threatened to crumple, but she held herself upright this time. Con sobbed into his hands.

'Shh,' Maya grasped his arm. 'Shh. Con, it's not Joe.'

The attendant at her other side moved closer to the window and beckoned. The officer came out of the room where the body lay and stood in front of Maya.

'Madam,' he said. 'Could you please repeat what you just said? Can you confirm that this boy is not your son?'

Maya ignored him for a moment while she pulled her husband's hands away from his face.

'Look at me. Con!' When he did, with haunted eyes, she turned back to the window for another, long look. Mentally superimposing the bloated face she could see onto that of the boy she had spoken to via the screen.

Hi, Mrs Galen.

'I can confirm it.' She spoke firmly. 'That's not my son. That boy's name is Nick. He was a friend of my son. I met him. . . I was introduced to him once on a video-call with my son.'

She straightened, relief and sorrow curdling in her stomach. That poor boy had a mother somewhere who had no idea that this was happening.

'His name is Nick,' she repeated, more softly. She turned to the officer. 'I don't know his family name. I'm sorry.'

Con insisted on upgrading them from the basic rooms Maya had booked and they were soon ensconced in a suite in a much more expensive hotel.

'You're all always nagging me about having a proper holiday,' he joked. 'I don't care if this eats into our savings. We're celebrating!'

His red-rimmed eyes were not the only sign of his recent, most terrible shock. When she placed her hand on his arm she felt a repetitive twitch beneath the skin. He also couldn't seem to stop clearing his throat. Secretly Maya couldn't help worrying.   Not that it mattered now because it hadn't happened, but the thought lurked at the back of her mind that if she hadn't gone in with Con to identify the body she'd be arranging a funeral for her son.   On top of this she suppressed an urge to go running back to the hospital and check one final time. What if it *was* Joe, what if she'd made a mistake? *Oh dear God*, had she been so certain because she hadn't wanted it to be Joe...?   But her immediate instinct on seeing the body was that it wasn't Joe...   it wasn't. If she'd never seen that camera swing onto the face of her son's friend on the second-to-last video chat she'd had with Joe, she could have been persuaded that the boy on the mortuary bed was him.   She'd have accepted it.   She remembered thinking at the time that the two boys had a similar appearance.

Again, the possibility of a mistake assailed her brain and she wanted to go back and check. Chills rippled through her body. There was no identification on the boy who was found. No rucksack, only a leather satchel slung across his thin frame. They'd been told it contained the Ziploc bag with the polythene-wrapped journal in it, the remains of some dried (rehydrated, Maya imagined) snacks, a pen and an Australian-network mobile phone which was currently being dried out to be examined. A canvas wallet with some coins in it but no cards... No passport. Deliberately no ID. *Dear God*, she thought again. It looked like suicide. Her heart cracked. He'd kept the journal safe so it could be returned to Joe. *Are you keeping warm enough?* There'd be dental checks, the officer had told her. They had a first name at least and would investigate records on Bali to start with.

'He had an American parent,' Maya said. 'That's all I know. I can find the original email from Joe if you want...' It would still be on her phone and also in a folder at home.   Don't worry, she was told, it would all be investigated.   Just for clarity's sake they would need to balance the dental findings against Joe's records too, since Joe was evidently a Missing

Person and the only clue to identification of the body lay in Joe's journal. *But don't worry, that's just procedure, it will be fine.*

They were to stay in Australia until Joe had officially been ruled out. *What if it is Joe?* Maya spent a restless first night in luxury at the hotel. Unable to sleep, she sat wrapped in a soft blanket in a cane chair on the balcony. She could hear the sound of a road close by and a variety of exotic animal and insect noises in the trees and surrounding air. She jumped when a large moth fluttered against her cheek before taking off towards a solar light, positioned above the doorway to the room. Through the multitudinous botany overhanging their tiny, private balcony garden, a rash of stars peeped down at the earth. Somewhere on this planet there existed her two boys. *Where are you both?*

Somewhere else there was a mother who was soon to learn the news of her son's death. Maya had been given a reprieve. And so had Joe's father. Despite his jubilation, Con had sobbed against her neck once they were settled into the new hotel. Money could buy all of this but it could never buy a dead son back, nor two missing ones. *What did we do wrong, Maya?* She felt nausea rising in her chest – he knew what their mistakes had been. If we can have him back – I promise I'll respect his choices in the future. *Empty promises, Con.*

Maya sat outside, wrapped in the blanket on her first night in Australia. Her twin daughters slept in one room and her husband slept in another behind her. She could hear Con's snores above the unfamiliar night sounds of a different continent. She had Joe's journal on her lap, miraculously undamaged by the water which had killed his friend. Though it was too dark to make out any detail she stroked the pages of the book with her fingertips, imbibing Joe. His fingerprints were all over these pages, invisible to her yet still detectable. She'd noticed the remains of powder earlier, from where prints had already been taken from it by the police. *Are you keeping warm enough, Nick?* She clutched the book tighter.

166

That poor boy.

Joe had mapped out his journey to the point at which he must have handed the book over to his friend. Denmark. What had made him stop? Where was Joe now? She'd only had time to flick through the pages, pausing briefly to scan the handwritten snippets amongst the maps, photos and tickets. The final handwritten entry had been made when he was on the boat in Copenhagen – from where he'd made his last video call to his parents. He was angry with them in the journal entry but she was moved by his feelings about his older brother, *I wish I knew this guy but I feel I've always been kept away from him. Well, kept from getting close to him at least.* She was moved, too, by Joe's idea that his mother would like to be set free.

She'd indulged Joe, always reflected back what he wanted to hear, and she'd done the same thing with Con. But perhaps Joe was right about the real Maya. . . Did she long to escape?

Were the clues to Joe's whereabouts somewhere in the journal? He'd last written in it more than a year ago. Maya closed the book and held it against her chest. She made a promise to Joe. *I'll find you.* And she would find herself, as well.

32

Jamie

Berlin, November 2016

Jamie rode his heavily-laden bicycle past the brightly-painted stretches of wall and into the labyrinth of industrial-looking buildings in Friedrichshain that housed most of his friends. His eyes watered from the wind and his legs felt stiff when he disembarked. He was out of breath as he hefted the bike up the concrete steps to their apartment block. He'd become out of condition. Too much sitting around, watching Electra with her Kindergarten pals. Perhaps he ought to spend those hours jogging around the perimeter of the playpark instead of sitting on a bench listening to music.

At the top of the steps he pushed the door open into the hall and bumped the bike over the ledge into the entranceway of their flat. Lugging the pannier of groceries over his shoulder he carried it down the dim corridor into the kitchen, the largest room in their two-level apartment. He bashed the rickety banister at the bottom of the stairs as he passed. Another thing to be fixed, it wouldn't take much to knock the whole thing down.

'*Depp!*' At the sound of his muttered self-curse, Electra came running out of the kitchen.

'Papa! Wo bist du so lange gewesen?'

'English, Liebling,' he reminded her.

'Where have you been?' she reached up her arms to him. 'Uncle Joe said you've been... uhm. He said you've been there and back to see how far it is.'

Jamie swung the pannier onto the kitchen table where it landed, splayed, like Bambi on ice.

'Eh up!'

Electra shrieked delightedly as he hoisted her into his arms. 'Your uncle was correct – and it was a long way there and back, and that's why I've taken so long.'

'You can take the boy out of Lincolnshire, but you can't take Lincolnshire out of the boy,' Joe remarked from the other side of the table. '*Eh up.* You sounded just like that motor-biking chap then, whassisname? Guy Martin. Anyway, *idiot*, you could have knocked my laptop off, or broken it. Be more careful, can't you? Or I'll refuse to babysit for you anymore.'

'And your bark's worse than your bite,' Jamie wagged his finger at Joe for Electra's benefit. She giggled again, playing with the ends of her father's hair.

In good spirits, Joe pushed his chair back, straightened and adjusted the pannier bag into an upright position before unzipping it and unloading the shopping onto the table. Jamie kissed Electra on the top of her head while she clung to him like a monkey, then he murmured some words to her and slid her to the floor. He handed her a packet of pasta and placed some further items in the top cupboard.

'Are you sure this is a sack of potatoes and not lead?' Joe pretended to collapse under the weight of the paper bag he was holding. Electra let out another musical laugh.

'Stop moaning,' said Jamie. Joe was right about Lincolnshire, though. It was still there in the nooks and crannies of his consciousness. But the more years that passed the harder it was to get back in touch with Mum and Dad. Inside his adult frame curled an abandoned child, arms shielding its eyes and ears from pain. *Pick me up.* Surely his parents could have found him if they'd wanted to? He bet they'd never even tried. He was a troublesome child, he knew that. Joe was another matter. His mother's golden boy. Joe had been disappeared for three years already. The lad knew how sad his mother would be about that. He kept promising he'd call home soon but then insisted he still needed more time. Surely he realised by now that time stretches so far it eventually snaps? It was all over for Jamie, he was well aware of that. He also knew that Joe wanted to finish his book before contacting their parents but still... he was playing a game of risk.

Sometimes Jamie jolted awake in the night after sitting at the kitchen table back home, watching his mother sobbing into a tissue. A dozen others were balled and strewn across the surface around her. He'd been sitting opposite her trying to console her but she couldn't see him. She'd fallen apart at the seams without her precious younger son to love and fuss over. Her hair had turned completely grey and was dishevelled from its usual neat style. There were swollen pouches under her eyes. Soon their mother would wither away and die and her boys would never find their way back to her.

How could she have let them both go so easily?

He closed the top cupboard door with a slam and forced a laugh as Electra copied him with the bottom one. Funny how he was able to live his everyday life with a completely different internal monologue alongside the biting sorrow whenever he thought of his mother.

'Don't let your mother see you doing that,' he warned his daughter. 'We don't want you to trap your fingers now, do we?'

'Reći ću majko. . . ' She clapped a hand to her mouth before switching to English. 'I'll tell her that you did it too, Papa.'

She spoke in three languages, his munchkin, whereas he'd

never managed to master her mother's native Bosnian. He picked Electra up again and tickled her. Writhing out of his arms she ran over to her wooden train set, laid out on the floor by the opening to the utility room.

'How's Lejla?' Jamie asked his brother. 'Still asleep?'

'I guess so. Haven't heard a peep out of her. I took Electra to the park earlier, she was so full of energy I was worried she'd wake Lejla up.'

'No chance,' said Jamie. How's the writing going?'

'Good,' Joe said. 'I'm three quarters of the way through, I estimate. It's the maps that're so time-consuming, but I didn't want to risk bringing one of them here and spreading it out on your kitchen table, not with the sticky-fingered munchkin around and the way *you* hurl things about. I'll leave them safely on my drafting table in the studio, thank you very much.'

'Is it warm enough over there, now the winter's coming? Don't you miss your sleeping-cupboard here? You can always come back, you know. You could babysit the new baby as well as our Electra here. At least you'd be warm.'

'You'll have me doing the breastfeeding next,' laughed Joe. 'Nah, thanks for the offer but I'm happy at the studio with the other guys, man. We've finished the internal walls now. We got some free fibreboard that the factory down the road was chucking out. It's amazing how much difference it makes to the place. Dividing the space off makes it much warmer. You'll have to come and take a look, you haven't been over for a while, have you? Yeah, yeah. . . '

Jamie had made a helpless gesture with his hands, encompassing in their span the kitchen, Electra and the ceiling above which Lejla slept. She was having a difficult pregnancy. And he needed to spend most nights at the club to make ends meet. 'Anyway,' continued Joe, once Jamie had made his point, augmenting his hand gestures with stupid facial expressions. 'Okay, enough already with your hangdog look. Apart from the insulation it's a matter of how many layers you can put on and still move around. And we have those gas heaters to huddle around in the work area. And fingerless gloves, of course.'

'Well.' Jamie dropped his hands, still doubtful Joe would last the winter at the warehouse. 'You know where we are if you need us.'

'Seriously? It's cool of you, man, I really appreciate it, but you're going to be up to your neck in nappies before long. And won't Lejla's mother be coming to stay again when the baby's born? Surely Lejla's going to need some extra care this time...'

'I just meant for the winter, mate, if it gets too cold over there. I mean it.' Jamie turned from the work surface where he was dropping teabags into a couple of mugs. 'I don't want you freezing to death. I feel kinda responsible for you, you know.' The kettle clicked and he poured boiling water into the mugs. His scalp prickled – there was an ominous silence coming from Joe.

'How the fuck do you figure that out?' Joe's chair scraped across the floor as he moved towards his brother and further away from Electra. She was engrossed in the little wooden people from her train. 'You feeling responsible for me? I was looking after myself for a while before I turned up in your nightclub, you know. I am *not* some helpless loser that everyone feels they have to look after. Haven't I proved that by now? You're happy enough to leave me in charge of your kid when it suits you!'

Jamie never failed to be surprised at the anger that could unexpectedly erupt from Joe. He just couldn't see where it was coming from. Had Joe been like that as a child? Maybe Jamie had blotted it out.

'Okay, calm down.' He made soothing hand gestures. 'If you want to know the truth I'm miserable as shit about the situation – about you not being in touch with Mum, I mean. She idolised you. It just seems a bit ungrateful if you know what I mean? She must be devastated...' His jaw tightened. Even while he said those words he wanted to hit something.

The worktop edge or his brother. Joe was spoilt, that was what it was. He could afford to keep their mother dangling like a fish on a hook because she would likely forgive him anything. Jamie took a deep breath. Saw how white his brother's knuckles were, bunched into fists at his chest.

'Okay,' he said again.

Joe's eyes were oddly empty of expression. Yeah, it was a bit weird, to be honest, how he could change from being so apparently happy-go-lucky to this. Like, when it came to himself, Jamie had never been happy-go-lucky in the first place, he'd just always been angry. But not Joe. 'Calm down, man,' he repeated. 'Look at Electra, you're frightening her.'

'I'm not frightened!' Electra piped up indignantly from the corner. 'Dämlich.' Her chin dropped back towards her chest and she caused one of her wooden trains to crash into the other. But it was enough to make Joe loosen his hands and let them drop to his sides. He stepped backwards until he was propped against the table edge, gripping it with his white knuckles.

'Okay. I'm sorry. Sorry, Munchkin,' he called to his niece. 'I don't know what came over me. I'm the stupid one, not your papa.' Her frown deepened and she gave her head a little shake but managed a small smile after he'd pulled a few silly faces at her.

'What was all that about?' Jamie's hands shook as he stirred the teabags in the mugs and then fished them out and poured in the milk. 'It's not like you to lose your rag like that.'

Joe folded his arms across his chest. His beard had thickened since he arrived in Berlin and now covered a good portion of his face, the colour of it deepened to a dark red. Their mother must have waved goodbye to a fresh-cheeked boy and would welcome back, if she ever got the chance, a fully-formed young man.

Jamie kept a picture of his mum in a plastic document wallet. It was of her with him at his eighteenth birthday

174

party, when she made him sit like a wallie in front of his cake while friends and family sang happy birthday. Although he'd hated the whole occasion, secretly her arms around his neck had made him feel special. She reached in front of him to hold the blazing cake out towards the camera. Her chin rested on his head. For that moment, apart from the cake, he'd had her complete attention. His sisters' excited faces were opposite him at the table. (The family was later arranged by the photographer around the cake for a professional photograph to mark the occasion – Jamie's 18th... done). The twins must have been fourteen then. He remembered the feeling like a bubbling pot inside him when his mates made inappropriate comments about them. He tried to picture Joe. *That's right, I remember him at the party. He was ten but he looked so young for his age.* Later, Dad was furious at Jamie's 'selfishness' for wanting to go out with his mates – the parents had paid a fortune to have the house and garden decorated with fairy lights and Chinese lanterns and Mum ended up in tears. Jamie stormed out, hating Mum for not sticking up for him to an audience of open-mouthed stares.

'So what's up, Joe?' They sat opposite each other at the table, both of them with their hands wrapped round mugs of tea. Electra had climbed up onto Jamie's lap and snuggled against him, drifting off if the way her head was sliding down his chest was anything to go by. He'd probably be in trouble with Lejla later when Electra was running around like a blue-arsed fly instead of going to bed but to be honest it was worth it for the chance to talk to his brother now. Absently, he stroked the black silk of his daughter's hair.

'Whassa going on?'

He got a long look from Joe. 'Sommat weird is going on, that's what,' he admitted. 'I dunno if I ever told you but when I was on the road I wrote this journal? I drew maps in it of all the places I'd been and I wrote a few diary entries but nothing that I absolutely didn't want anyone to see – so if I ever lost it

I wouldn't have to be embarrassed about anything personal if you know what I mean. But it was kinda special. It's what I'm basing my book on but I'm having to do it all from memory, which is a pain. I was hoping to have the journal back by now. I lent it to someone. It was never meant to be a gift, only a loan.'

Jamie took a long gulp of tea, holding the mug away from the top of Electra's head. As he placed the mug back on the table she twitched in his arms, her small brown hand loosening its grip on his thumb. He could probably still wake her up at this point if he tried hard enough but why shouldn't she sleep if she wanted to? It wasn't as if he was at the club tonight, and if she got too much for his poorly wife to cope with later he could take her in the studio with him. She liked it when she was allowed to put his old headphones on and mess around on the broken mixing desk he kept for her to play with.

'So who did you lend it to – the journal?'

'The guy I walked across Germany with. Nick, his name is. We both stayed on that houseboat in Copenhagen for a while, and then... you know... there was the misunderstanding with Will.' The visible parts of Joe's face reddened. 'So I said I was leaving. I told Nick I was going to find you. So he decided to try and make it up with his own family, back in Bali.' Joe gave a short laugh. 'I was turning my back on our parents but Nick was going to make up with his. But he said he would do some hitching in Australia first. He'd already applied for a visa.' Joe twiddled with a Lego brick he'd found on the table. Then he put it down and opened his laptop, started fiddling about with the keys. 'I wish I hadn't done it now because I want my book back. It had all sorts of stuff in it. I was stupid to lend it to him. But he promised to send it back to me wherever I was living once he'd finished using it – following my trail, if you see what I mean? It was like a guide, especially the maps. And I kinda liked the idea of the book revisiting the places we'd been together. Also he could give me feedback on whether a finished version of it would be useful for rookie travellers.'

Jamie nodded. He couldn't help kissing Electra's silken hair as he shifted her slumped weight onto his other knee. 'So what happened?'

'He kept in touch until about, let's see, I guess it was about a year after I got here. I remember how cold it was turning and thinking how warm it would be in Australia where he emailed me from. He said he'd been in touch with his parents and they weren't very welcoming. They told him their lives had moved on.' Joe glanced at Jamie as if he was harbouring the same concern about their own parents. 'Nick seemed a bit down but he hoped they'd forgive him once they'd got over the shock of hearing from him again.'

Joe sat tugging the skin around his thumbnail with his teeth. Jamie glanced at the darkening window, ghosts of themselves reflected in it, superimposed over the dim outlines of trees in the communal garden. It was getting darker in the kitchen, too as afternoon segued into evening. Lejla had slept a long time but she didn't sleep much at night. It wasn't only because of pregnancy – the nightmares of her past still haunted her.

Jamie hugged his daughter tighter. 'So, you didn't hear from him after that?'

'No. That was the last time, now I think about it. I did message him but I got no reply. I thought maybe it was because he'd lost the journal and was too embarrassed to tell me. I asked a few mutual acquaintances from our time on the road to see if anyone had heard from him but they hadn't.' Joe's eyes hardened. He turned his laptop around so Jamie could see the screen. 'And then today I found this... Shit, man. I think someone's stolen my journal and now they're impersonating me.'

33

November 2016

"The Blog of Joe"

Tags: *Vagabonds*, *Travellers*, *On the road*, *Worldwide*, *Maps*, *Spain*, *Mothers and Sons*, *Family*

Hi Folks

As you can see from the photo gallery, I'm now in Lleida in Spain. It was originally an ancient town: dominated by the tall tower of La Sue Vella, the former Roman Catholic cathedral. There is also a "new" cathedral, which was built in 1761. And then there's the modern city sprawled out below, full of hotels and restaurants and shopping centres. I went and got myself a mild case of heatstroke today but I'm all right, no need to worry! People are kind. I picked the wrong spot to busk in, I'm afraid – though I started off in the shade the sun soon made its way around the corner of the cathedral wall and found me – and I'd forgotten my hat. As you can imagine I have a rather nasty case of sunburn on top of the heatstroke. My nose will begin to peel in a few days! I met a Swiss couple who walked back down the hill with me and bought me some water and food. Then I had a sleep under a tree in a small park and after that I took a paddle in the river with this dog that follows me around everywhere! I'm in an internet café right now and have 20 minutes left. Send in any comments about the photos, guys, and I'll try to answer them next time I'm online. If there's anything you want to know about this area of Catalonia, or anything about walking the Camino de Santiago as well, (thanks for all the previous comments on your Camino experiences) I'll do my best to help.

Later I'll go back "home" to the wonderful community I've been living in since I finished my walk on the Camino. I jumped off the trail at Leon and made my way back east using the easy method – by car and truck rather than on foot – through Burgos and Logroño, through Puente la Reina as far as Jaca. Then it was a series of small lifts and long walks – with lots of sleeping under the stars – that brought me to Lleida, where I decided to stay for a while. Well, near Lleida, anyway. A friend I met on the Camino told me about the community of tramps and travellers in the woods on a hill. But I can't say any more about it than that, guys. If you ever come out this way you could make some enquiries. You need an invite to get in.

It's good to sit around the fire at the end of the day, sharing a communal meal, playing music with my companions. There's always a guitar or two and some sweet voices singing and the murmur of convivial conversation... I've been a solitary star for a while now and maybe I'm just a little tired of being alone, you know?

Write in and tell me if you're a fellow vagabond, and if you've ever started to feel you want to travel in company rather than on your own.

It would be great to get your stories about life on the road. I don't get much internet so yeah, it's nice to be in a proper town at the moment and have access to facilities like Wi-Fi and a public convenience. I come to the Biblioteca Pública, here on Rambla d'Aragó – where I was able to spread out my drawing stuff and update the map of my recent travels. If you haven't done already, you could take a look at my 'Maps' archives page and see the drawings of my earlier journeys from the beginning of my life on the road in Australia up to my time in Iceland and Denmark – where I lived on a boat for a while. Click HERE.

As for photos, well, they're not perfect because I use the camera on my tablet, but every time I find a good Wi-Fi source I'll post more pics of the places I visit. If anyone wants to post any pictures in the comments, feel free. Pics of your home or your back garden, the view from your window – whatever you like. Let's share how we all live on this planet of ours. Yeah, I miss my home sometimes, although that's beginning to dim – but the feeling still sometimes rises unexpectedly. I haven't seen my mum for a good while now and I'm sure she misses me like crazy. I bet my sisters do too. But I guess they all know that a man's gotta do what a man's gotta do and they'll be understanding when I return home...

Time's running out on the internet, guys. Thanks for all the comments I've already received on the photo gallery. I'll try and respond to them next time. You're all awesome! *Freedom is wonderful, solitude is bliss, but we humans were born to communicate and be part of a pack. Or is it that we always want what we haven't got?*

34

Jamie

Berlin, November 2016

Joe chewed on his knuckles. 'That's the most recent post. I've never even been to fucking Spain. Although to be fair I was planning to after revisiting Germany.' He picked up the Lego brick again and fastened it on top of another one which had emerged from under a tea towel draped over the edge of the table. 'I was going to continue from here to France. I wrote about my future plans in the journal. But then I found you, and I seem to have lost the will to travel.'

Jamie shuffled his chair closer to the table, holding Electra securely in his other arm. He leaned forward to examine a couple of the gallery photos. 'Okay,' he said slowly. 'So, it's called, weirdly, *"The Blog of Joe"* – it's even more weird that the title's got quote marks. But what makes you think this person's impersonating you? There must be hundreds of travelling Joes. What's got you so hot under the collar?'

'Because I've read back through the whole fucking blog!'
Joe clenched his jaw so tightly he could hardly get the words
out. 'They're impersonating me, all right. They've copied my
journal entries word for word – apart from maybe what they
thought were the slightly-too personal ones. But they've got
all my travel notes on here and they've scanned all my hand-
drawn maps! It's plagiarism, that's what it is!' He dropped the
bricks and scratched frenziedly at his forearm. Good job his
nails were bitten down.

Jamie settled both arms more comfortably around Electra,
who snored softly. There was a slight bump from the ceiling
above, which must be Lejla waking up at last. She'd probably
have a bath before she came downstairs, usually preferring to
transition from sleep to wakefulness through the medium of
water. She said it was her time for communing with their five-
month-old foetus but it was also a ritual from her childhood,
when the nightmares were so bad – after they escaped – that
her mother bathed her in the night to calm her down. Jamie
swallowed and kissed the top of Electra's head. Lejla had only
been a few years older than their daughter when. . . He forced
his attention back to Joe.

'Seriously? They've copied your actual motherfucking
journal word for word?'

Joe rolled back his sweater sleeve. His skin was scratched
raw. 'Yup. Fucking bastards. Look in the archive section and
you'll see.' He shoved the laptop closer.

'Do you think it could be your friend, what did you say his
name is. . . Nick?' Jamie scrolled back through the previous
posts, reading his brother's travelling tales as transcribed by
a stranger. Clicked a few buttons and scrutinised the blog's
stats. 'Look at this, Joe. The blog was only set up six months
ago, yet the earliest posts are marked 2012.'

'That's because they're copied,' Joe repeated. 'Whoever
wrote this blog definitely has my journal. Fuck. I want my
book back! Someone's taking the piss!' He screwed his fists
into his eyes like Electra when she was having a tantrum.

All these months while Joe had worked on his manuscript from memory, somebody else was holding his first-hand material hostage. Merrily posting it all over the web. But why – what did they want?

'So, do you think it could be Nick?'

'Nah, I. . . I just don't know. Why would he do that? He has a travelling life of his own. . . He would've written more about Australia – carried on from where I left off. There'd be no need for it. I don't know. How do I get my journal back and stop this crap? How do I prove that they've stolen from me and who can I report it to?'

'Crazy that they've continued your journal past the time when you handed your book over to your friend,' Jamie mused. 'Like they're inventing your future or something. It's pretty fucking spooky.'

The pipes on the wall rattled as the boiler kicked into life, presumably providing hot water for Lejla's bath. On his lap Electra stirred and stretched awake. Her eyelids flickered and she smiled, first at Joe who was in her line of sight and then, twisting her neck around, up at her papa.

'I'm thirsty.' Her mouth opened in a cat-like yawn and he admired her pearly, tiny teeth.

'Okay baby. Papa will get you a drink.' He stood up stiffly, tucking Electra against his side with one arm, bending to collect his and Joe's mugs from the table with his other hand. 'I should get supper on. You'll stay, won't you Joe?'

'Here's one from a few months back. These are strangely addictive, to be honest. Maybe because it's supposed to be me.'

September 2016
Hey Guys!

I'm at a very nice Albérge which has free Wi-Fi, lucky me.

185

Earlier, I walked into the outskirts of León with an elderly couple and their grandson, who's only fourteen. The boy's grandfather is blind and he walks with his hand on his grandson's shoulder. The boy describes everything to the old man as they walk. I've got to admit that the bond between them brought tears to my eyes.

'Brought tears to my eyes,' scoffed Joe. 'I would never write that on a blog. They're fucking crap at impersonating me!'

I carried the grandmother's pack (on my front, because I had my own bag on my back – I'm amazed at how physically strong I've become in the years since I started this) and the couple were so grateful. They insisted on giving me some money because they said they had so much and they could tell I'd been living on so little.

'So grateful! You won't be bloody grateful when I get hold of you.'

I think I'm going to get the bus 50km ahead so I can meet up with some other new friends later, because my knees have not been good these past two weeks. Age taking its toll, ha ha – well, you know what I mean. If anyone has any tips for natural remedies I'd be grateful to hear them.'

'Natural remedies? I'd die of embarrassment if anybody actually thought that was me!'

How's it going out there in the rest of the world, anyway? Post me a message and let me know. If I don't catch your responses while I'm here I'll reply to you another time.

So, let me tell you about León. It's a beautiful city, especially the *casco antiguo* (Old Town) with its ubiquitous cathedral. If only I had the tools to draw it. León's one of the most famous way-stations on the holy Camino to Santiago de Compostela. You should see the old San Marcos Bridge, crowded with pilgrims as they make their way out of León. This suburb is on a hill, so when you stand at the top you get an epic view of the whole city spread out below.

> I love it here but hey, I'm a vagabond – I can't hang around
> in one place forever. Summer is drawing towards its end
> now. I don't think I can do winter up here.

Jamie studied his brother's face. They'd cleared away the supper pots and Joe had the laptop open again on the kitchen table. The stark kitchen lightbulb (Jamie needed to remember to buy a new paper lampshade for it – he'd torn the old one last time he changed the bulb) cast spooky shadows into the corners of the floridly orange walls. They sat in a pool of sallow light. Lejla was putting Electra to bed upstairs, they could hear his baby girl's occasional excited shouts and Lejla's low-toned pleas for her to go to sleep. Jamie tapped his fingers on the table. He wouldn't go up yet. Lejla would think he was suggesting she couldn't cope. He glanced at Joe, who scrolled down the screen again.

'What's eating you now?'

'Vagabond,' said Joe. 'There's something self-conscious about the way the writer uses it. I dunno. Can't explain. Let me try and figure it out.'

> I crossed out of Provincia de León into a land called Galicia.
> It has its own dialect. All the Albérges are built by the local
> government so they are very modern. Has anyone else ever
> visited this part of the world? Be good to hear what you
> think. Any other Pilgrims out there, get in touch, I'd love
> to hear from you. Hey, I'm finally leaving the mountains.
> Go me!

'What?!' spluttered Joe. 'Who talks like that?'

Jamie had to laugh, his brother reminded him so much of himself in the past. How was it that he and Joe had such different experiences of childhood – albeit with the same parents – yet they turned out so similar? Pity he hadn't bothered much with Joe when he was a little kid, they could've kicked a ball around together, he could've taught him how to play guitar. Ah well, better late than never...

'Listen. Let's mull on this some more another time. I've gotta get into the studio – AKA the cupboard – and work on

187

some tunes. From the lack of sound upstairs, I guess maybe Lejla's dropped off to sleep with the little one. Good job I've got you to keep me company. You're not rushing back, are you? Wanna join me?'

'What? Yeah, in a minute. This is a load of rubbish but it's genuinely quite addictive. And there're some good photos. Spain looks brilliant. When I've finished my book I may take off there myself. We could all go.' Joe's cross expression transformed into a hopeful one. 'We could all go – in a campervan! We could do one of those vanlife vlogs, maybe we could get sponsored by some company or other. Electra could be the star of the show – she'd love it.'

'Yeah and I could run a pop-up outdoor nightclub,' Jamie contributed to the fantasy. He grabbed a couple of beers from the fridge. 'Long as I can fit my decks on board I'm happy to go anywhere. We could even have solar-powered disco lights. Cool. Anyway, must get on. Meet you in the cupboard in a few mins, mate.'

'Yeah, I won't be long. . . '

Does anybody reading this blog fancy meeting up sometime? Am vagabond – will travel, if you know what I mean.

Anyway, so, guys out there in the world outside of "The Blog of Joe", let me know what you think in the *comments* section. Looking forward to hearing from you when I next check in. Over and out! TBoJ.

Jamie returned to the kitchen for the bottle-opener and found Joe still had the laptop open.

'I'd put that away now, mate. We'll have a think about what to do about it later.'

'It's a bit weird though, don't you think?' persisted Joe. 'This inauthentic voice, together with the fact they reproduced half my journal at the beginning. I wonder if they always meant to carry on with this blog after they finished the journal, or just got kind of, you know – carried away with the whole thing. Hey, maybe I inspired someone to travel!'

188

Jamie shrugged and gripped the bottle-opener. He hesitated in the doorway before continuing back through to his studio-cupboard, keen to lose himself in his own pursuit. But Joe didn't follow him. He took a few deep breaths and returned again to the kitchen. This thing was obviously bothering Joe and it probably wasn't a good idea to let him brood alone. He stared at the screen over Joe's shoulder. Joe rattled on. 'The photos are real, this person is genuinely travelling, man. But it can't be Nick. What would be the point? He has enough backstories of his own, he doesn't need to steal mine. And he wouldn't do that to me, I know he wouldn't. I'm kinda spooked.'

35

Maya

Paris, May 2016

On the Champs-Élysée, Con had held Maya's hand while he attempted to lure her into an expensive hairdressers.

'Once you've had your hair cut,' he said, his voice tight, 'You can let me buy you that dress I liked.'

The hairs on Maya's arms prickled. She resisted the pull of his hand and continued moving forwards.

'Where would I ever wear it?'

Con swallowed. They took a few more steps. Turning her head towards him, at the level of his throat she watched his Adam's apple bob up and down. She faced forward again. He stopped walking and by default she did, too.

'Here, tonight,' he said. 'With me. I love you. Aren't I worth that much to you?'

Her mouth felt dry. 'You've been a star this past year and a half.' She hesitated, thinking what to add. 'I love you too, honestly I do. But what would happen to the dress after this weekend if I let you buy it for me?'

People swarmed past them in both directions along the famous avenue.

'I'll save it for you.' He put on a brave voice. 'I'll take it home with me in my suitcase and hang it in your wardrobe and when you come back to me – we'll go out to dinner in the village bistro and I'll show off my beautiful wife to everybody.'

She sucked in her bottom lip.

'They all think you've left me, you know,' He twiddled the button on his green linen jacket with his spare hand. 'Everybody in the village does. I notice their pitying smiles if I ever have the courage to attend one of their functions. Daisy's good, she often accompanies me. And sometimes Lola does, too, although she hates *dos*. But our friends – your former friends – they don't think you're my wife any more. You *are* still my wife aren't you, Maya?' He tightened his grip on her hand. 'I know you have your mission in life, darling, and you don't want to abandon it. But I could hire a private detective instead. We could find the boys that way.' He gave her a searching glance. She stared back, narrowing her eyes. 'I want to find our sons as much as you do,' he said lamely. Now they'd stopped, her feet felt cold in the flat gold sandals. She felt her nostrils flaring.

'I fear you may have been watching too much television.' *Private detective!* She pictured herself back in the kitchen at The Cottages. Her fingers turned numb in Con's grip. 'And as for the dress... Come on, it's not really me anymore is it?'

She touched her scarf-wrapped head. Con released held breath, assessed her headdress, his lips pursed. 'You could have all of that cropped off. Why not? It suits you short. And it would be easy for you to look after. Remember when you had it cut very short on our twentieth anniversary cruise? It looked so beautiful curling around your ears.'

The ground of the Champs-Élysée rocked under Maya's feet as if she was back on the cruise ship. She and Con had modelled the characters in the film *Titanic* – as most couples their age did – standing one behind the other with their arms outspread, swaying in the wind at the bow of the ship.

'We're not those people anymore Con,' she said, recovering French ground beneath her feet. 'I can't imagine anything I'd rather do less than go on a cruise now. And if I have my hair cut it will only start knotting again in a few weeks' time. Keeping it brushed and free of tangles on the road is a constant battle. That's why I let it grow into dreads in the first place.'

'Dreads... will you listen to yourself.' Con loosened his arm from hers. 'This is the truth,' he said at last. 'I can't see anything left of my wife.'

Roaring filled the air, or at least Maya's head. She felt his fingers digging into her shoulders, pinching and prodding as if she was Hansel or Gretel. Was she ready for the oven, yet? Power rushed through his fingertips into the muscles of her arms, he could hurt her if he chose – so succinctly, right here in public. A vibration went through her. When she looked up into his eyes, their dark centres had turned cold.

'You can't do one little thing for me, can you?' his voice was emotionless. 'Not one thing.'

'But Con...'

'Shut up, for once in your life. I want you to give me a chance to say how *I* feel. It's always about you, isn't it?'

She opened her mouth to speak again but his narrowed gaze quickly closed it for her. She knew from past experience to allow his rare rage to run its course.

To anyone walking by, she thought, they might look like a couple on their second honeymoon. She wore an old-fashioned muslin dress, hair wrapped in an old but exquisite cream scarf. She was brown-skinned, but a white woman. Her reflection in the jeweller's window by which they'd stopped told her she looked like an actress. Con was tall and dark-haired – good-looking in a reserved sort of way, he looked the type to have good manners. Good manners were important, everyone knew that. He stood with his hands placed on her shoulders, gazing into her eyes. As if he was about to serenade her. From the corner of her eye Maya noticed a cluster of people – possibly an extended family – gathered at a respectful distance, watching them. Waiting for something to happen, probably. They must look so romantic. He placed his face closer to hers.

'I hope you know how much you've hurt me,' he muttered through clenched jaws, his breath hot on her face, smelling of garlic from their recent meal. 'You've let me down, do you know that? It's not fair. You've made a laughing-stock of me in our village. But not anymore, oh no. I'm not going to let that happen to me anymore. We'll finish this holiday together, as I've told the girls. And then you'll come to London with me as planned. That's for the girls after all. You've let them down enough already, as well as me. Then after that, Maya, I'm washing my hands of you.' His fingers gripped tighter. 'You needn't bother to text me or offer to Skype, however regularly. I know how much you hate doing that anyway, don't think I haven't noticed. I know you find my life boring and uninspiring. But I *like* my life, I've realised that. I like being the boring fart you think I am. So if you don't like it anymore then that's your problem. After this holiday you're on your own and I hope that makes you happy – I really do.'

He took his hands from her shoulders. The small knot of watching strangers remained in place for a moment. When nothing much else happened, the knot broke up and dispersed into the milling crowds. A cold rush of air poured into the space between her and Con.

36

Maya

Lleida, Spain, December 2016

Kofi had stopped to listen to her one afternoon when she was busking below the walls of *La Seu Vella de Lleida*. From the corner of her eye she'd registered him trudging up the steep, paved walkway towards the cathedral. Coins falling into her guitar case from a sweet elderly couple, holding hands as they made their way down the path, distracted her. She smiled and thanked them. When they had moved on she looked up again and saw Kofi there. He stood in front of her, blotting out the sun and tapping his foot. There was a slightly lopsided smile on his face when she briefly met his eyes. He moved to one side of her, allowing the sun to flood back into the spot he'd vacated. He bent to pat her dog, who lay on Maya's jumper in the shadow of the old stone. Kofi wore a leather hat with a floppy brim, along with a checked shirt and a denim waistcoat that looked hand-sewn. His beard was black, wiry on his jaw and chin and his eyes were keen and intelligent. The kind of guy she was attracted to when she was a student, when she played the guitar at a folk club. He positioned himself half in front of her again, resting on the low wall that bordered the path. She finished another song and was thinking about moving to a busier spot by one of the shopping centres in the city, when he straightened his shoulders and stepped forward. 'Kofi,' he offered his hand. 'How are you? Fancy some company?' He brought out a harmonica.

The sun was behind him and behind the sprawling view of the city. Its blinding light threw his features into shadow again. She sensed the dog shifting and felt it nudging the back of her legs as if to urge her forward.

A reverberation rang through the body of the guitar as she accepted his firm handshake and gave him her name. He proceeded to put the harmonica to his lips and played an intro. She smiled, recognising it immediately. Tapping her foot, they performed Dylan and Baez together. Followed by Neil Young. Kofi's knowledge of the music of her childhood was impressive.

She'd played the same songs on her guitar for Con when they first met. He'd always found it hard to let himself go, whereas this young man closed his eyes and had no self-consciousness. A couple of songs later, he took the harmonica away from his lips and contributed a vocal harmony to her melody – singing as though he'd written the words himself. His voice was hauntingly deep. She recognised the danger in it, found herself craving his company for another song and then another, even when the flow of tourists dried up. Her fingertips tingled – not only from the reverberation of the guitar. It was the first time she'd felt real for a while. *I'm tired*, she thought. *I've been searching for two years and I haven't found what I'm looking for.*

She pulled the guitar strap over her head. Felt her body sagging.

'I'm ready to call it a day.'

'Oh, right. Okay, that's fine.' Kofi pocketed his harmonica and slid down the wall beside her. The dog nestled closer and laid her head in Maya's lap. Maya pushed her fingers into thick, white fur and felt the dog's skin beneath.

'She's a lovely dog. What's her name?' his fingers touched the dog's head, their colours starkly contrasting.

Maya laughed. 'I don't know, she hasn't got one. I just say, "here girl" when I want her to do anything. She follows me everywhere, but she's not really mine, she just kind of picked me up.'

'That's sweet. Have you been around here long, then?'

'A few months. Staying at a place out of town.'

He cocked his head enquiringly but she wasn't allowed to give anyone the community's location. After an increasingly awkward pause he chipped in with, 'I'm at a hostel-cum-hotel place called Terraferma. Single room, shower and all that. It's a luxury after the road, certainly.' His laughter boomed.

There was another pause. Maya dragged the guitar case towards her with her foot.

'I should split the takings with you.' She sorted through coins and notes with both hands, laying them into two piles. 'They're quite good.'

'Oh right. Oh, no, of course not. I didn't hang around for that, certainly I didn't. I hope you don't think I—'

'Of course I don't,' Maya said. But it was a joint effort. I hardly had anything before you arrived. Here.'

She handed over a carefully counted-out portion of the money, which he accepted into his cupped hands, grumbling faintly. She scooped the rest into a cloth purse and stuffed it back into a cotton bag with thin straps.

'I'm hungry, I need to be heading back down into town.'

'Goodness, I'm hungry, too,' said Kofi. He laughed again. 'Is there anywhere in particular you'd like to eat? I know of a great outdoor place near where I'm staying.' He glanced at the dog, catching scents on the air with her twitching nose. 'The

197

dog will be fine, there. Do you fancy joining me? We can split the bill from our takings, hey?'

'You really like that stuff don't you? You are a vegetarian?'

'I have been for the past two years.' Maya licked the side of her hand. 'Mainly because carrying non-meat food on the road is easier – safer. More hygienic.' She couldn't help still sounding like a mother sometimes. 'And yes, I do love this bean stew. Not to mention the *tostadas* con *tomate. Mmm.*'

Kofi squinted at her. His face, despite his young age (she guessed no older than thirty) was deeply lined around the eyes and nose. It looked as though it could do with a wash but then so could hers. He wolfed down the final third of his *jamon* sandwich.

'It resembles a dish that is popular in tourist restaurants in Ghana,' he said, studying the remains of the food in her bowl. 'They call it *Red red.* I believe they make it from beans and plantain. I tried it once, but in the village I come from there is no such thing as a vegetarian, and I prefer a good goat stew.'

Maya wiped her mouth with the back of her hand. His voice felt hypnotic. Perhaps it was due to her tiredness.

Kofi studied her more intently. She felt her face turn hot, hoped the shade of the *plàtans* surrounding the outdoor restaurant would mute her high colour.

'Hey now. What's a woman like you doing on the road anyway?' (A question she'd been asked so often it was boring.)

Not answering, she continued to dip her spoon into her bowl, raising one eyebrow.

'I see,' said Kofi. 'You are obviously a woman of mystery, I like that.' Maya's hand loosely stroked the dog's head on her lap. She focussed on her food, lulled by the sound of his voice, saying something else that she missed, but didn't ask him to repeat. Kofi used his fingers to scoop breadcrumbs from his plate, licked them and then wiped his hands on his jeans' legs. Still she said nothing, swallowing the thick sauce that coated the beans. He scrunched up his eyes, cleared his throat.

'I also enjoy watching you eat,' he said. 'Bit of a turn-on, to tell you the truth.' She'd half-closed her eyes and was holding the taste of tomato in her mouth, but almost choked on the bubble of laughter that rose in her throat.

'Now you've spoilt it for me, and look what a mess I've made!'

She dabbed at her shirt and the tablecloth with her napkin.   Before this, she hadn't eaten since leaving her accommodation that morning and she'd wanted to make the most of it.

'Damn.' But she was still laughing. Lifting her spoon again, she continued scraping out the bowl.

He reached across and used the tip of his little finger to wipe at the corner of her mouth. An electric jolt went through her. She blinked, and straightened on the stool. Laying down her spoon, she picked up the last of the tomato bread and mopped her bowl; looked pointedly away as she enjoyed the flavours on her tongue.

From the corner of her eye she saw him rub his nose with the back of his hand. Turning back to him, she reached over to his plate and grabbed a scrap of remaining meat, which she fed to the dog. Kofi laughed. He fed the dog another scrap. The animal licked her lips and fastened her eyes on him. A silence grew between Kofi and Maya, while they focussed on the dog.

'There's usually a story behind a woman of. . . a woman of, let's say forty. . . or perhaps a little more. . . ? Travelling alone, as you are,' Kofi finally said.

'Oh, puh-lease,' Maya laughed. 'Flattery will get you nowhere. I thought there was more poetry to you than that, boy. What with the Bob Dylan and all that. I believed you had some imagination, at least.' It was a shock to hear herself sounding very much as if she was flirting. Her body showed signs of it as well, angling in a particular way towards him. But why not, anyway, if she was truly free, as she was attempting to be? It was as if Con was in her mind, on the other side of a closed, glass door, but only his shadow. His features had become indistinct.

'You are a sexy woman, did you know that? And I think your hair's great, by the way. Would you mind if I touch it?'

She swallowed. 'Go ahead.' People often asked that, but mainly children. When adults did she usually hated it but she didn't mind him. Felt honoured, in fact. She controlled her breathing as she unwrapped the scarf from her hair. By this time they'd consumed most of a bottle of wine as well as the food. She was unused to drinking and the effects were rapid and powerful. Her stomach tensed as Kofi tugged one of her dreads, winding it partially around his hand, something a child of hers would have done had they still been young enough. Was it a sense of mothering she was seeking with Kofi? Why did she have to question herself all the time?

'I considered keeping my locs but I decided I would travel light. They weren't that important to me.' Maya noticed the sweat-circle under his raised arm as Kofi ran his spare hand over the back of his shorn head, and she imagined what his hair would feel like. His hat lay on the table beside him. He leaned in closer.

'I must say, I've never met a woman like you before, Maya.'

This was someone else's son. And the sensations she'd begun to feel were not motherly. She could barely remember what they were called. The roots of her hair tightened. She felt sharp tingles over her scalp and they ran down the back of her head to the top of her spine. Kofi used his grip on her hair to bring her face closer to his. She could have stopped it at any time. But there was something about the tension in his beard, the way the black strands seemed to stand more stiffly to attention. His rapid breathing. Their lips touched, and she allowed his tongue to probe her lips open. *What was she doing?* She thought of Con again but he was only a cardboard silhouette. A rush of too many feelings to examine wrapped themselves around her and she stroked the younger man's knotted arm.

Whenever any kind of emotion took hold of her it quickly turned to sorrow, but she wouldn't allow sorrow to engulf her on this night. That was why she gave herself permission to grasp an unknown young man's wrists and pull his hands further down her body to her waist. They'd turned to face each other on the bar stools, their knees pressing together. The sky had begun to darken and stars shone with unremitting hardness, halos flickering around each one. It was going to be a cold night. She ought to be pulling on warmer clothes – she should be catching the bus for the long walk back to the community. She backed away from Kofi, *it was sweet while it lasted*.

'I've got to. . .'

'Why don't you stay with me?' Kofi interrupted. 'I've got a room in that hotel place just up the road.' His laugh sounded embarrassed, close to her ear, his breath tickling her neck.

It wasn't the first time someone had asked her. She'd come close to kissing another man, earlier that year – an older man who was recovering from testicular cancer. Their paths had kept crossing in various Albérges and campsites, or in shops selling bottled water. They ate lunch together on the first day they met. He had silver strands of hair mixed in amongst the black, a life story etched on his face. A hunger about him had attracted her – a hunger for a life that had almost been snatched away. Threads of similar sorrows connected them. Fred, his name was. Maya and Fred had walked together for a few days on the *Camino de Santiago* and deliberately stayed in the same Albérges. They had linked arms on the road, given each other hugs at the end of their walking days, but their lips had never touched. So what was it about Kofi?

She wanted to say yes. The thought of walking into the violet dark with her dog. . . then fumbling with a torch and cold fingers. The layers of clothes she must put on when she arrived back at her scant shelter. Perhaps she was too tired to continue with this way of life.

I'm losing myself, she thought. The controlled, determined Maya I've turned into since I said goodbye to my family in Australia, I'm losing her. *Maybe I've been doing this too long.* She suddenly craved the company of this young man with whom she had things in common that they could talk about. She wanted to hold and be held by someone who had a singing voice – and speaking voice – which turned her insides to liquid. Someone who spoke to her as an equal – and who desired her. She wanted Kofi's company.

She couldn't blame the drink. She knew what she was doing when she walked away from the market with him – the dog trailing close at her heels.

37

Maya

Lleida, Spain, December 2016

Despite his wiry beard and the lines around his eyes, the carpet of hair on his chest – he still seemed a boy to her in the stark light of morning.   She was so accustomed to belonging to a peripatetic, mainly youthful community that she'd stopped thinking of age as significant. Now her old self elbowed its way into her head and berated her with what felt like a wooden spoon bashing her brain. Head pounding, she lay squashed next to Kofi on the narrow bed, thinking about what they'd done. She tried not to imagine the disgust on her daughters' faces if they ever found out.

Propping herself up she studied the contours of Kofi's face before he woke, the way his cheekbones rose into mounds above the darkness of his beard and how his unusually long lashes clustered together in delicate points on the bruised-looking skin beneath his eyes.   He was probably about the same age as Jamie. Maybe? Oh, God. This was her first sexual transgression since her marriage began, *thirty-one years ago.* She struggled into a sitting position and waited for the cacophony in her head to ease before pushing back the blanket and releasing the scent of their sex into the room. Breathing shallowly, she swung her legs to the floor.

'Wait.' Kofi stirred and stretched. His fingers trailed the outside of her thigh. 'No need to go yet,' he said, but she moved away from the bed anyway, causing his hand to fall back onto the sheet. He sighed. 'Where are you going?'

'I need to shower.' She bent from the waist to lift her flannel shirt from the floor, shrugging her arms into the sleeves and crossing them over her body. 'Thanks for, you know.' *What?* Glancing at him before turning away, she gritted her teeth.

He had the look of an eager puppy.

'You're welcome. Are you sure you have to go? Maybe we could hang out together for a while. What are your plans for the day?'

'I can't leave the dog any longer, she'll need feeding. And I have some writing to do.' She could do with earning some money too, later in the afternoon – having spent more than she'd meant to on the previous night's feasting. And the wine. She would try a shopping centre she knew of, across town from here. Locals returning home from work or tourists from an afternoon's shopping would willingly empty their pockets of change for a lone woman busker. Especially when she sang sad ballads. And today the sadness hurt, a pain high in her chest. She glanced over at her guitar in the corner.

'Writing?' said Kofi. 'What about?'

'Oh just a journal. Keeping a bit of a record, you know. Places I've been, people I've met.' She glanced at him sideways, holding the edges of her shirt together with tense fingers.

'I never get that. Unless you're writing a song. It makes a lot more sense to put it in a song. Songs are for sharing.' He rambled on, scratching his beard. Leaning over to rummage in his backpack which leant against the side of the bed, he brought out his *doings*. Began to roll a joint on a cardboard inset from a packet of biscuits, still muttering. Maya swallowed disappointment. He seemed like a different person from the night before and their shared experience felt less profound than it had.

She gathered the rest of her clothes into a neat pile outside the door of the cramped bathroom, tucked in next to the wardrobe. The back of her neck prickled. Finding a towel that lay crumpled on the desk chair she wound it around her waist and took three steps back across the room to accept a toke of the joint – thinking of how his unwashed fingers had manipulated the Rizlas. She also thought briefly of Con, of the soft flesh of his upper arms and of the way he so carefully considered her in bed. Or used to. She hadn't seen him for over six months. She wondered what he was doing now – working diligently at his desk, she imagined. He would not even consider that his vagabond wife might recently have had sex with a man who was possibly around the age of their oldest son, or that she was currently standing in a stuffy room in Spain half naked, smoking a joint.

She felt a popping sensation inside her and something bubbled up until there was no space left for anything else. She handed the joint roughly back, dropping ash on the edge of the sheet. She heard Kofi curse and caught sight of his flapping hand from the corner of her vision as she edged into the bathroom and stripped the towel from her waist – but she was too busy containing the thing inside her to pay proper attention.

Grabbing the edge of the stuck shower door, she squeezed through the gap and turned on the pitiful spout of water. She hoped the pipes made enough noise to cover the sound of that great thing erupting from her ribs, choking out of her throat.

'Hey, are you all right in there?' his concerned voice rose above the sound of the water, the growling of pipes and her own snotty outburst. She coughed a glob of mucus into the drain and held her face under the water, rinsing snot from under her nose and tears from her eyes.

'Yeah, be out in a minute.' Before emerging from the bathroom, Maya wrapped the towel around herself, suddenly conscious of the impropriety of her nakedness. Almost as if the old version of herself had fully taken over.

'Hey now,' said Kofi. He gave in to a coughing fit. Recovering, he held out the end of the joint. 'You look sad, Maya. Want this?'

'Nah. And I'm fine.'

She kept her head down, dreads dangling over her face while she dressed with swift and efficient movements. As she pulled her t-shirt over her head she noticed yellow stains under the sleeves and the strong scent as it covered her nose. *Damn.* She found the roll-on deodorant in her bag and applied it to both armpits. She'd need to wash her clothes in the stream later.

She wedged her feet into her sandals and picked up her tote bag. Stumbled as she straightened and looked round the room, feeling dizzy. *Don't forget your guitar.* Leant down again, holding onto the corner of a small table for balance, zipped up the guitar case and shouldered it. She stopped at the door of the room. Kofi lay back on the pillow, a frown between his closed eyes and his face wreathed in smoke. Pinching the roach of the joint between his finger and thumb.

'I'm off now,' she said as lightly as she could. 'See you later maybe.' *Or most likely not.* 'I've gotta hit the road.'

He looked young with his eyes closed, especially compared to her – despite his abundance of facial hair. Perhaps he'd thought it cool to be messing about with an older woman. But it hadn't felt so. He lifted a hand from his stomach in a lazy wave, opening his eyes to lizard-slits. Faintly regretful she let her eyes fall to the line of hair trailing from his navel to the folds of sheet that covered the tops of his thighs. Straightened her spine. She closed the door quietly behind her, memorising word-for-word certain things he'd said, and mentally rearranging the pattern of others, to make them flow more smoothly when she wrote them down.

206

38

Maya

Lleida, Spain, December 2016

Shame nibbled her insides. She may be a thin fifty-six year old who could pass for someone in their forties – and anyway the children of the road counted age in experiences, not years – but still she couldn't help thinking of herself as the dumpy housewife who'd struggled to lift her rucksack off the ground two years before. The woman who'd been determined to find her sons.

Perhaps she could pretend the aberration had never happened. Bury it inside her deep, sweet sadness. *The end of her marriage.* How could she ever have thought it would work – that she could one day go back to that village in Lincolnshire and resume life with Con as if it had never been disturbed?

The faint winter chill brought Maya out of her reverie as she descended the steps from the Spanish hostel to the pavement below. The dog rose from the porch where she'd slept the night, nestled into Maya's jumper. She wound her wraith-like body around her chosen human, whimpering sounds coming from her throat. Maya pushed her fingers through the dog's thick coat and laid them on her warm skin. 'You're a tough girl, aren't you?' she murmured. 'C'mon, let's go and get some breakfast.' She gathered up the jumper, shaking off the hairs and rolling it tightly. Stuffed it into her bag and straightened her back. 'Good girl. Come on,' she said again.

Later it would be warmer and she'd take up her spot in the square. She'd play some more tunes and this time, if Kofi stopped in front of her, tipping his wide-brimmed hat in a vagabond's salute, she'd only smile enigmatically. The tips of her fingers tingled on her left hand in anticipation of reuniting with the guitar strings. The skin on those fingertips had hardened to callouses now, though it had taken weeks of dedicated practice to get them into playing condition at the beginning.

The streets were quiet but the library would be open by now. She had some writing to do and there was a sheltered spot on the veranda of the bakery next door, where she could get breakfast. The owners loved the dog and fed her scraps of bread. The dog was good and waited for Maya however long she stayed in the library. Instinctively Maya felt for her tablet. She was tired. Her body felt unfamiliar from the recent sex. Her sandals, which had been fixed up at an old-fashioned cobblers' shop in this very town thudded dully on the pavement as she walked into the more commercial area, the dog's claws tapping beside her. She could store her guitar in one of the lockers in the library's basement while she carried her tablet to the upper floor, where there was free internet. Her brain ticked over, wondering if and how she could use her recent experiences to reach out to Joe.

39

Maya

Lleida, Spain, December 2016

In the late afternoon Maya and the dog returned to her temporary home: a house made of sticks at the transient community in the forest. The dog polished off the bowl of kibble Maya poured for her, then whined quietly. She seemed restless, turning on the spot and poking Maya with her long, pink-tipped snout as Maya rummaged in her rucksack.

'What's up, girl?' Scrabbling about under the rudimentary kitchen worktop, the dog finally flopped onto her stomach on the makeshift bed of hessian and a threadbare blanket. She let out a heavy sigh. Maya crouched down to ruffle her fur, adopting her usual murmur for the dog. 'Good dog.' This would be her final evening at the community. Maybe the dog somehow sensed she was leaving. Maya stroked her harder. 'I'll miss you, I really will.' The dog lifted her head, gave Maya that uncannily perceptive stare she'd become familiar with.

Standing and stretching, she paused in the doorway. None of the other community members seemed to be around. Maya

209

followed the path to the stream with an armful of clothes. She used soap that she'd watched Wild Eric boil up from, amongst other things, the fat of a roadkill goose that must have fallen foul of its programmed migration. Eric had thrown some wild herbs in for the essence of a scent. The goose must have flown alone and confused, in search of its kin. Her fingers tightened around damp cloth. She scrubbed her few items a final time, rinsed them and hung them out to dry in the sun on a particularly obliging branch angled alongside the path. Back at her house she decided to crawl into bed for an afternoon nap with the aim of being alert later. A delivery driver at the small supermarket in the village between here and Lleida had promised her a 100km lift the next morning. It meant getting up at 5am to walk the two miles there but it would be worth it for the long stretch of road she'd cover.

The itinerant community were so easy to get along with. They had no expectations of each other apart from that everyone must participate in food hauls and general housekeeping. It would have been tempting to stay. She was close, in particular, to a young Spanish girl named Valeria, who had asked her to stay longer. Valeria once accidentally called her Mamá. But she wanted to reach Barcelona by Christmas, still hoping to persuade her own daughters to fly out and meet her. *Perhaps even Con.* Would he be able to forgive what she'd done? They hadn't spoken for six months. It would hit harder at Christmas. She sometimes dreamt that Con was accompanying her on the road; it had happened a lot when she was walking the Camino, in the months after their parting in the spring. There were parts of the trail that she hadn't yet walked – they could walk it together... if only Con would just, well – *let go of his hang-ups.* Now she wasn't so sure that he would.

'We're like chalk and cheese,' Con once said to her in the early days of their relationship. He called her a wild, hippy girl, although she didn't feel she was. That was more her sister, Jen. Lying now in the stick house Wild Eric and his

210

partner built when they first set up the community, the still-warm sun painting stripes on her sleeping bag through the gaps in the walls, Maya considered the qualities of his two options. Which one of them was which? So far they'd both remained firm to their resolve – Con refused to respond to any contact from her and she wasn't planning on running home to appease him – she could never be that housewife again. She did not want to have the rats' tails (his final insult) on her head nicely lopped-off to suit a prescribed image.

Perhaps he'd believed himself to be the cheddar and her the chalk. In the early days of their relationship Maya was perhaps *something* of a wild child, just less so than Jen who had gone travelling in a gypsy caravan with her older boyfriend. Back then Maya wore flowing cheesecloth dresses similar to Daisy's now. She played the guitar and sang at a weekly folk-club, which was how Con accidentally found her one evening. He'd opened the door of what he mistakenly thought was the chess club. She'd been the one to lay down her guitar and lead him along the corridor to the room he was looking for.

Con enjoyed brass band music and Maya liked Joni Mitchell. Maya was convivial and friendly to acquaintances and strangers alike but Con was more of an introvert, or simply downright suspicious. So what had drawn them together?

They explained it by how they completed each other's personalities, but in truth it was sex that bound them. Thinking about it, Maya's hand unconsciously trailed from her neck to her stomach over the surface of the sleeping bag. Her fingers circled lightly so that she could only just feel their touch through the fabric. Until she met Con she hadn't known the kind of sex they had was possible. She only realised soon after they started sleeping together that she'd never completed an orgasm before. During sexual communion she yearned for them to transgress each other's physical boundaries and become one being. *That* was what

211

bound them together.

The sun was warm and no-one was around, apart from the now-snoring dog. Maya unzipped the sleeping bag and pushed both hands inside, one gently stroking her breasts inside her shirt, the other pushing down beneath the waistband of her harem pants, over the loose skin of her stomach and between her legs. She closed her eyes and conjured a younger Con into the narrow bed with her. The thick, dark hair flopping over his face, the guardedness in his eyes slowly melting. *That was what turned her on so much.* She heard the catch in his breath that meant he was about to come... Grabbed his hand and pushed it between her legs with her own, watched his eyelids flickering and his mouth opening into an 'O' – felt her back arching. *Con.*

———

She woke to the sound of voices by the stream. She stretched and climbed down from the sleeping-platform, a slight ache in her hip. Perhaps the day she'd be forced to return to "society" would be when her body started to feel its age. Up to now she'd been lucky to escape arthritis and asthma and type-2 diabetes – conditions that had inhibited her mother's lifestyle from her early fifties onwards. Or maybe it was as much to do with state of mind as genetics. Perhaps the illnesses would have claimed her too, if she hadn't got away from London.

The air had cooled considerably but it wasn't yet dark. She washed perfunctorily with the water she kept in a basin on the countertop and pulled on a long sweater, miles too big for her – that she'd gained from a clothes swap at the last hostel she was in. Rolled up the sleeves. She looked around for the dog but she must have left the shack a while ago – when Maya pressed the back of her hand to it she found the dog's bedding had cooled. She felt her way out barefoot, knowing by now where the sharp stones were, and down the track to the main part of the commune. All the buildings on the land had been constructed by hand from recycled and

212

natural materials. Valeria and a Danish boy were washing pans in the stream. 'Hi, Maya,' called Valeria, scrubbing vigorously with a scouring sponge woven from tough grasses. Her dark hair was twisted into a knot at the back of her neck. *The way she does her hair reminds me of Daisy.* The boy turned his head and offered Maya a grin.

'Are you on cooking rota tonight? We won't be long with the rest of the pans.' His blue eyes were honest and friendly. It was a family of sorts that Maya would be leaving behind but she'd made that kind of break before. . .

The youngest member of the group was chopping wild garlic and onions on a felled tree-trunk by the path to the fire. Maya half-slid in a puddle created by a dripping pan, balanced on a grid of branches at the edge of the track. She laughed and smiled at the English boy as she held onto a branch for steadiness. Not for the first time she wondered if his mother knew where he was. But it wasn't her business. *Not all vagabonds are castaways*, she recalled a conversation with a pair of young vloggers during a stop-over at a wild campsite after she left the Camino. They chided her for assuming they'd run away from their parents.

She'd been advised on arrival at the commune not to ask personal questions or try to take on any kind of motherly role. Everyone was equal in status, each a free spirit. The truth was she had taken more from these young people than she'd given them in return. They didn't need looking after, only to be allowed *to be*. It hurt that she hadn't understood this from raising her own children.

Anxious Lola would benefit from this kind of existence, she thought as she approached the blaze. An Irish boy and an Italian woman who probably wasn't much younger than Maya were busy straightening a metal grill over the flames, ready for the pans. Maya hadn't heard from her more tumultuous twin daughter for a while and was trying to ignore her steadily brewing disquiet. *Lola's a grown-up, she needs time to discover herself, without me interfering. But I should have sent emails when I was at the library this morning,* another part of her protested. Instead, her time on the internet had been taken up with the feverish and dedicated activity that consumed her lately. *Something's going to happen.* An impending resolution. She stood for a moment, gazing around her at the welcoming fire, the sheltering trees and the focussed activity of her fellow humans, all working together towards a common aim. Warmth flooded her chest but at the same time, tears pricked behind her eyes. *This was all I ever needed, why couldn't I see that before?*

40

Maya

Lleida, Spain, December 2016

Faces glowed around the fire as the community gathered for dinner. She'd learned so much from the gentle travellers that surrounded her. Her boy would be all right – his attachment to her had once been strong and she trusted now that he would one day follow his umbilical cord back to her. As she explored the faces of her companions she acknowledged that she mustn't let her own need dictate when the reunions with her sons would occur. Sitting within reach of the flames' warmth it became clear what she must do – stop posting on *"The Blog of Joe"*. Delete it altogether. Shame flushed her cheeks – what damage might she have done? If Joe ever found out it could be irreparable.

She took the newly-sharpened knife and chopped the salvaged carrots and home-grown potatoes from the basket the Italian woman had brought her into cubes. As usual, it was Joe she'd been thinking of whilst at the library. But now a sudden urgency pricked her to connect with the twins.

Perhaps they weren't all right after all. The feeling of disquiet about Lola strengthened. She steadied her trembling hands before beginning on the red peppers. She would email her daughter in the morning. Well, once she had access to the internet. *A time for everything and everything in its time. . .*

Maya stirred the dumpster-dived vegetables into a stew with the wild foraged garlic, onions and greens. *Something was going to happen.* She'd spent some of her busking money on salt and pepper, rarely found in the dumpsters. She added sprinkles of each to the stew. She'd leave the condiments behind as a thank you gift. There was a bustling sound and her companions around the fire shifted as someone arrived with an armful of crusty bread that had been salvaged that evening by the second dumpster-diving crew. A perfect accompaniment to the stew.

'Oh my God!' Maya was startled by Valeria, jumping up from her tree-stump seat opposite. 'They've brought custard. *'Eso es fantástico!'* Eyes widened as the dumpster crew unloaded twelve cartons of past-date but still perfectly edible custard from a cardboard box. Valeria clasped one dramatically to her chest. Maya smiled across the fire at her. Living on salvaged food made the sweet things even sweeter.

The sky was truly dark and breathtakingly clear. A twinkling chain of fluorescent stars clustered in the gap between the trees and the dark flanks of the mountains rose behind the trees' tall trunks. She drank in the contented faces and it felt as if the earth was turning inside her.

The children here were independent of their parents. They existed as their true selves. Hers and Con's manner of bringing up their children was based on ownership, she saw that now. They'd created a prison of love from which their sons had escaped. She was sad for all the parents, like her, who believed they'd lost their children. If she was patient, if she was calm, if she lived the most honest life she could—. But the first thing she had to do was let go.

Nature and humanity. It was enough. And animals. Wild

Eric had told her the white dog had haunted the place like a ghost for months before she came, not completely trusting anyone. *As if she was waiting for someone special.* Now Maya heard a faint rumble from the dog's throat as she nosed her way between the English boy and the Italian woman on Maya's left and moved past the fire to press her head against Maya's leg. Maya's stomach wrenched at the thought of leaving this trusting creature behind. *But she was good at turning her back on those she loved, wasn't she?* The voice of her insecurity re-arose and beat against the calm promises she kept making to herself about acceptance and understanding.

Laughter boomed from the other side of the fire and her heart pounded. She suddenly felt displaced. The stew bubbled in the pan, emitting the pungency of garlic. Witching scents. Her inner layers had been exposed – *Maya the fake.* Here she was, pretending to be a natural nurturer, when she'd driven away two of her own children and deserted those that remained. She wiped her brow with her sleeve and stirred the pot to hide her confusion. The white dog turned her liquid eyes up to Maya, sensing that something was wrong. The dog's eyes were dark-shadowed, as if she was wearing make-up. Maya stroked the soft head with her spare hand, before leaning towards the bubbling pan with the spoon and scooping some stew from the edge.

'Who wants to try?'

'Me,' the Danish boy was sitting on her right. He blew on the food and then sipped it from the spoon, moving it around in his mouth, keeping her waiting for his verdict.

She avoided his eyes, uncomfortable. Only that morning she'd woken up in bed with a different young man of around the same age.

'Det er lækkert!' The Danish boy pronounced.

She pulled herself together. 'Good. Ah, good. That sounded positive to me. Ready to serve, then.'

They held their metal bowls out and she ladled the food in.

Resettling one at a time, they cradled the bowls on their laps around the fire.

After food and conversation came music. She'd left her guitar in the stick house and was happy to listen and join in with the choruses, which became rowdier as home-made cider was passed around, culminating with a particularly cacophonous rendition of *Wild Rover*.

Wild Eric, community founder, no longer lived up to the wild part of his name. She'd noticed him leaving the fire circle some minutes earlier and was afraid he might have gone to bed if she didn't move soon. She wanted to ask if she could borrow the Dongle he kept in the main hut in case of emergencies. Once she was on the road tomorrow she didn't know how long it would be before she had internet access again. She had such an urge to tell the girls how much she loved them, beg them to meet up with her in Barcelona for Christmas. Filled with the warm glow of resolve as well as two portions of stew, custard and cider, Maya helped gather the pots and load them into the metal washtub full of stream-water that was boiling in a large saucepan over the fire, before walking up a narrow track through a thick cluster of trees. The dog pressed close to her thigh as usual, while she knocked softly, her tablet tucked under one arm. Eric agreed to her request and took time to tell her that that the community would miss her. Then he left her alone. Sitting in the cosy space of the community's office, off which were Eric's private quarters, she drafted a series of emails before connecting to the Dongle, so as to conserve data. The dog hampered progress by nudging her arm repeatedly but eventually she was finished. Keeping the email to Daisy short and hoping it would adequately express the depth of her feelings – of gratitude as well as love, for she knew it was Daisy who kept things on an even keel at home – Maya had followed it with a draft to Lola. Her tone in this one was more brisk in nature. Lola wouldn't be able to handle the kind of emotion she could communicate to Daisy. Finally, Maya had

218

drafted an email to her husband.   *Please meet me in Barcelona. I know you said you wouldn't have any contact with me until I was ready to come home, but I need to talk with you some more. Please, Con. I promise this will be the last Christmas I put you in this position.* With some kind of a promise made, Maya clicked on the internet icon and waited for an available connection to appear. But the list was empty. The Dongle must have run out of data. The emails would have to wait until she reached the next Wi-Fi location, or until she could get a signal on her phone.

41

Jamie

Berlin, December 2016

Lejla was feeling better now she was in her sixth month of pregnancy. She'd even returned to work at the club two nights a week, and at the weekends she stood again at her market stall. Jamie wasn't that happy about the club, worried it might affect the baby's hearing. This second pregnancy felt more tenuous to him than the first.

'Don't talk crap, Jamie,' Lejla brought him down to size, aiming a swipe at his shoulder. 'I told you – the baby, he likes dancing to the music. He's gonna be a little rapper-man, aren't you, baby?'

'Nah, he won't,' said Joe. He'd accepted the warehouse was too cold a place to sleep after all, now the bitter December winds were blowing through the gaps in the window frames. His three flatmates had all moved to warmer accommodation too. For rent Joe babysat his three-year-old niece. He settled Jamie's guitar on his knee and picked out an introduction to a song. 'He's gonna be into Bob Dylan and Neil Young, I'll make sure of it. Like our little Electra.' He strummed a few more chords while Electra sang in her high voice, about how times were a' changing.

They were clustered as usual around the table in the kitchen. The smell of paint was still strong but the fumes were worth putting up with for the apple-white walls. There was also a new shade softening the bulb – made of pale green glass instead of paper. The previously-purple corridor had been similarly transformed. The place looked less like a seedy bar. It now had the wholesomeness of apples. Having Joe to stay had been advantageous in more ways than one. Joe strummed the guitar more raucously as Electra's voice became shriller.

'Okay, shush now, let's get back to the business. C'mon, please,' Lejla flapped a hand in front of her face. 'We're doing this for you two, you know, not for me. Now. We have to come up with a suitable name. Put on your thinking caps, everybody, and behave yourselves.'

The pause lengthened while they all wore their thinking caps. The child propped her chin on her hand in a similar way to her mother, her eyes flicking mischievously between the adults. The silence was broken by Joe, twanging the strings of the guitar.

'Please, miss, I have a suggestion.'

'Yes?' Lejla spoke like the stern teacher she had trained to be before dropping out to become a *badass DJ*. 'Okay, tell us your answer, please.'

'She was just singing it,' Joe pointed to his niece. 'It's a Bob Dylan song.'

42

Maya

Barcelona, December 2016

'Our German Shepherd had to be put down,' said the mother, twisting around in the front seat. 'We are all still very sad.' She said they would be visiting an animal shelter to choose another dog as soon as they felt ready. Meanwhile she rummaged in the glove compartment and found some dog treats that her daughters fed one by one to Alicia, amidst shrieks and giggles. Alicia's ears twitched and she flinched at the sudden noises. Maya made shushing sounds. 'She's very nervous,' she explained when she had the girls' attention. She searched for words in Spanish. '*Se amable con ella.* You need to stroke her gently and whisper in her ear. She likes that.' Shortly afterwards, when all the treats were gone and the girls were sucking lollipops their mother had passed over to them, Alicia settled into sleep with her nose tucked under Maya's arm. With her other hand, Maya circled her fingers in the silky hair at the base of the dog's neck. The creature could do with a bath and some grooming. *Now you won't*

223

have to live on the outskirts of a community, or wait outside
buildings for me on the off-chance I might come back.

The commune were vague about where she came from. Gaby, the Italian woman, thought she was one of the puppies that had been born on a farm a few miles away but didn't know how she'd become a stray. 'She only started hanging around here full time once you settled in,' Gaby said. Maya now had vets and vaccinations on her mind. She'd have to delve into the bank account she'd barely touched since flying to Europe.

She leaned forward in the car, careful not to disturb the sleeping dog or the drowsing girls, their fingers relaxing on the lollipops resting on their lips, their eyes glazed. The mother turned her head enquiringly at Maya's hand on the back of her seat.

'Can you recommend me a veterinarian in Barcelona?'

'Of course.' The mother rummaged in the glove compartment again and took out a creased card printed with a graphic of a dog and a cat, the line-drawn figures running into each other. She smoothed it with a finger before handing it to Maya. 'This is the vet we used for our Enzo. They will sort out Alicia for you.'

An hour later the girls' father stopped the car just before a junction of two busy roads. Both he and his wife got out. The wife opened the door and took the dog's lead while Maya encouraged her past the smaller child's feet, sticking out from her car seat. The girls were fully awake and waved their lollipops and cried, not wanting Maya or the dog to leave. Their father handed Maya her rucksack and guitar from the boot. He spoke in halting English.

'Thank you for keeping the girls entertained during the journey. We didn't have to bribe them with a DVD at all.'

'Thank you for the lift. Your daughters are wonderful.' Maya swallowed. While the woman still held the lead Maya shrugged her arms into the rucksack and swung the guitar strap over her shoulder. 'I hope you feel ready to get a new

224

dog soon,' she said to the woman as her husband got back in the car. 'I wish I'd allowed my children a dog when they were small.'

The mother smiled. 'Goodbye.'

'Goodbye, and thank you again.'

The children waved as the car drove off. It was early evening already. The city, even on the outskirts, felt like a concrete jungle after the mountains and small town Maya had inhabited for three months. In her tote bag she carried water and a spare pack of sandwiches that the family had bought for her earlier, and some biscuits for the dog. She stood, getting her bearings. Looking southwards she faced the city and westwards she looked back at the slopes of a hill. Alicia pressed herself tighter against Maya's leg, frightened by the heavy traffic. Maya felt herself trembling, too. She touched the dog's head.

'Come on then, baby. One more night in the wild for us. It will all be fine.'

They climbed the hill. From the top Maya looked down on an incredible view. The city appeared jam-packed into the space between the sea, glimmering in the distance at its foot, and the mountains behind it. An orange haze muted the tightly-packed buildings and streets on the sloping plain that led to the Catalonian foothills. Maya had an odd sensation of drifting. She had to check that her feet were still on the ground because her senses were still permeated by the motion of travel. Alicia pulled on the lead, whining faintly. She seemed to be aiming for a small copse of trees partially bordered by a low wall. Maya scanned the close vicinity. A few picnickers; a family with small children and a little way off, a group of teenagers, were ranged on the slope below. It felt likely they wouldn't stay on after dark. Maya walked into the trees with the dog. In the copse she looked around for a safe-looking place to spend the night. She let Alicia off the lead while she scanned the bushes for a place to briefly call home. A few minutes later she saw Alicia squatting in a deep pile of leaves. Maya moved closer and kicked a layer of mulch over the dog's deposit. Pressing her tummy, she was grateful she'd had the opportunity to use flushing toilets a little over an hour before.

It wasn't too cool yet but it would definitely become much colder overnight. Maya opened her rucksack and put on her thick jumper, removed her cargo trousers and pulled on a pair of leggings, replacing the trousers over them. She also unstrapped her walking-sandals and pulled on a pair of thick socks. Her eyes continually flicked in all directions, checking to see whether anyone else was about. Having walked the Camino, mostly in company over the preceding months, followed by the few months of living in the commune – she now felt unaccustomed to sleeping out on her own. *Oh, God, what did I do?* The memory of sleeping with Will seared through her body. She must bury it as she had done the dog's poo.

'Thank goodness for you, Alicia.' She wrapped her arms around the white dog's neck and the dog leaned into her. She kissed Alicia's fur, thinking of how disgusting the old Maya would have found that.

Why hadn't they had a dog while the children were growing up? She pictured Jamie as an eight-year-old, introverted and difficult. Why hadn't she responded when he begged for a Jack Russell puppy, bred by his friend's mother? All she could recall was terror at the thought of the dog chasing the girls' guinea pigs and rabbits. And the poo, ugh. *Poor Jamie.* But maybe? She'd said to Con. We could buy a dog-proof pen for the guinea pigs. And a pooper-scooper. I wouldn't mind the walks. But Con said the boy didn't deserve to be rewarded for his bad school report. *A dog might have helped Jamie. He would have learned to take care of something.* 'I can't imagine not having you,' she said to Alicia. Alicia swung her head round and nibbled at the fur on her back.

The landscape beyond the trees had dimmed to an opaque

blue – the sun was in its final stages of setting. She could still hear children's voices, chattering and laughing on the slope below, but the sound was diminishing. Perhaps the family was moving down the hill. She spread out her tarp, pushing the dog away as Alicia repeatedly stepped on it while she worked. Eventually she was happy with the results of her efforts. She'd looped a section over an overhanging branch like a child's play-tent and laid out her mat and sleeping bag on the lower portion, which covered the softly-piled leaves on the ground. If it rained she'd stay more or less dry. And Alicia would help keep her warm. Now it was time to eat.

When she and the dog had finished their supper of sandwiches and biscuits, Maya stood up and then bent again as she crept under branches, ploughing a channel into the undergrowth behind her makeshift camp. The dog followed her and pushed past, moving ahead. Maya felt the rumble of her own laughter as they both squatted and urinated into the leaves. Memories of years of visiting the *Ladies* in pairs or groups turned the rumble into a choke. 'Watch it!' she warned herself aloud as she struggled to control her stream of urine. Alicia peered at her through the darkness, flinching slightly at a particularly loud cry from Maya's throat. While Alicia's hindquarters rose gracefully, tail high, when she was done, Maya was forced to stand and wrestle with her annoying layers of clothes. The dog led Maya back through the tangles of undergrowth to their camp.

Maya pictured the village hall in Navengore, the glitter of jewellery at expensively-moisturised throats. The scent of hairspray. Slashes of bright lipstick on smiling mouths, the boutique dresses, as the women made their way back from the toilets to their one hundred pounds per place charity-ball tables. It all seemed so far away in place and time, and ridiculously meaningless. She crawled into the sleeping bag under the tarp, and curved her body to make room for Alicia, on the mat beside her.

43

Maya

Barcelona, December 2016

Alicia licked her awake the next morning, whining softly. 'Ugh.' Maya wiped away the saliva with her hand. 'I hope you haven't got any diseases.' She squinted at the rising sun through the branches as she transferred dog-drool onto the sleeping bag. 'Visit to the vet's for you today, I think.' She struggled out of her sleeping bag and they visited their makeshift lavatory again. This time Alicia did what the children used to call a 'number two' and Maya covered it over with leaves. She herself would wait until the next supermarket or petrol station, a good reason to get moving early.

She ripped open a packet of wipes and gave herself the once-over before putting on clean underwear, replacing her layers of clothes item by item. The used wipes went into a plastic bag containing the rubbish of their previous evening's meal. She stuffed it into a side pocket of the rucksack. She would treat herself to a room in town later, if she could find somewhere that would take the dog. The vet would know. Then she could wash and dry the remainder of her clothes at the facility's laundry. She tied a clean scarf around her hair, checked that the sleeping bag and tarp were packed into the bag as tightly as they could go, swung the bag and the guitar up onto her back and clipped on Alicia's lead, receiving a look of reproach from the dog.

'Sorry,' Maya said. 'We're going into society now and we need to look as respectable as we can.'

They emerged from the woods, walked down the hill and set off along the awakening street towards a huge supermarket.

Later, on the crowded, scenic avenues of Barcelona, she felt like a visitor from another planet. Alicia walked close to Maya's hip and Maya kept bending to rustle her fingers in the fur of the dog's neck for comfort. If Daisy and Lola had been with her they would have stopped at every souvenir shop and Christmas display – the *Fira de Santa Llúcia* was the second Christmas market Maya had spotted already, in the Gothic quarter, by the main entrance to the cathedral – they would have wanted to taste the artisan ice-cream in sumptuous displays in a nearby shop window. But after the isolation she'd become used to, the visual and aural richness surrounding her was overwhelming. Artists and human statues performed in front of the clothes shops and bijous restaurants. Maya had to fight hers and Alicia's way through the crowds gathered to watch the performers. Tall, historic buildings loomed on both sides of the street. Maya's head whirled. She stopped to study the hand-drawn map the woman in the car had given her, and pulled in deep breaths.

The vet's receptionist (who thankfully could speak passable English) asked Maya to bring the dog back the next day for her vaccinations. Maya had to fill in a temporary registration form. On her computer, the receptionist also pulled up a list of Airbnb's that were pet-friendly and went as far as to book Maya and Alicia into one. 'Thank you so much, we'll see you tomorrow.' Maya returned the smile of the youthful-looking

Spanish woman who'd helped her and given her a breather from all the exotic culture on the streets.

Emerging again into the bright sunshine, Maya squinted against the glare. Keeping Alicia on a short lead she frowned down at another hand-drawn map, this time from the receptionist. The Airbnb was only a few streets away, on the *Avinguda de l'Estadi.* Maya's tired brain took in a sign to the MNAC which she knew was the National Art Museum of Catalonia, because the mother of those two little girls had told her she worked there. Looking down at the dog, Maya noticed Alicia's eyes were red-rimmed. The dog must be even more tired than she was. Alicia panted heavily as they stood together on the doorstep of their next temporary home.

'I know,' said Maya, stroking her head. 'It's all a bit scary, isn't it?'

Their host was named Katya. She welcomed Maya and bent to give Alicia some fuss. Apologising for the piles of flattish boxes in her airy downstairs entranceway, which Maya guided the dog around carefully, Katya explained that she worked as a seamstress. The boxes contained an order of bridesmaids' dresses for an upcoming wedding and she would be going out that afternoon to deliver them.

Her small house felt warm and friendly, painted white and with terracotta tiles on the floor of the one, split-level room at street level. Worn but brightly coloured rugs dotted the floor and were spread over the low sofas. Maya and her host shared a lunch of soup and bread at a white table, indulging in simple getting-to-know-you conversation. Later Katya offered Maya the use of the enclosed, red-tiled back terrace for Alicia. Maya followed the dog around, brandishing a poo-bag from a roll purchased at the vet's and careful to avoid the heavy pots of geraniums. Alicia took her time finding the exact, correct tile on which to place her deposit. Having bagged and binned, Maya excused herself and took Alicia up the shallow staircase to the privacy of their plain but comfortable room. Armed with a Wi-Fi code, she checked her inbox, at the same time watching the messages she had composed before leaving the commune wend off on their ways.

44

Maya

December 2016

Email from: Maya_Lifeforce@dmail.com
    To: Daisy Galen
    Subject: Love you

Darling Daisy,

I've been sitting around a fire, sharing a meal with a group of lovely young people here in the mountains of Spain, and I thought about you. Not that I don't think about you most of the time, my lovely girl, but tonight was different. I was thinking about how caring the young people I've met on my travels are, and it occurred to me that you're exactly the same. I shouldn't have needed to travel the world to find that out, but there you have it. Don't think I don't appreciate everything you do at home, Daisy. I know you look out for your sister and Dad, and I hope that you get time to have some fun yourself. I hope you find what you need out of life. I just wanted you to know how much I love you.

Darling girl,
Love, Mum xxxxx

Maya watched with satisfaction as the emails she'd composed in Wild Eric's hut finally left her outbox. She clicked on an email from Daisy, the only thing in her inbox. Lola must still be sulking at her mother's refusal to return home. Vague discomfort nudged at her insides but she ignored it and concentrated on what Daisy had to say.

Email from: Daisy_halfcrazy@dmail.com
To: Maya Joy Galen
Subject: none

Mum...
I know I don't give much away in my emails, you must think I live in a kind of vacuum of feeling – well, I know if you could see me you wouldn't think that, but you can't – so you might. But this time I'm going to tell you.

I feel lost and scared. I'm betraying one of the people I love whatever I do now, so I've made the choice I think will be the best. Lola's probably going to kill me but I can't do this anymore. I'm overwhelmed. I've got her staying in my flat at the moment because she's split up with her boyfriend, Steve. You knew about him, right? Yeah, I remember, Lola was going on and on about him when we met up with you in May. But I know she hasn't told you this...

She's having a baby, Mum.

Lola's having a baby. Really, really soon. Like, after Christmas.

She made me promise not to tell you because she's mad at you for not coming home. It was hard for me because I've felt like I've been betraying you by not telling you – although we haven't shared so many emails lately anyway what with you being off-grid so much – and Lola says you won't care about this thing but I know you will. I begged Dad to tell you because

234

then I wouldn't be breaking my word to Lola – which she kind of forced out of me – but he's acting all high and mighty and refusing to get in touch with you, too.

So it's all fallen on me as usual and I'm fed up with it. The heating in my flat's broken and they're taking forever to send someone out to fix it. My cat, my lovely Tink, she went missing when Lola turned up in floods of tears and she didn't come back for three days, bedraggled and hungry. Now she skulks under the sofa and only comes out when Lola's in bed and she knows it's safe. And I can't even *get* in my own bed because Lola's taking it up – and she steals all the pillows and lazes around all day while I go to work and then come home and cook for her – and then she eats and goes back to bed. *My* bed.

Sorry for telling you everything this way but as you can imagine, the responsibility's getting on top of me.

Lola and I are going to have to move back in with Dad – I can't cope with her in my flat anymore and she says she won't leave unless I do, too. I feel like my independence has been sucked away.

I just thought you should know.

Tell me about your adventures. I envy you.

Love, Daisy xx

The shock of what she had just read turned Maya's lips numb. Her fingers and arms tingled and a hollow pit opened in the centre of her body. *She was going to be a grandmother!*

Lola, with a baby. On her own.

She needed to get home.

Oh, God.

She couldn't ignore the rising nausea when she pictured the sprawling house in Navengore, though. She couldn't live there, she couldn't. Not in the long term. There must be some compromise she and Con could make. She pressed one hand to her stomach and the other to her mouth. Sitting on the edge of the bed, she sagged at her core as though a tensioning string had been snipped. The dog rose from her place on the floor and nudged Maya's knee.

Fingers trembling, Maya quickly typed a reply to Daisy, who would think her mother had been ignoring the tumultuous news she'd sent a few days ago.

She needed my comfort and I wasn't able to give it.

Email from: Maya_Lifeforce@dmail.com
To: Daisy Galen
Subject: I'm sorry, love

My dear Daisy,
You've probably only just got my previous email, sorry about two together, but I wasn't able to send the first one when I wrote it. You see I haven't had a signal for the past few days. You must have thought it an odd reply to what you've told me. Oh, Daisy...

I'm sorry you've been feeling so lost and lonely but I'm here now, I promise.

Wait. I want to rewind and tell you about my trip before I even try and sort out my thoughts about that momentous news... My wonderment and worry... Oh, God. But perhaps I can cheer you up a little, while I try to sort out my own thoughts...

So. I (well, me and my companion, but I'll tell you about that in a minute) were in a truck on our way to Barcelona. The truck only took us part of the way and then we got a lift in a car with two young lads who had no money left to buy fuel. We all had our fingers crossed that we'd make it to the next petrol station because if you've got to break down anywhere that would be the best place! Anyway we just managed to roll onto the forecourt before the last drop of fuel in the tank was used up. Luckily the lads were buskers like me, and between us we were able to put on quite a show and earned enough money to fill up the tank again. My companion and I travelled another hundred kilometres with them and then we had to part ways because they were going in a different direction.

I had to sleep in some bushes overnight and it was a little unnerving because there seemed to be some sort of rave going on nearby. But – and this is the best bit – I now have a dog. Can you believe that? When I left the place I've been staying at, a small community in the foothills of the Catalonian Mountains, this dog that had been living there followed me. She adopted me a while back and I started to look after her. She's white, about collie-sized, I'd say, and I've called her Alicia. What do you think of that? It suits her perfectly. Anyway, she followed me down the road to where I was getting picked up by the truck and the driver said it was all right to bring her with me. So it seems I'm now a dog-owner. The morning after the dog and I slept in a bush, we woke up and walked down the road to a petrol station. Thankfully they had a bathroom there with a shower, the kind where you put a coin into a slot and get three minutes of hot water. I had to leave Alicia tied up outside, of course, using one of my long scarves. But she's used to that. So I decided to buy her a proper collar and lead at the petrol station supermarket. Amazing, the variety of things you can buy in those places. Then my dog and I got a lift in a family car. I was glad I'd managed to have a wash because as a primary school teacher you know how honest children are when it comes to smells – and other things like a person's weight, of course. The children were very interested in my hair and I had to explain how it came to be that way. I liked the fact that their parents didn't try to stop them questioning me.

It's quite unusual for a family with young children to pick up a hitchhiker but they must have thought I was safe because I'm a woman. It was possibly because of Alicia, too. She's an unthreatening-looking dog, you see. There were two little girls in the car – not twins – but they did remind me so much of you and Lola. They loved my dog, made too much of a fuss of her in fact and I had to ask them to calm down.

Why am I going on about this when you've told me something so much more important?

I suppose I'm scared...

I need to get to the point of your email, don't I...?

I suppose I've been avoiding it because it's so overwhelming. Well of course you know that, you poor thing. I'm sorry I wasn't there for you. Lola's having a baby, you say? *Next month?* Oh, good lord, I can't take it in. Why didn't she tell me? I can understand why you didn't if she made you promise not to. And I'm sorry. I'm sorry to both of you for putting you in the position that you feel you couldn't confide in me. She probably didn't even know she was pregnant when I saw the two of you in London in May. Is that right? Or maybe she was keeping it to herself even then. But thank you, Daisy, for letting me know. I appreciate it must have been a hard decision.

So, that's me decided. I've got a few plans to make and I'm waiting for an answer from Dad before I can tell you what I'm going to do – but don't worry. You did the right thing by telling me. I'll see you soon.

I love you,
Mum xxxxx

45

Maya

Barcelona, December 2016

'Don't worry,' she leaned forward and patted the white dog's head. Alicia had laid her nose over Maya's shins where they were stretched out on the bed in front of her. The tablet was propped on her stomach. 'You're my dog now. Navengore won't know what's hit it when the two of us arrive there.' She sucked in a trembling breath. Black-encircled eyes stared soulfully back into hers.

She pulled herself further upright on the woven, patterned coverlet, dislodging Alicia. Resettling herself at the bottom of the bed, the dog sighed and propped her chin on a hard cushion instead, her eyes sliding towards the window which framed the outer branches of a Spanish fir tree. Suddenly alert, her head popped back up and Maya noticed a wagtail-like bird briefly alighting on the windowsill before taking off again. Alicia lowered her chin back to the cushion and Maya thought of her twin girls chasing a robin in the garden at home when they were little. An English Christmas awaited her, and two grown young women who had both kept a secret from their mother. She couldn't help wondering if Con had been gloating all this time.

Would Lola, who'd been through her whole pregnancy without her mother, ever trust Maya again?

Oh, there was no point dragging it all up again now. She could only move forward. She was going home to spend Christmas with her... husband but more importantly her daughters, and Lola would soon have a baby. A grandchild to bring the family back together, or as much as it possibly could without her sons returning home.

Around the campfire at the commune she'd felt great hope that her sons were well and living fulfilled lives out in the world somewhere, but now the horror of her loss struck again. Two boys that she had given birth to had disappeared from her life completely. Some of the kids that passed through the community in the mountains were in the same situation as her boys – out of touch with their families – and she'd felt sympathy for each of those young people. She'd been on their side. Had Joe been mothered by another woman somewhere? Perhaps he was now living with a partner whom she might never meet.

Maybe he was living in some transient community such as the one she'd briefly been a part of. *Where was he?* Her chest ached at not knowing. And Jamie, he'd been gone so long. She shivered as an image of Joe's friend, Nick, flooded her mind. His cold, white face. His closed eyes. What if another mother, in a different country, had been called to wrongly identify her son's body and it had been Jamie lying there, unloved and unsought? Never claimed. *No, no.*

The dog edged up the bed, pressed herself closer to Maya's side. Maya stroked her repeatedly as the tears continued to spring from her eyes and snot streamed from her nose. Choking ravaged her chest. She mopped her face with a handful of tissues from the box that had thoughtfully been placed on the bedside table, thankful she'd heard the homeowner leave the house earlier.

Just as she managed to bring her emotions under control a second time, the dark-screened tablet pinged and flashed up a message notification from the contact form on the blog. The blog she needed to delete. Numbness spread through her insides, at least it was a distraction from the pain. She quickly keyed in the password and clicked on the message.

From a publisher of travel books – *Changing Times*. The representative informed her that they'd been following "The Blog of Joe" and would like to set up a meeting with Joe Galen. They wished to discuss the possibility of publishing a book based on the blog.

Oh God, what have I done?

After showering and changing into the clothes she'd washed in the stream at the commune, Maya and Alicia left their room and went downstairs, Maya carrying an armful of laundry that earlier Katya had said she could put in the washing machine. The downstairs room was cheery in the light of a coloured glass lamp.

'I fell asleep,' Maya told Katya. 'The bed is so comfortable.'

'Thank you. My mother sleeps in that room when she comes to visit, and she's very particular about her comfort. Ah, I see you have your laundry. Let me show you how the washing machine works, you have to jiggle – is that the correct word to use, jiggle, yes? – Jiggle the dial in a certain way. There. You will be able to take fresh clothes away with you when you leave.'

They ate supper together, a paella that Katya had cooked to a recipe passed down from her grandmother. 'I went to the market after I dropped off the bridesmaids dresses,' she said. 'The fish was caught only this morning.'

Maya put her hand on her chest, moving her head from side to side. 'It's delicious. I can't tell you how spoilt I feel being looked after like this.'

Alicia shifted on the tiles under the table, probably watching out for any spilled morsel of food.

'I enjoy cooking very much,' Katya said. 'I enjoy having company, too. Often people want to book an Airbnb that is unoccupied but I had a spare room so, I thought I would try. It means I meet a variety of new friends who are prepared to socialise and you are an especially interesting guest to have. Tell me more about your life on the road. And please, have some more wine.'

'I have to admit to being unaccustomed to drinking, these days.' The room lurched when Maya moved her head too quickly. When it steadied again she dabbed her mouth with the linen napkin. She smiled at Katya across the light of the twinkling candle. 'Just one more, then.'

'What do you think I should do?' she asked Katya a while later, surprising herself with her readiness to pour out the story of Joe, which, in effect, was what had become the story Katya was so interested in. 'They want to meet Joe Galen because of the blog, but it was me who created the blog, and I don't know where Joe is. I suppose I hoped that he'd be the one to discover the blog and through that discovery, reach out to me. He was always into his computer. Will I get in trouble for what I've done?' Her words slurred in her mouth. She twiddled the stem of the empty glass on the table cloth.

Katya's dark eyes widened. She poured more wine into both their glasses and Maya didn't object.

'Oh my God.' Katya's English was heavily-accented. 'What you gonna do? My God, I don't know.' She took a solemn sip of her wine. Maya stared into the red pool in her glass, the edges of her vision blurred. If the *Book of Joe* was published, it would surely come to Joe's attention at some point, even if the blog hadn't. But it would be a crime to use his name, surely? Imagine a court case in which she was prosecuted by her own son's lawyers. Heat pressed behind her eyes. She stroked Alicia's silky head, now resting on her knee. Alicia's eyes were closed. The dog had long, pale eyelashes which rested on the

242

black smudges beneath her eyes. Maya had an idea. She still kept in touch with Aiden Wilde, the boy she'd met along with Ned and Jodie. He was back living in Newcastle.

'What?' said Katya; 'What you thinking, eh?'

'I could ask someone to pretend to be Joe.'

She and Aiden could pretend the name Joe Galen was a pseudonym.

'What do you think, Katya? Would that be very wrong of me?'

Katya pursed her lips and moved them from side to side. 'Let me see now. My God, I don't know. You have to look into your heart, Maya.'

46

Maya

Barcelona, December 2016

The vet examined the dog thoroughly and pronounced her
mainly fit and well. Alicia stood frozen, a continuous stare of
betrayal in her eyes. The vet smiled.

'Those eyes, they have the sorrowful look of a Bassett
Hound. You could get her DNA tested, you know. Find out
what mix of breeds she has in her.'

'Uhm,' said Maya. 'I'm not sure. I kind of like her being a
mystery. Like the way she magically appeared in my life.'

Completing her examination, the vet concluded that Alicia
was about a year old and had some muscle wasting on one
hip, which would explain her tendency to a slight limp after
exercise. She'd probably been kicked or knocked over by a
car at some point. Maya looked into Alicia's unbearable eyes
and pushed down the grief of the world. She stroked Alicia
and held her still while the vet inserted a microchip under
the skin between her shoulder blades. For registration, Maya

reluctantly gave her address in Navengore. Finally Alicia was given a series of vaccinations, including rabies.

'These tablets are to kill the fleas and the worms,' the vet said. 'Not that I have noticed any evidence of either, but it is important. You will need to bring her back to be given another dose before she is allowed to travel to the UK and you must wait for three weeks before then.' Maya felt the muscles in her face loosen.

'Is there a problem?' the vet asked.

'Yes,' Maya said. 'I was hoping to take her home before Christmas.' The word home felt bitter in her mouth.

'I'm sorry, that will not be possible. If you need to leave before then, I can give you a list of kennels that will look after her for you. We have our own boarding kennels attached to this practice, as a matter of fact. We could also arrange her transport back to the UK.'

'Thank you.'

Wandering back to her Airbnb, weighed down with concerns, Maya felt Alicia pulling backwards on the lead. As if she could sense the plans Maya was making for her.

Con was due to arrive in Barcelona the following week. They'd discussed a plan of action via email. *We need to talk about how to present a united front to the twins*, Maya had written, not mentioning the humiliation she felt that he'd been aware of Lola's pregnancy and not broken his silence to her. *I think we should take a short holiday together, first*, had been Con's response. *Let's find out how we feel about each other after our break and discuss the possibilities in moving forward. Then we can fly home together.* Maya came to a standstill on the street, trying to catch her breath. She was a butterfly, about to be pinned down. The door of The Cottages would lead to anaesthetisation and the potential impossibility of escape.

She inserted her key in the lock of Katya's house. The walls pressed around her and she could hear her own breathing, harsh and fast. She couldn't control it – soon all the rushed-

246

in air would make her explode!

Alicia whimpered, pushing Maya's hand with her nose.

'I know.' Maya steadied herself with her hands on the cool walls. 'We need to get out of here.' Walls were traps. She missed her house of sticks, the freedom of the mountains. On the hall table was a note from Katya, saying she'd had to go out. She told Maya to help herself to anything she wanted. The woman and dog climbed the stairs together. Alicia seemed to be keeping guard by the door as Maya reached for her possessions and packed them hurriedly into the rucksack, snatching the dried, neatly-folded washing that Katya had left on a dresser in the corridor outside her room and stuffing it in with the rest of the clothes. Before disconnecting her tablet from the charge-point, Maya touched it into life and brought up a map of the local coast. She took a screenshot of the area she was interested in. Then she hurriedly typed an email to Aiden, asking if he'd be prepared to stand-in for Joe in the case of a potential meeting with *Changing Times*, the book publisher.

With her breathing calmer, her racing, scattered thoughts came in to land. She read through what she'd written, pressure mounting again in her chest. Looked down at her finger, hovering over send. *What was she thinking, asking a young man to lie for her?* Maya pressed delete instead. She shut down the tablet, slid it into its embroidered sleeve and wrapped it carefully within her soft, flannel shirt in the centre of her packed bag. She sat cross-legged on the bed in the room Katya had prepared so lovingly for visitors, stilling her limbs, breathing deeply. After Christmas she would email the publishers and admit what she'd done, explain that she'd been hoping to find her son. Perhaps they could put out some kind of appeal for the real Joe. *But no.* For now it was important to come to terms with the fact that Joe, like Jamie, had severed contact with his family for a reason. Both she and Con had to take responsibility for their parts. Maya's own vagabond journey, her unwillingness to return to

247

what she thought of as captivity – had led her to understand that *there is pleasure in the pathless woods, there is rapture on the lonely shore* – as the poet Byron would have it. She could only hope that time and lived experience would lead her sons to forgive their parents. Maya saw that her role now was to practice patience.

All I have to do is remember the face of that dead boy. He could have been my son, but he wasn't. My boy is alive. Both my sons are alive, I'm certain I would know if they aren't.

That was all that really mattered.

Maya hitchhiked out of Barcelona, having accepted a lift from a skull-faced man who didn't speak apart from a reticent 'ola' and his grunted acknowledgement of her introduction in broken Spanish. It took some encouragement to get Alicia to jump into the cab of the truck and sit on the seat next to the driver. Maya lugged her rucksack into the footwell, then climbed into the cab herself – angling her knees towards the door. She slammed the door closed, keeping her feet tucked in. She was out of breath and glad of the driver's silence once she'd given him the name of the coastal town she was heading for, *Canet de Mar*. She travelled with her arm around her dog, the driver's stale breath filling the space in the cramped cab.

That night she slept on the white-sanded beach, at the base of a cliff, just outside the mouth of a deep cave. The tide was out. Atop the cliff, mansions overlooked the sea. She discovered that an overhanging bush on the grassy clifftop intermittently dropped its spiky leaves to where they embedded themselves into the sand below. She tucked her camp neatly against the cliff-foot, out of reach of the occasional rock or stone which also fell onto the sand. Her skin tingled within her layers of warm clothes. *Freedom.* One night in a house had been enough. 'How are we going to cope, back in England?' she whispered into the dog's familiar-smelling fur. She shut out the waves of imagined fear Alicia would feel at being confined in kennels. She closed her eyes and allowed the far-off waves to lull her.

It grew cold in the night. She slept on the folded tarp, curled in her sleeping bag around Alicia, who snuffled in her sleep. Perhaps the vaccinations were working their way through her blood.

Maya woke three times. Each time she remained awake for a good while. It felt like a privilege to witness the secrecy of the night-beach. The dog scrambled into a sitting position by her side and they sat with their backs against the damp cliff. Primeval and alert, Maya's every sense tingled, all the way to the tiny hairs on the backs of her fingers. It was liberating to be free from the walls of Katya's house, however welcoming they'd been.

It no longer seemed desirable or even normal to crawl into a bed at night and not wake until the next morning, oblivious of the time that had passed during the lost hours. Sometimes she lay down, curling again against the dog and sometimes she fell into short periods of slumber still sitting up against the cliff. On the land above people must be snuggled into their beds; the walls of their individual rooms enclosed within the outer casings of their houses, layers of barriers surrounding them. Between Maya and the stars there existed only the purity of sea-tinged air. Her sleeping bag and her dog were all she needed. At that moment, Con would be sleeping within the same physical and emotional barriers as she imagined the people in the cliff-houses were. He had no idea of the richness of her experience and she wished deeply that she could share this night with him. The rhythm of the tide was a soothing lullaby. A breath of breeze sifted fine grains of sand onto her cheeks. *Mr Sandman.* She felt her eyelids closing. Each time she came back to consciousness, the stars had moved in the sky and the moonlit shadows of the multitudinous troll-like rocks on the beach had formed alternative silhouetted countenances on the cold, white sand. Silently, throughout the night, the rocks' shadows laughed and cried and appeared morose in turn and each time she looked, she felt her face mirroring their expressions.

47

Maya

Barcelona, December 2016

At the end of this long, miraculous night of drifting, Maya woke properly. She blinked and digested the truth of her existence which was, simply, *to be*. She knew this by the fact that she had nothing apart from the means to keep warm and more-or-less dry. Enough food to eat and now the deeply-felt connection with the dog. And it contented her. All the detritus of her former life as Mrs Galen must have sat uselessly in the wardrobes and on the dressing table in the bedroom at The Cottages, Navengore, for the past two years, ignored. Meaningless. She wished Con had thrown out every trace of her from the house. She wished he could join her in watching the sunrise.

The tide had receded and the sky was slate grey. As she watched, it turned blue and then pink. The pink slowly transmuted into orange and the orange spread itself more thinly into lemon-yellow, finally opening out into full daylight. She shifted herself once more into an upright position and unzipped the sleeping bag. Alicia struggled against the jumper Maya had fastened loosely around her and soon freed herself. She shook herself and went careering off down the beach with an open, laughing mouth. Maya allowed herself to become warmed by the strengthening sun before forcing herself to move. Nearby, on an ordinary rock, which the night before had seemed to be a weeping face stretching across the sand in a dancing response to the movement of the moon, she spotted a little lizard, no doubt with the same idea as her of warming itself.

Maya shook her legs free of the sleeping bag and stood up slowly, flexing her back. Her feet were cramped and she exercised them by raising herself up and down on her toes. She also raised her arms to the sky before performing a series of side-bends. She didn't feel over-tired, though back in her old life she would have felt resentful and deprived by such a night of fitful sleep. Pulling off her thick socks she burrowed her toes into the sand – already warm on the surface but damp and cool underneath.

Barefoot, she walked along the base of the cliff until she found a spot sheltered by an alcove. There was also a natural recession in the sand. Glancing around, she hooked her thumbs into the waistbands of her cargo trousers, leggings and underwear and pulled them down to just below her knees. She urinated and remained squatting, glancing repeatedly from side to side, while she allowed herself to drip-dry. Standing, she quickly rearranged her clothes and kicked sand over the puddle she'd made as she watched the moisture soaking into the surface.

She walked down the beach until she found a series of rock pools and washed her hands in saltwater. Walking back up towards her camp she called Alicia. The dog came into view, looping huge circles of joy on the wide expanse of washed-clean sand.

Maya threw her head back and laughed. 'Alicia,' she called again, lengthening the word on a sing-song note. Her voice calling the dog's name against the cliffs on the empty beach echoed back to her. The dog charged across the sand towards her, tongue lolling. Maya poured some water from her bottle into one of the dog's two thin plastic bowls and placed a handful of biscuits in the other. Her chest felt empty of the pressure of the previous day. She examined the backs of her hands and turned them over to inspect her fingers in the clear morning light. *These are magical. I can do anything.* She unwrapped a croissant from a paper napkin and used her penknife to cut a slice of cheese, which she inserted into the croissant. It felt like a day for making coffee on a beach, so she unstrapped the tiny, stick-fed stove from the loop on the side pocket of her rucksack and poured a cupful of water into her miniature pan. Stabilising the tiny appliance with a border of sand she pulled the box of matches from the pocket of her shirt and began to feed the stove. There were enough twigs and driftwood slivers, not to mention dried seaweed and vegetation sprouting from the sand at the top of the beach – all within reach of her ranging hands – to keep the stove going long enough to boil one tin mug's-worth of water. She poured it slowly over the strainer containing a spoonful of precious coffee, and watched the black beads of liquid dripping through into the mug.

While Maya sipped with her eyes closed, suffused by a sense of well-being, Alicia scoffed the last of her biscuits. Finishing, she sniffed around for a moment or two before checking the bowl again. Finding it still empty, she slumped onto the sand next to Maya. 'Sorry,' Maya said. 'Got to conserve rations.' The dog's damp breath misted on her wrist. Gulping the final mouthful of coffee, she examined the grounds at the bottom of the mug. A picture emerged, suggesting a forest with a dark pool at its foot. At the lower right corner of the picture she imagined she saw three wise women stirring a pot. Behind them, emerging from the depths of the forest, she invented a figure carrying a baby. If Maya had intended to post any more on "The Blog of Joe", it

253

might have been the picture in the mug. She would have interpreted it as a plea for contact. Instead she laughed and poured the coffee grounds into the sand. She covered them using her cupped hand as a spade. She wiped the mug clean with the paper napkin and fed the napkin to the dying embers in the stove. It flared up, briefly.

Asking herself what she wanted to do next she unzipped her guitar case. She softly played Simon and Garfunkel, losing herself in the chords and her own voice. Half-an-hour later, she heard the tinkle of coins on the case and felt the cool of moving shade. Alicia scrambled to her feet with a 'woof' and a scattering of sand, stumbling slightly on her weak hip.

A dancing shadow blocked the sun – that of a man conjoined with a dog. Maya looked up and saw a black Labrador bouncing around while a man stood in front of her, smiling.

Alicia barked a few times, before running off to frolic stiffly with the long-legged Labrador.

Maya cleared her throat. 'Hello.'

'Hi,' the man leaned down, his hand outstretched. 'I'm Bernie.'

'Pleased to meet you. I'm Maya. I hope my caterwauling didn't disturb you?' As soon as she'd said it, she wished she hadn't. She had a pleasant voice, she'd been told often enough. 'I apologise for the self-deprecation. Thought I'd got over silly stuff like that.'

Bernie lowered himself to the sand beside her. 'Takes longer than you think. We British, it's our default setting.'

'Ah, so you're from the UK?'

Bernie had long, grey hair and a thick, well-groomed beard. He rolled himself a cigarette, offered the tin to her but she shook her head.

'A vice I've managed to stay clear of, I'm happy to say.' *Did that sound rude?* 'But please,' she gave a small wave of her hand. 'I didn't mean... Go ahead.'

Bernie smiled, lit the cigarette and posted it between his lips. He tapped his jeans-clad knee with a long finger. 'Yes, I'm from the UK, mostly. But I was taken to Africa as a baby. Brought back and finished growing up in Liverpool. Lived in Catalonia for almost thirty years, now.'

'It's beautiful here. Was that what made you stay?' Maya lifted the guitar off her lap and laid it carefully in its case. 'Do you have work here?' she felt around her for the various objects that had strayed from her rucksack, and began packing them away. Alicia was nosing at the shoreline with the other dog.

Bernie blew out smoke, his head turned away from Maya. 'I was travelling through Europe as a young man, when I met a beautiful woman named Caterina. Shortly after that she became my wife. We travelled on and off for a few years before we came back to settle here. Now we have a ten-year-old daughter.' Speckled grey-and-black hairs hugged the contours of his cheeks and his eyes had a raven-like appearance. They scanned Maya's face and looked away again, at the silver line on the horizon. A companionable silence ensued, Maya soaking up the strengthening sun. After a while he turned to her again. 'And you?'

'Me? Oh, I've only been travelling for two years. My children had all grown up, and. . . ' She dug her fingers into the sand. It was too complicated to explain.

'Well, it's a great way to spend your retirement,' said Bernie, shifting his weight, leaning forward and propping his arms on his knees. The burnt-down cigarette dangled from his fingers. 'You must have had your children at a much younger age than me, and you still have years of adventures ahead of you now.'

Maya lifted a handful of sand and let it slip through her fingers.

'Uhm, yes. Although I have to go back to the UK for Christmas and a while longer at least. My daughter's expecting a baby.' *Breathe, Maya.* Fixed Bernie with headlight-eyes. 'I've only just found out.'

'Hmm,' he said. 'Tell you what, would you both like to come back to my house for coffee?' He nodded at Alicia who was chasing the black Labrador in circles again. 'My daughter would love her and I think our Riley does, too.'

Maya's hand hesitated in the front pocket of the rucksack, into which she was fitting Alicia's feeding bowls. Walls would be around her again. But she wouldn't have to stay long.

'Thank you,' she said. 'I'd like that.'

'I have another reason for asking you,' Bernie told her as he helped her fold the tarp and stuff the sleeping bag into its drawstring sack. 'I'm a musician and I was wondering if you would play some music with me. I have a roomful of instruments and I like to record passing strangers in my recording studio.'

48

Maya

Barcelona, December 2016

He insisted on shouldering the rucksack as they walked together along the beach to where stone steps were set into the cliff. The black dog and the white dog cantered ahead of them.

They left the beach and entered town, turning up a sloping, cobbled street. Bernie led Maya up a flight of steps to his house. His daughter emerged from her bedroom wearing shorts and an oversized t-shirt at the same moment as Bernie ushered Maya and the dogs into the open-plan living space. The girl rubbed her eyes, uttered a small cry and pounced on Alicia, who trembled, pressing herself back against Maya's legs.

'She's nervous,' Maya explained, making calming motions with her hands. 'She's not too used to people, or to enclosed spaces.' She realised she was talking about herself, too. But the girl became gentler and Bernie's Liverpool accent was soothing, and soon both Maya and her dog relaxed. The girl's mother, a ceramicist, was away at a craft convention in Madrid.

The girl stretched out on the floor on her stomach, kicking her legs behind her and stroking and crooning to both dogs, who lolled about and licked her face and tugged playfully at each other with soft growls. Maya accepted a mug of rich coffee and some freshly-baked bread, heady with the scents. She learned that Bernie was born in Liverpool and spent some of his childhood in Nigeria. He'd hitchhiked around the world as a young man and arrived in Spain to study the language.

'But Caterina captured my heart and I stayed, and look what I was rewarded with.'

He smiled at his daughter, Sofia. She rolled her eyes. He crinkled his at Maya. Guilt swilled into her stomach with the bread and coffee – Bernie had given up his travelling for a family and she had given up her family for travelling. He now taught at the university and translated English and Catalonian manuscripts.

Bernie asked Maya if she was in a hurry to go anywhere and she said no. So he would make her some lunch. Sofia re-emerged from her bedroom dressed in a short denim skirt and a peasant-style blouse which looked much too big for her. Maya guessed it might be her mother's. She crept up next to Maya where she was half-dozing on the comfortable leather sofa while Bernie worked in the kitchen.

'M'agrada el teu cabell,' the girl murmured. Maya struggled to interpret. 'I like your hair,' Sofia repeated the compliment in English. 'May I... err, *puc jugar amb ell*? Play with?'

'Of course.' She leaned forward so that the girl could plait her ropes of hair together and rearrange the scarf around her head. Bernie called from the kitchen. Over lunch, Maya let out some of her own story.

'So I'll have to put her into the kennels at the vets when my husband arrives,' she said of the dog. 'It breaks my heart, but she'll have to stay there until she's allowed to travel to the UK after Christmas. They said they'll arrange transport for her. A van, I think.'

Sofia's eyes widened. 'Una gossera, no! Not kennels for her! May we look after her?' she asked, glancing from one to the other of them. 'Please Dad, please?'

Bernie brought his brows together, looking thoughtful. Sofia wrung her hands together. 'If your mother doesn't mind,' Bernie said at last. When they'd finished eating he went into another room and closed the door while he spoke to his wife on the phone. 'She says that it's fine,' he said, returning. 'No, honestly, Maya. She loves dogs, like Sofia. She said as long as Riley's happy.'

They all turned to observe the two dogs, curled together on the rug before the unlit fireplace. 'I think Riley's happy,' Bernie said. 'So that's settled, then.'

They went into Bernie's studio, leaving the dogs on the rug. Maya recorded a Joni Mitchell song while Bernie played a gentle rhythm on a box-drum. The girl sang a surprising sweet harmony. Bernie promised to email the music to Maya once he'd mixed it. Sofia's mother wasn't expected home until the following evening and the child wanted Maya and Alicia to spend the night at their home. Maya glimpsed a reflection of the twins at her age in Bernie's daughter's face, as she did in every female child. She felt herself softened by loss. The dilemma of family. But Alicia was prowling and sniffing at the door and Maya found herself longing again for Byron's *the rapture of the lonely shore*. She hugged the girl and Bernie and thanked them for the day, and then she and Alicia walked out into the dark, back to the magic of night on the beach.

49

Maya

Barcelona, December 2016

Maya's eyes were still red from saying goodbye to Alicia. It felt like a part of her was missing. She'd dropped the dog off with Bernie and his wife and daughter only two hours before and taken the train back to Barcelona. Alicia whined as Maya hurried away from their house. *Her Collie-shaped dog with the Bassett hound eyes.* But at least the dog would be in a family home for the three weeks until she was reunited with Maya. She scrubbed her face with a paper towel in the airport toilets and went to meet her husband.

'Darling, darling!'

Seriously? Con had wrapped her in his arms and kissed her exactly as though they hadn't recently been estranged. He tried to hide the slight flare of his nostrils and his drawing back with the guise of scratching his nose but she noticed anyway. He stepped away further to take a better look at her and she clenched her jaw before speaking.

'I've been sleeping on a beach for the past few nights.' She had sand in her dreadlocks and inside her shirt, too. 'But hey. We're about to check into a fancy hotel so I'll be able to have a long soak in a bath and then I won't smell anymore. I'll even put a dress on for dinner, how's that?' She forced a red-eyed smile and managed a playful nudge with her shoulder.

'Is it so bad?' Con put a finger gently up to her cheek and it came away wet. 'To see me, I mean? I promise not to put any pressure on you, Maya. It was wrong of me to try and impose my own desires on you last time.'

She felt a rogue tickle in her belly and flushed as her lone lovemaking in the stick-house came back to her. It seemed so long ago already. And that had been a controllable fantasy of Con, not Con himself. Now he stood in front of her with longer hair than she could remember seeing on him since the 1980s. He wore a long-sleeved, finely-knitted grey top she'd never seen before – something a younger man might choose. Or someone – perhaps a woman – who knew about fashion. A flare went off in her chest. While her own life had been in turmoil, so had his. Had someone...? She chased the surge of possessiveness away. It could have been one of the twins who bought him the top, anyway. Or his sister. And what did it matter who he might have been with? They were both here now.

Perhaps the two of them could still work as a couple...

There is pleasure in the pathless woods... No sense trying to pre-empt what was going to happen. She took his hand.

'It's not you, it's just... oh, let's wait until we get to the hotel. I have so much to tell you.'

50

Maya

Navengore, Christmas Day, 2016

During the previous days she'd tried more than once to have a conversation about Christmas with Con.

'Why don't we open the house up?' Perhaps it would make it feel more like her own home, she was so used to sharing. 'We have so many unused rooms. We could host a Christmas dinner for homeless people – young ones. There's a charity that deals with that sort of thing. We could make people happy, even if it's only for a short while.'

'Good idea,' Daisy chipped in. 'This house is so big. I never realised how privileged I was when I was a kid. But some of the children I teach have no. . .'

'But what about me – I mean, I'm pregnant.' Lola interrupted. She stroked her belly and looked put-out.

'What about it?' Daisy snapped. 'It wouldn't even have to affect you. Half the house is basically uninhabited anyway.'

'It's too late to organise anything like that.' Con said hurriedly. 'We've already invited half the village to come round for drinks on Christmas afternoon.'

'What? You never told me that!'

Maya wanted to curl in on herself like a hedgehog.

'It's what we always do, darling.' He kept talking as if the past two years had never happened. He really did seem to believe they were picking up where they'd left off.

'Oh, Maya,' later when they were in bed he stroked her hair. Or rather his fingers caught in the ropes and twists that she'd freshly coconut-oiled. He buried his nose in the coils. 'I could get used to this hair, you know. I'm sorry I wanted you to have it all cut off. Oh my God, not to mention this body of yours. I can't believe I went six months without seeing you. Oh, Maya.'

'Con, what do you really think about the idea Daisy and I had?' She held him off with the palm of her hand on his chest. 'It would be a lovely thing to do, wouldn't it? Perhaps after Christmas. Give something back to the community. Should I get in touch with that charity I was talking about? For homeless young people. Say we can provide a meal and at least a couple of rooms overnight?'

If she could do *something, anything* to reconnect with the person she'd been trying to become before she was sucked back into the vortex of comfort and materialism. She might feel real again.

'You know what the answer is,' Con said after a hurt pause. 'We've already discussed it.' He continued stroking her ropes of hair. Her scalp tensed. Her neck was stiff from the position she was lying in, on her side facing Con. 'We couldn't do something like that. It's not just me – and Lola's about to have a baby. It would totally freak her out, you know that.'

Their queen-sized bed stood in the middle of acres of carpet. The bedroom was almost as big as a twelve-bunk room in a hostel. Maya slid out of bed and tiptoed across the floor when Con fell asleep. She sank to her knees by the tall window, propping her arms on the sill and her chin on her arms. She missed Alicia's warmth at her hip and the snug security of her sleeping bag. Few stars were visible above the glow of electric light coating the base of the Lincolnshire sky. In the distance she could see the lit-up cathedral, a building she'd once been in awe of. She pictured herself busking in its shadow but could only remember the cold wind that always seemed to blow around it. She felt she could hear the buzzing of civilisation – over-intense and penetrative – seeping through the walls of the house. She gripped her elbows with locked hands, terror flooding her that she would never again escape into her most basic self.

Who knew that a heart could feel so heavy? Maya's lungs felt starved of oxygen but she carried on breathing as evenly as she could, while her family opened yet more presents. She'd begged them not to buy her anything but inevitably a mound of goods lay piled on her lap. She was already being sucked back into the vacuum she'd escaped two years before. She would donate the gifts to a charity for the homeless as soon as Christmas was over.

Lola sat resplendent in the red velvet armchair Maya had once paid a lot of money to have restored. Lola's belly was an earth-like orb, throbbing with life. Maya clasped her hands around her knees. She tried and failed to imagine the real, living baby that existed beneath Lola's grey jersey dress, safe within her layers of skin and muscle. Lola had allowed Maya to kiss her in Christmas greeting that morning but pulled back short of a hug. Maya counted to ten in her head as her daughters exclaimed over a pair of animal slippers one had given the other, the cost of which she imagined would have covered two nights in a hostel. The house echoed around them.

Later that afternoon the villagers – *their kind of people* as Con called the select invited – would arrive at The Cottages open house as they had in Christmases past. Maya was the curiosity they would all be coming to see this year. She missed Alicia.

51

Jamie

Berlin, Christmas Day, 2016

The apartment was crammed with people. Jamie's mother-in-law, Amina, had brought her fiancé. He was a stooped, shy man who'd arrived in Germany at the same time as Amina and Lejla. His family had been lucky to remain complete throughout the Bosnia-Herzegovina war but Tarik had now been a widower for six years. It was a constant source of sorrow to Lejla and her mother that the body of Amina's husband – Lejla's father – had never been discovered. Twenty-two years hadn't dampened Lejla's nightmares. Jamie caught his wife's eyes and blew her a kiss. Tarik's son and daughter were also present at the party, along with the upstairs neighbours and Joe's mates from the warehouse in the less-gentrified area of Kreuzberg. The doorbell rang again. Jamie squeezed a pathway for himself down the crowded corridor to answer it. It was a couple with two children around Electra's age. He heard

Electra's squeal of delight as the children tunnelled their way into the kitchen ahead of their parents.

Everybody had brought food to share and an eclectic feast was laid out on the long table in the kitchen. Jamie watched with interest as his brother interacted with Tarik's son. The tilting of the two young blokes' heads echoed each other as did their sudden flashes of smiles. Joe had flushed cheeks. Jamie nodded sagely to himself. Perhaps he had at last got over his feelings for the boy on the boat. *About time.* Joe was finally coming out of himself – in every way, Jamie reckoned.

Electra had a new remote-controlled car and was whizzing it around the kitchen floor between legs and bumping it into everybody's ankles. Jamie wasn't alarmed therefore, when he heard a sharp cry from Lejla, the other side of the crowded room. She must have got hit again. He carried on talking to Tarik. Then he heard raised voices. 'Where's Jamie?' They were shouting. 'Jamie, get over here, something's wrong with Lejla.'

He focussed on Lejla through the parting crowd. She was doubled over, her face streaked with tears. 'It hurts,' she whispered through gritted teeth, when he managed to get his face close enough to hers to hear what she was saying.

Lejla needed to stay in the hospital for two days. After an examination and an ultrasound scan she was put on a drip for rehydration. She needed to spend regular sessions with a baby-heartbeat monitor strapped to her belly.

'The baby's fine,' Lejla reassured Jamie. 'But the doctor says I have a – now what did he call it? – Ah, a low-lying placenta, whatever that means. I must need to be careful from now on.' She had been instructed to rest more and stop work altogether. 'From now on until the birth of our baby boy I am required to have double the amount of check-ups. Ah. *Bums.*' It always made Jamie laugh when Lejla used the word Joe had introduced to Electra when she'd started swearing. He squeezed Lejla's hand tighter. 'They say I might have to give birth by caesarean if the placental position doesn't improve.'

He brought her home from the hospital. Joe had earlier taken Electra to the zoo and brought back some poinsettia, Lejla's favourite flower. The vase was new, or rather, second-hand. Joe said he'd bought it from the *Prinzessinnengarten Flohmarkt*. Jamie remembered hearing that Amina's stepson-to-be had a stall at that very flea market. He might quiz Electra later about who she and Joe had been talking to that afternoon.

Joe cooked supper while Jamie got Lejla settled into bed with a hot water bottle and a book. When Jamie came down Joe was wearing his *I've got something to tell you* expression. In fact, he was practically wetting himself with excitement if the way he was bobbing up and down was anything to go by.

Jamie wasn't in the mood.

'Spit it out, then.' He felt tired. So tired. He grabbed a bottle of beer from the fridge and knocked the top off on the corner of the table. Joe gulped too fast from the bottle he was already holding in his hand and sprayed beer from the sides of his mouth.

'Sorry.' He wiped his mouth. 'It's not really spitting-out material, even though I almost did, just then.' Jamie couldn't even summon up a smile. Joe's eyes were unnaturally bright.

'You'll never guess.'

'I wasn't trying to guess.' Jamie moved to the doorway that led through the scullery to his studio, where there was a small television that Electra was allowed to watch occasionally. 'Turn it down a bit, Lecky,' he yelled over the noise of a cartoon. His kid had been playing up a bit lately – not surprising really, what with the upheavals over Christmas and a new baby on the way. The noise continued to blast untempered through the utility room. Jamie took a deep breath before measuring his steps towards the tiny studio. Electra seemed to have grown bigger over the past few days – she looked much older than three, when he peeped his head around the door to tell her off. She'd squashed herself into a corner of the compact leather sofa, a pile of records towering on the seat cushion beside her. She had her knees drawn up to her chin, her arms wrapped tightly around them. She shifted her gaze onto him briefly and then back to the TV, her mouth turned down at the corners.

'Whatcha watching?' It felt too mean to tell her off. She answered in German, an indication that she wanted to be left alone. She'd be tired from the zoo, he supposed. A fresh bout of weariness weighed his own shoulders down.

'Okay, baby. You can watch for another half-hour and then it's bath-time, all right?'

She dug her chin further into her knees and a muscle on her cheek flickered. 'Right. Well. I'll come back and fetch you at bath-time. Half an hour more. Enjoy your programme.'

His head ached. The TV remained at the same volume. Beer might help.

'It's been a difficult couple of days for her,' Joe said when he moved back into the kitchen. 'She's such a good kid usually.'

'Yup. I know.' Jamie's beard itched. Lejla was always going on at him to use moisturiser. She was away a couple of days and everything went to pot! He scratched at his face and gulped a half-bottle's-worth of beer. Tapped his fingers on the table.

'So have you chewed this item of news enough to spit, yet, mate? Coz I'm not in the mood to guess.'

He glanced at Joe's face and nearly got sucked into the vortex of his brother's eyes. The beer sloshed in his stomach.

'What? What is it?'

'We got an email back from the person who's been writing "The Blog of Joe",' Joe's face underwent a curious transformation of expressions as he spoke. 'It's, I don't know how to say this...' He sounded breathless and looked about to burst into tears. Jamie took another gulp of beer, felt the cold trickle down into his stomach and join the whirlpool that was spinning there. *His brother's face...* Joe continued to speak but Jamie had lost the thread of the stuttered words. He couldn't seem to make sense of them. The words ran on and on.

Was Joe actually saying what Jamie thought he was saying?

'Stop!' the sharpness of his voice surprised them both. 'Slow down a minute. Tell me slowly, so I can be sure of what I thought I heard you just say. Who's the person who's been plagiarising your journal and pretending to be you? Say it again.' Silence. 'Say it again, Joe!'

He held his breath then let it out again through numb lips. Joe appeared to be doing the same.

'You did hear correctly.' Joe finally said. 'It's Mum. It's fucking Mum who's been impersonating me. *Our* mum. She confessed it all to the fake publisher. She said she only did it to try and make me get in touch.'

After Joe had finished speaking he closed his mouth. Then he opened it again and a hoarse, racking sob fell out onto the table.

52

Maya

Maternity Hospital, Lincoln, January 2017

No wonder she hadn't been able to picture the baby before it
was born: she could never have imagined a child as perfect as
the one Lola had given birth to. Or the power of the primeval
forces that propelled Elijah into the world. Even though she
had performed this act herself for the very girl who had now
become a mother. *Grandson.* She rolled the word around in
her mouth.

Steve, Lola's ex-boyfriend, came to the hospital. Maya
congratulated him and watched him disappear behind the
bed curtain while she stood by the window that overlooked
the car park, watching hungrily as Daisy rocked her new
nephew in her arms. Daisy had been Lola's birth partner.
Lola consented to Maya being present in the visitors' room,
on standby, for when Daisy needed to use the toilet or to get
something to eat. This had given Maya isolated, precious
hours with her during the night, whispering and comforting
and encouraging her to lean forward over the beanbag. But

Lola hadn't wanted both of them in the delivery room at the same time. *She still hasn't quite forgiven me for not somehow sensing she was pregnant.*

Behind the curtain, she heard Lola agreeing to allow Steve full access to his son.

Maya had never met the man until this day. He had moved back in with his *previous* ex-girlfriend, who had two young children of her own. Daisy had confided to their mother that Lola had made a deliberate effort to "lure" him away from this woman in the first place. 'I warned her at the time,' Daisy said. 'I told her she'd only end up getting hurt.' This was during the time Lola was being examined on her admittance to hospital. 'I can't believe she's actually having a baby, though.' Daisy said. She looked wistful. Maya marvelled at the life of her daughters that had taken place during her absence.

'Elijah,' she heard Daisy whisper by the window, with the newborn in her arms. Maya moved closer and stood gazing at the baby with the same rapture as his aunt. His skin was coffee-toned. He forced his liquidy eyes open in response to Daisy's voice. Daisy stroked his cap of finely-knitted hair with a curled forefinger. 'You are such a beautiful boy.'

Maya put her arm around Daisy and pulled her in closer, noticing how her daughter's eyes were set in dark hollows.

'You must be exhausted,' she said gently. 'Why don't you go home for a sleep? I'll get Dad to drive you. He'll be back in a minute.' Con had gone to find someone and ask when Lola could be discharged but they were expecting her to be kept in until at least that evening.

Daisy's lip trembled. She hooked a loose strand of hair behind her ear, already expert at balancing the baby on one arm.

'I can't. Lola needs me and so does Elijah.' She shifted enough so that Maya felt forced to withdraw her encircling arm. She folded her hands across her stomach. *Not surprising that my daughters have closed ranks against me. I've missed the most important few months of their lives.*

'I was the first person to see you,' Daisy whispered to the baby. 'Before your mother, even. You heard my voice first, didn't you?'

Elijah blinked as his mouth opened into an O shape. He looked as if he was talking back to Daisy. He had a blister on his upper lip from his first feed at his mother's breast. 'You'll be home with us soon,' Daisy said in her normal voice. She settled him more snugly into the crook of her elbow. 'We're having the first floor of Grandpa's house made into a flat especially for me and you and your mummy. Grandpa's old bedroom will be our living room and the middle bathrooms will become our kitchen. When you're big enough, you'll have mine and your mummy's old bedroom, all for yourself.'

Grandpa's house. Maya watched Elijah spread his starfish fingers as if in a wave of approval. Daisy lifted him closer to her face and giggled. 'When you grow into a smelly teenager, you can have a bathroom of your own, too, and you'll have to clean it yourself.' Elijah burbled in response. Daisy continued murmuring, describing their future. Maya's gut twisted. 'Your Grandpa will be on hand downstairs whenever we need a babysitter,' Daisy continued. 'You'll like that, won't you? Funny Grandpa. I bet he'll spoil you rotten, down there in his Grandpa-flat.' She took a shuddering breath and paused before she turned to face Maya and briefly met her eyes. She focussed her gaze on the baby again. 'Perhaps you'll be able to take exotic holidays with Gramma.' She planted her lips on the baby's forehead for a long moment. 'Wherever she happens to be at the time, although your accommodation probably won't be too exotic! Take your own tarp, me-boy. Oh yes, you'll need to take your own tarp when you go and visit Gramma, won't you?'

Maya saw how her daughter's body automatically took up a rhythm: bend and stretch, her hips swaying in a circular motion as Elijah in turn stretched and yawned in her arms. She didn't know where Daisy had learned to rock a baby like that but her actions appeared to come naturally. Maybe she *was* a natural. Maybe one day soon she would have a baby of her own in her arms. Daisy continued as if she was telling Elijah a bedtime story.

'Grandpa doesn't need that whole ground floor to himself, does he, Elijah-baby? No he doesn't. So do you know what Auntie Daisy's going to do? She's going to run her own little nursery-school in those silly rooms that we used to call the *boot* room and the *ironing* room and the *office* that nobody ever went in. What do you think about that, eh? And then if your Mummy wants to go back to work when you're a big boy, you can stay downstairs with Auntie Daisy, in *Daisy's Day Nursery*. Won't that be lovely, eh?'

Something about Daisy's monologue felt wrong but Maya couldn't work it out. She was tired. They were all tired. Mesmerised by her daughter's swaying and rocking, the sounds of the ward melted into the background. She slumped against the windowsill. A metallic clanging, as if something had been dropped, startled Elijah into a high-pitched, lamblike bleat. Maya jolted back to her senses. She saw the baby wriggling in Daisy's arms, his fists pumping as the volume of his cry increased.

From beyond the curtain came the sound of Lola's new mother-voice, commanding the return of her son. Steve pulled the fabric to one side, smiling. His eyes landing on his baby, he had the same besotted look on his face as Daisy and the one Maya could feel on hers. Elijah's head was now swivelling from side-to-side, his mouth rooting for his mother. Daisy reluctantly let him out of her arms as Lola unfastened her nightgown and brought out a blue-veined breast which she fed into her baby's mouth. He fastened on as if his life depended on it. And of course, it did. Daisy, Steve and Maya exchanged glances of admiration for this new, grown-up Lola. They settled into the bedside chairs to watch the newborn's jaw, working with machine-like precision.

53

Maya

Maya and Con were busy emptying the row of wardrobes in what used to be their bedroom.

'I can't believe the workmen are coming later to rip this whole place apart,' Maya said. 'Remember when we had that ensuite put in?'

'I do. It was your idea, if I remember. You were always wanting improvements.' He straightened his back and tilted his head to one side. 'We were pretty proud of it though, weren't we? Not having to walk out into the corridor and go to the bathroom next door.' His single laugh seemed to set off an answering peal. Maya studied him, feeling a bubble ripple up in her own body. Soon her stomach muscles were aching.

'Stop, it,' she said, wiping her eyes. 'It's insane. That's what it is. Whatever possessed me?'

Con sobered. 'I suppose you were lonely and bored. I'm sorry.' He chewed at the inside of his lip.

'No really, I'm sorry. It was me who broke the, you know, the status quo and all that. But what's done is done, as my granny used to say. Probably everyone's granny, for that matter. But it *is* done. New plans have been made. At least you won't be lonely in this house.'

'Hmm,' said Con. 'I don't think I'll get a chance.' He looked as if he had something else to say but she sensed that their recent hilarity was in danger of becoming maudlin.

Maya threw a sock at him.

'Oi, watch it,' Con growled. He tried to lasso her with a tie.

'Okay, okay, I give in!' Maya laughed. 'Let's finish up here before the girls get back.'

Trunks and suitcases laid out on the floor overflowed with discarded clothes.

'This is going to take three trips to the charity shop – in an articulated lorry,' Maya laughed, depositing yet another little black dress onto the pile. 'Why did I have so much stuff?'

Con picked the dress up and ran his hand over the flimsy fabric. 'Is that the one you wore on Christmas afternoon, at the gathering? I thought it looked rather fetching in combination with your dreadlocks.'

'Yes it is, and I'm not sure Susannah Metherington would agree with you on that,' Maya answered, folding a blue angora cardigan and tucking it into a gap at the edge of the case. 'Or the other Sue – or either of the Carolines. I thought they were all going to faint when they saw me. Or at least drop the expensive dishes of food they'd brought. Anyway, the dress does rather hang off me now.'

'Well I thought it looked lovely. Do you know there were several people at that party who actually didn't recognise you?' Con added another silk shirt to his charity shop pile. 'I mean, genuinely. I saw John at the newsagents this morning and he asked if I'd heard from you recently. When I told him you were at the party he said he'd spent the whole afternoon at our house and left without even knowing you were there. It was bloody funny seeing the look on his face when I explained that the skinny brown woman with the thick ropes of hair was you.'

'Ha-ha. Serves him right,' Maya said with satisfaction. 'At least he didn't get a chance to pinch my bottom. Not that I have much bottom anymore. I can't believe I used to put up with that crap. And if he ever laid a finger on my girls. . . ' She pulled the last dress off its hanger and closed the wardrobe door. 'Con – you will keep an eye on them, won't you?'

'Of course I will, love. And you will come back regularly to visit, won't you? Especially now that you've been revealed to the village in your true plumage.' He knelt to zip up the holdall he'd been filling and straightened stiffly into an upright position. 'Nothing to be frightened of anymore. Nobody's going to try and clip your wings.' He sucked in his cheeks, familiar and alien at the same time. Something bubbled in Maya's chest. He noticed, took a step forward and clumsily drew her against him. She allowed herself to fall. He held her tight for a moment while her arms wound around his back and her hand stroked his spine through his jumper. When he pulled away, she saw that his lower lashes glistened. She wiped a finger under her own eye.

'I'll definitely visit, darling. I'm just not sure how regularly. I've decided to go over to Greece and help at the refugee camps for a while. I know some people who've been working there for the past year – they told me they desperately need help on the ground – you know, cooking and setting up facilities for the families.'

She was looking forward to spending time with Jodie and Ned again.

Con took a tissue from the box that sat looking rather lonely on the built-in dresser between the wardrobes. He blew his nose and looked around for the bin but it had already been moved downstairs to his new bedroom, the back half of the enormous through-lounge on the ground floor. Con stuffed the used tissue in his pocket and bent to pick up the zipped holdall. At the door he paused and looked back at Maya. His mouth opened and closed.

'What is it?'

'You could take Daisy with you.'

'Pardon?'

'Take Daisy with you. Encourage her to get away from here. She's already given up her job and her flat. She's basically intending to become a surrogate husband to Lola. It's not right. She's too young to devote her life to someone else.'

'But her nursery. . . '

'Do you really think that'll happen, Maya? She'll get bogged down in Lola's needs. She's besotted with Elijah and she's already worn herself ragged fetching and carrying for the two of them. Take her away for a bit, show her there are problems bigger than her twin sister's rather enviable ones. Lola and the baby will be fine here. I'm not going anywhere. Not once I get back from our trip, anyway.'

Maya stood still in the middle of the empty bedroom floor, pondering the situation of her daughters. Lola would depend on Daisy – she always had – Con was right. Daisy should experience more of the world before getting embroiled in *any* binding relationship. She could always come back and set up her day nursery once she'd stretched her wings. Had time to consider the *truth of her existence. . .*

Daisy – as Maya had, as Maya intended to continue doing – needed to find herself in her most basic human condition. Lola might kick up a fuss but she had her baby to think of now. It was time Lola stepped up to the mark and she might never do that if she used Daisy as a permanent crutch.

Maya dropped the lace slip she was holding and moved quickly across the expanse of carpet towards Con. She slid her arms around his waist again and rested her cheek on his chest – holding on and letting go at the same time. In the mirror she saw their chalk-and-cheese reflections: the dark-haired man in his Marks & Spencer chinos and lamb's wool sweater and the smaller, nut-brown woman dressed in combat trousers and a loose shirt. Her mass of dreadlocks was tied at the back of her head in a tasselled scarf. She could hear the heart of her husband and feel his broad hand on her back.

Pushing away, she looked up through a film of water into his eyes. 'Shall I speak to her before we go, or...?'

'I think it's best to wait. I'll have a word with her, tell her not to start making any arrangements for the nursery yet because I've got a surprise for her when I get home. I'll tell her to concentrate on Lola and the baby for a couple of weeks until I get back. No sense in upsetting Lola just yet, is there?'

He was sparing her. He kissed her on the nose and turned for the head of the stairs with the holdall over his shoulder and the heaviest suitcase in his hand. She heard the emotion in his manufactured cough and was glad Daisy and Lola had taken the baby out to visit one of their friends.

Maya used the condemned en-suite bathroom for the last time, revelling in the luxury of peeing in ceramic. As she washed her hands she studied the deepening lines on her face in the mirror. Then she switched off the light and moved back into the bedroom where she fastened the catches of the final suitcase. Her knees creaked as she rose again to her feet. She would soon start to feel her age...

Alicia greeted her frenziedly at the bottom of the stairs. Maya calmed her down and sank to the bottom step with her nose buried in the dog's fur. Alicia already smelt different – from being in houses too long and, at Con's insistence, having been professionally groomed.

'I must smell the same as you,' Maya sat up and sniffed her own skin. 'Too chemical. The sooner we get back on the road, the better.'

Con came in through the front door and lifted the suitcase. He paused for a moment to watch the dog giving Maya's face liberal kisses and remarked, 'I won't miss that animal's hairs all over the floor, that's for sure. Daisy's cat is bad enough but at least I can get the girls to keep it upstairs. Right. I'll just put this one in the van and then we'd better gather our

281

things. Has she done her business?' he jerked his head at Alicia. 'If not you'd better take her outside first. We don't want any mess in the van – there'll be a penalty.'

Maya shook her head at him and his eyes crinkled at the corners.

'We can drop the charity stuff off on the way through Grantham,' he said. 'You did say your goodbyes to the girls and Elijah, before, didn't you?'

Maya swallowed hard. *No more tears.* She lifted her chin from the dog's shoulder and bravely nodded.

'Yup, I said my goodbyes. It's not as if I haven't done it before, is it?'

But never to a brand-new grandson.

'Anyway, if Daisy agrees to our plan – I'll be seeing her again soon, won't I?'

'Of course you will. I'm certain Daisy'll agree. Anyway,' he echoed. 'Let's look forward to where we're going now, Maya. That's all that matters at the moment.'

54

Jamie

Berlin, January 2017

Jamie was shitting himself. Literally. He'd had to go to the toilet half a dozen times already and it was only ten in the morning.

'Is Uncle Joe here yet?' he asked Electra when he opened the door onto the landing, again. His daughter was jumping up and down outside the bathroom, clutching between her legs.

Jamie had missed Joe since he moved back to Kreuzberg. There were other reasons Joe hadn't been hanging around *chez Jamie* as much, but Joe was still slightly shy about mentioning Amar. Electra urgently tugged at Jamie's jumper.

'Papa, get out of my way, please, I need wee-wee!' She bumped past his hip, pulling her leggings down and hitching herself up onto the toilet just in time by the sound of it. The look of relief on her sweet little face. But then, 'Eueww, Papa, it stinks in here. Why are you doing so many poos?'

'Because I'm scared, baby.'

He was nothing if not honest. Electra jumped off the toilet and washed her hands. Drying them, she asked, 'Why are you scared?'

'Grown-ups get scared about all sorts of silly things.'

He scooped her up. Her legs wound around his waist and she tucked her head under his chin. It only just fit now. He noticed that the texture of her hair was changing, firming-up, like the rest of her. She was changing from a baby-faced toddler into a streamlined little girl, just in time for her baby brother to be born. Jamie remembered his parents coming home from the hospital with his twin sisters in their car seats. His Granny had travelled to London to look after him while his mother was away at the hospital. When he examined the faces of the babies that had been deposited in the middle of the carpet, he felt panicky that he would never be able to tell them apart. He also remembered the overwhelming sense of responsibility. Everybody repeatedly told him he would have to be a grown-up boy now that he was a big brother. He didn't want Electra to feel loaded down like that. He placed her on her feet in front of the sink.

'I'll brush your hair.' He took the wooden-backed brush and began drawing it through the thick strands. 'Do you want it up in a ponytail? Remember we have some very special visitors coming today.'

Electra tilted her head from side-to-side, considering her reflection. Her hair had grown out of its customary bob and now hung to her shoulders, a thick black fringe above her eyes. Apart from her darker skin she reminded him of his sisters. At least of his memory of them. While she deliberated he swallowed the indigestion that always came along with excitement and anxiety.

'No, Papa,' Electra decided, bobbing up and down on her toes. 'I want to leave my hair down for the special visitors. I want them to see how long it is on its own. Can I show them my remote-control car?'

'Of course you can.' His daughter's hair slipped through

284

his fingers as she charged out of the bathroom to fetch her most prized possession.

He replaced the brush in the cabinet above the sink. Downstairs, he could hear Lejla welcoming Joe into their apartment. He checked his watch again. Time for a final evacuation of the bowels...

———

Electra sat on the woman's lap, pretending to ring bells with the thick ropes of her hair. The woman had wrapped her arms tightly around Electra and she kept burying her nose in his daughter's neck. Electra appeared to be loving the attention. *The woman.* It was impossible to think of her as his mother. Perhaps recognition would come in time – there was a particular way she laughed, for example, that he remembered. Jamie felt coldly distant, as if he was hovering above the kitchen.

When she first greeted him at the door he'd been unable to hide his shock. His fantasies of the sobbing mother at the kitchen table were blasted to pieces. Joe didn't seem to have any such problem relating to the traveller, though. He'd shoved his chair as close as possible to Maya's and was rubbing his cheek on her shoulder like a kitten.

'Silly Uncle Joe!' Electra batted her uncle's face with a dreadlock. 'Get off my gramma!' That was how Maya had introduced herself to the child.

'She was my mummy before she became your gramma!' Joe stuck his tongue out at his niece and she batted him again, then fell against Maya's chest, claiming resident's rights. Jamie felt something twist inside him.

'You're too big to have a mummy, isn't he, Gramma?' pleaded Electra. Tilting her head upwards, giving Maya her cute-eyes.

Maya rewarded his child with a squelching kiss.

'Nobody's ever too big to have a mummy.' She turned her head to give Joe a quick kiss too, right in the middle of his

285

forehead. Jamie was surprised Joe hadn't melted into a puddle on the floor by now, he looked that love-struck.

Parts of Jamie were being etched away. He was happy for Joe – he'd been encouraging his brother to get back in touch with their parents for the past three years after all. But he didn't know if he could cope with being an outsider all over again. He raised his eyes from his tightly-furled fingers on his lap to see that Maya's gaze was resting on him. What was it he could read in her face? Rawness, like an overexposed film. Meeting his gaze, her face lit up from inside like a blinding light.

He felt as if he was wading through sand in an arid desert. He watched Maya take his daughter's face gently in her hands and angle it towards him.

'That man,' she said. 'That man over there. Your papa.' She hesitated. Could it be that she was struggling to overcome tears? 'He's my baby as well, you know. He's my very first boy and I'm so proud of him. I bet you are, too – he is such a great papa, isn't he?' Electra nodded solemnly, her lower lip jutting out. She laughed nervously.

'So you see,' Maya continued. 'Nobody is too big to have a mummy, not even your papa.'

They heard voices and Lejla came in through the flat door with Dad, bumping down the corridor with boxes of fresh pizza. Lejla rested the ones she was carrying on her tummy. Electra squealed as the boxes were opened on the table. Meeting her new gramma seemed to have regressed her into babyhood, but that was okay because she had such a short time left to be the baby of the house.

Con was much the same as Jamie remembered, only softer, somehow. Perhaps he had more grey in his hair and deeper lines on his face but he had stayed living the same life, in the same place, unlike his wife. Jamie had always seen his father as a stern man. But on arrival Con had at first gripped the hands of both his sons, then pulled them individually into manly hugs, then enveloped them both in a bear hug at the

286

same time. Jamie couldn't remember ever being hugged by him before.

It was crazy that their ma and pa had travelled all the way through Germany together in a camper van – a luxury one, it had to be said, but a pretty cool way to travel nonetheless.

'Your mother wanted me to take early retirement and travel around the world with her in an old hippie van,' Con laughingly explained. 'But it's not really my thing. I might persuade Lola and the baby to come on a campervan holiday with me in the summer, though, now that I'm used to it. Her nipper should be big enough by then. We could bring him here and introduce him to his cousins, couldn't we?' He slapped his hands on his lap. The white dog barked in shock and cowered under the legs of Joe, whom she seemed to have adopted. Electra gave Con a suspicious look and buried her head under Maya's chin. Lejla put her hand on her stomach, exclaiming that the baby had jumped. Con looked embarrassed. Now that Jamie was a father himself he found some empathy in his heart for the man who seemed to struggle with the role.

Jamie was still trying to get used to his mother being a hippie. And his sister Lola having a baby! But he supposed she must be equally as surprised about her waster of an older brother being a dad. There was a lot for them all to catch up on.

Later that evening, Lejla persuaded him to play some of his music to his parents. His mother listened with her eyes closed. He could tell she was crying. Jamie could have been knocked down with a feather when Maya got up and headed for the door, leaning back into the room to say – 'I'm just going to fetch something from the van. Won't be long.' The dog crawled out from its hiding place and made to follow but Joe soothed her back into restfulness. Maya returned, carrying a scuffed, brown guitar case. Then Jamie had a vague memory of her playing and singing to him when he was a small child. The picture came into focus and he could see her face as she

287

leant over the guitar. A battered, blue guitar she had then, with stickers all over it.

She caught his eye and began to strum the chords to *Jamaican Farewell*. It had been his favourite, while the twins had preferred *The Raggle-Taggle Gypsies*. Maya kept her eyes on him as she sang the chorus out loud, nodding her head. Eventually he joined in, more for Electra's sake than anything – understanding that it was his mother's way of truly saying sorry.

Author's note

I was greatly helped in writing this book by two young people who have extensively travelled many parts of the world alone. I feel privileged that they have shared some of their insights and experiences with me in order for *The Vagabond Mother* to have some authenticity.

The final paragraphs of this collection of thoughts are my own, written when my youngest son set off on his very first vagabond journey.

Tracey Scott-Townsend

The Vagabond Guide

Travel— Make the most of the vast network of motorways that stretch across Europe. It's often possible to cover huge distances in a short time.

You need to be strategic. Often if you wait at the last gas station before a major highway entrance, there will be many cars about to go on long distance trips. *Hitchwiki.org* is a great resource to find good spots for rides.

It's useful to study the roads before departing and learn the names of all the gas stations between you and your destination. Let's say you're in Germany – hitching out of Frankfurt and going to Freiburg – a man stops but he's only going to a small village outside Heidelberg. You ask if he will take you to a gas station on the south side of Heidelberg on the A5. From that gas station you get all the traffic from Frankfurt and Heidelberg going south, this puts you in a better position for getting to Freiburg, a good stopping point on the way to France.

Hop on and off hitching is perfect for short journeys or in places with simple road systems. Iceland for example is a place where you can get out of the car anywhere on road 1 and expect another to pick you up sooner or later. The same goes for Tasmania and even the pacific highway that runs from Sydney to Brisbane in Australia. For this you don't need to worry about highway exits and entries or gas stations.

In Germany the autobahns – minimum two lanes a side – are well maintained and mostly have no speed restriction. All even-numbered autobahns run roughly east and west, all odd-numbered ones run north and south. Non-A roads are smaller and you can hop on and off and hitch from the side of the road – but long distance journeys will take much longer this way and you will easily get lost. Three-digit-roads are all connecting roads, they either link two roads together, or they link a highway to a town. Never hitch on a three-digit-road in Germany without knowing where it is going.

Where to sleep— When entering an unfamiliar town, I make note of the time. If it's before midday I'll relax and not worry about where to sleep. In general it really doesn't matter until it starts getting dark, so there's no need to stress. Enjoy the place first! It's a good idea to ask people in the street about parks in the city – they're often the best place to find a good spot to squat – then explore to get a feel of the town. Abandoned buildings can be perfect, but approach them with caution. If the building is being renovated and has construction materials lying around it can be great, because people don't go in much. You can sleep there and get out early in the morning. Bushes are also good hiding places and even when next to a pathway you can sleep there without being disturbed. You may be surprised to know how often you're walking past someone's temporary bedroom!

If you don't feel like sleeping in a park, architecture from the post-war era can be a promising place to look. Town halls often have raised concrete walkways and stairs you can hide beneath. In summertime, security will be more vigilant but in winter no one expects anyone to be crazy enough to sleep outside, especially in places like this.

It's important to get a good feel about a place before setting up for a night. Look around, if there are lots of bars then people will be out late and can disturb you. Trust your instincts.

How to Find Food— Table diving. Go to food courts in malls and train stations – they're the best places because of their high concentration of food outlets. Try and raid the trash racks before the staff clear them off. And try to be discreet so the staff don't become more vigilant. You can also check regular bins on the street.

Dumpster diving is the most effective way to find food and it's very possible to eat a better diet than the average consumer in this way. Supermarkets discard food every day and it can stay in perfect condition for up to a week in the trash container. In Europe the best time to dive is after the shop closes but in Australia, the earlier you go, the better haul you'll get. Most dumpsters are frequented by several crews as well as lone divers, so try to find the best time to get the best haul. Be aware that sometimes there are dry periods in dumpster diving in some towns. The best way to get free food is a healthy mix of table diving and dumpster diving.

Money— Never pressure anyone into giving you money.

When busking, choose a spot that's not too noisy but has a decent amount of pedestrian traffic. There are three types of people who give money to buskers

1. someone who enjoys the music and would like to support the busker.

2. someone who wants to feel good or be able to tell themselves that they did a good thing today.

3. someone who wants to empty the small change from their pocket and will pick the coins of least value.

There are always dry periods. That's important to know.

Observations— A cold street over a warm bed is a choice made by many but understood by few. We travellers are not obliged to anyone but ourselves. To perform arbitrary 'work' for a bed when you can build one for yourself seems a bad deal once you've made your own bed more than once. But the road can be a lonesome place. Most of us are motivated by our pathological need for comradeship.

I *choose* to stay here. Our hardships are usually self-imposed in some way. I'm growing comfortable in an uncomfortable life.

ZS, aged 22

I grew up in Germany but I left there soon after my high school graduation. I spent all my savings on a round-the-world trip. Since then I haven't really gone back "home".

I had become more and more disgusted with my consumerist lifestyle and my departure from that was a welcome opportunity to sort out the important stuff. Still, my backpack was heavy and a total pain in the ass to carry around.

The first time I hitchhiked was in the countryside of Galway when my friend and I were lost and wanted to get to a paintball game we'd signed up for. The second time was when I wanted to do the Golden Circle in Iceland. I even made a sign back then – something I don't do anymore because without one it is easier to decline people with a "bad" vibe – although I only had to do that twice in the almost-four years since I've been hitchhiking.

I wouldn't pick vulnerable as the word for how I feel travelling alone as a woman. I feel jealous of my male friends, as they seem to be able to do things I don't really feel comfortable doing simply because of my sex. I meet a lot of guys who've slept in city parks and streets and subway lines; something I could probably do as well, but the chance that I might get raped or mugged simply because a woman seems to be an easy target are, I think, higher for me.

I trust my gut feeling when it comes to people. What I've learned is that there are a lot of real, genuinely nice and compassionate human beings out there. The world is *not* full of serial killers or thieves, as some people seem to think.

On my own I've travelled in Ireland, Iceland, Singapore, Australia, New Zealand, New Caledonia, Japan, Spain, Germany, Switzerland and Morocco. Before that I travelled around France and Scotland quite extensively with my family.

The first time I slept truly in the wild on my own I camped out in a place called Paradise, Glenorchy on the South Island of New Zealand. I got eaten by sand-flies and mozzies. It was next to a beautiful, glacial stream in the middle of an enchanted forest – they filmed Lothlorien from The Lord of the Rings trilogy there. I just wanted to be alone in the bush so I'd hitchhiked there without really knowing where I'd end up.

Back in those days I actually carried a hammer with me everywhere I went: not too big, not too small – enough to seriously hurt someone if I smashed it in the right place – it made me feel a bit safer than only having my pocket knife. So after crossing that glacial river, which turned out to be quite treacherous in places, and hiking upstream for a while, I finally found a flat area of forest clearing with easy access to water and I simply pitched my tent and read for a while with my hammer next to me.

I like the simplicity of this way of life, and that I constantly have to figure out new ways of getting to where I want to be. You have to either work with the things you have or find out how to get the ones you need. The prospect of having an actual pension that you can live on when you're old is becoming slim for my generation. I'll work until I'm seventy or eighty anyway so why not do it anywhere in the world? I didn't used to have a lot of faith in the good things in the world. Following the news can be depressing. But all the random acts of kindness, generosity and love I've met along the way – they really restored my faith in humanity – that's one of the reasons I chose this life. Good things come to you all the time, and when you don't own a lot of things that would distract you from them, you start to realise it.

It's hard to stick a label on myself. People are never just one thing – you're made up of a bunch of traits that all come together in the grand, colourful picture of you. I may be an adventurer at times but there are also weeks when I consider my adventure to be my trip to the grocery store or the beer in the pub when I meet up with friends after whatever job I'm doing – rather than climbing some mountain and nearly losing my shoe during a river crossing.

Funny story? There are heaps of them but if I have to choose one it would be when I was hitchhiking in the middle of nowhere in Northern Iceland. Suddenly this massive red jeep, splattered with mud, stopped next to me. I was trying to get back to Reykjavik that day. The driver rolled down his window and told me in very broken English (over a lot of weird sounds coming from inside the car) that he could only take me to the next intersection. In these cases, when you're out in the countryside on the only road there is – a short distance is better than nothing so I opened the door, put my backpack in and climbed up behind it. It turned out that there was a big fluffy sheep in the back seat, fully fastened in with the seatbelt. It was bleating at full force because this was evidently not its preferred mode of transport. The driver had found his neighbour's missing sheep and was taking it home. He picked me up along the way because why the hell not?

JG, aged 21

On the Camino, an Englishman has given him ten euros, a Spanish woman has given him forty.

He walked eighteen miles after the sun rose this morning and rested by an icy pool, his view enclosed by mountains.

He has cooked food for other pilgrims. He ate with a German couple along with three new Spanish friends. The table was candle-lit and they sat under a forest canopy.

Tonight he sleeps in a makeshift camp, in company. Knowing this – I will sleep well in my own bed.

He is sixteen. This is only the beginning of his journey.

I wave him off at the station for the second time.

He's still only sixteen, a slight boy who carries a heavy bag.

This time he's going for an indeterminate period. He's carrying dried food, a gas canister, a tarpaulin. He's a boy who has not been at school for two years now – instead, he's been sitting in a dark room hatching plans.

A ray of sun glances off his face, lights up his pale skin. I hope he remembers to buy a hat.

I wish people would stop saying I'm brave for letting him go.

The Mother

Acknowledgements

The larger part of my acknowledgements go to to Zak, for the initial inspiration behind this book. Thank you for allowing me to borrow some of your experiences, the tales of your travels and even, at times, the voice of your youth.

To Jacky, for answering my questions and providing stories about travelling as a lone female.

To Ruben, for the Bali chapter, including the rich descriptions of the old town of Kuta Bali.

To Felix, for the tales of Bundaberg, and Faye, for recollections of your trip to Barcelona, and all of you for telling me about Berlin.

Thanks to my early readers of the manuscript: Zak Scott, Sarah Carby, Bruford Low and Jacqueline Goede, for your suggested improvements.

Thanks to my editor Sara-Jayne Slack, for the hand of consistency throughout the manuscript, and to S.B. for the reader's report.

Acknowledgements are due to the following books and films:
Everett Ruess, A Vagabond for Beauty by W.L. Rusho (Gibbs Smith, 2007)
Into the Wild by Jon Krakauer, (Pan, 2007) [and the film, 2007, directed by Sean Penn]
Wild: A Journey from Lost to Found by Cheryl Strayed, (Atlantic Books, 2013) [and the film, 2014, directed by Jean-Marc Vallée]
The Way (film, 2010, directed by Emilio Estevez)
Eat, Pray, Love by Elizabeth Gilbert (Bloomsbury Publishing 2007) [and the film, 2010, directed by Ryan Murphy]

All of these explore similar themes to those within *The*

Vagabond Mother, and the eternal questions, I think, at the heart of us all.

To Luna, my dog-soulmate, for being the model for Alicia in the book.

As always, thanks to Phil in your diverse roles as husband, co-publisher, and campervan driver on our many and varied travels and adventures together.

About the Author

The Vagabond Mother is Tracey's sixth novel, inspired largely by the travels of her four grown children, and her own resultant burgeoning sense of adventure. Together with her husband, Phil and their two rescue dogs, she spends a lot of time travelling at home and in Europe in their camper van.

Her novels explore the pressing themes at the heart of human existence. Sense of place is also important, and each new novel reflects the locations she has recently travelled to.

Tracey is also an artist and poet, and a grower of food on her allotment.